MODERN CARPENTRY

A PRACTICAL MANUAL

A new and complete guide containing hundreds of quick methods for performing work in carpentry, joining and general woodwork, written in a simple, every-day style that does not bewilder the working-man, illustrated with hundreds of diagrams which are especially made so that anyone can follow them without difficulty : : : : : : :

REVISED AND ENLARGED

BY

FRED T. HODGSON, ARCHITECT

Editor of the NATIONAL BUILDER, Author of "Common Sense Handrailing," "Practical Uses of the Steel Square," etc.

ILLUSTRATED

Fredonia Books
Amsterdam, The Netherlands

Modern Carpentry:
A Practical Manual

by
Fred T. Hodgson

ISBN: 1-58963-615-5

Copyright © 2001 by Fredonia Books

Reprinted from the 1917 edition

Fredonia Books
Amsterdam, The Netherlands
http://www.fredoniabooks.com

PREFACE

"Good wine," says Shakespeare, "needs no bush," which of course means that when a thing is good in itself, praise makes it no better. So with a book, if it is good, it needs no preface to make it better. The author of this book flatters himself that the work he has done on it, both as author and compiler, is good; therefore, from his standpoint a preface to it is somewhat a work of supererogation. His opinion regarding the quality of the book may be questioned, but after forty years' experience as a writer of books for builders, all of which have met with success, and during that time over thirty years editor of one of the most popular building journals in America, he feels his opinion, reinforced as it is by thousands of builders and woodworkers throughout the country, should be entitled to some weight. Be that as it may, however, this little book is sent out with a certainty that the one and a half million of men and boys who earn their living by working wood, and fashioning it for useful or ornamental purposes, will appreciate it, because of its main object, which is to lessen their labors by placing before them the quickest and most approved methods of construction.

To say more in this preface is unnecessary and a waste of time for both reader and author.

FRED T. HODGSON.

PREFACE TO SECOND EDITION.

MODERN CARPENTRY.

VOL. I.

The necessity of preparing a second edition of this work has become so urgent that its publication cannot be longer delayed. The demand for it has almost outgrown our means of production, and our supply is about exhausted, so we hasten to take advantage of this condition to enlarge and improve the work and render it more acceptable and valuable than ever. The additions and improvements now made to the work, are of so very useful and practical a character, that we are sure they will prove of benefit to the workman, and to the general student of the carpenter and joiners' art.

It is hardly necessary for me to indulge in a long preamble setting forth the good qualities contained in the contents of this work, as all this has been before the people now for several years; all recent developments in the carpenter trade, however, have been added, so that the present volume will be found to contain the very latest practice of doing things. The additional matter and diagrams will, I am sure, commend themselves to the workman, and will, I hope, prove a help to him in his everyday labors.

FRED T. HODGSON.

MODERN CARPENTRY

PART I

CARPENTER'S GEOMETRY

CHAPTER I

THE CIRCLE

While it is not absolutely necessary that, to become
a good mechanic, a man must need be a good scholer
or be well advanced in mathematics or geometry, yet,
if a man be proficient in these sciences they will be a
great help to him in aiding him to accomplish his work
with greater speed and more exactness than if he did
not know anything about them.   This, I think, all will
admit.   It may be added, however, that a man, the
moment he begins active operations in any of the con-
structional trades, commences, without knowing it, to
learn the science of geometry in its rudimentary
stages.   He wishes to square over a board and employs
a steel or other square for this purpose, and, when he
scratches or pencils a line across the board, using the
edge or the tongue of the square as a guide, while the
edge of the blade is against the edge of the board or
parallel with it, he thus solves his first geometrical
problem, that is, he makes a right angle with the edge
of the board.   This is one step forward in the path of
geometrical science.

He desires to describe a circle, say of eight inches
diameter.   He knows instinctively that if he opens his

compasses until the points of the legs are four inches apart,—or making the radius four inches—he can, by keeping one point fixed, called a "center," describe a circle with the other leg, the diameter of which will be eight inches. By this process he has solved a second geometrical problem, or at least he has solved it so far that it suits his present purposes. These examples, of course, do not convey to the operator the more subtle qualities of the right angle or the circle, yet they serve, in a practical manner, as assistants in every-day work.

When a man becomes a good workman, it goes without saying that he has also become possessor of a fair amount of practical geometrical knowledge, though he may not be aware of the fact.

The workman who can construct a roof, hipped, gabled, or otherwise, cutting all his material on the ground, has attained an advanced practical knowledge of geometry, though he may never have heard of Euclid or opened a book relating to the science. Some of the best workmen I have met were men who knew nothing of geometry as taught in the books, yet it was no trouble for them to lay out a circular or elliptical stairway, or construct a rail over them, a feat that requires a knowledge of geometry of a high order to properly accomplish.

These few introductory remarks are made with the hope that the reader of this little volume will not be disheartened at the threshold of his trade, because of his lack of knowledge in any branch thereof. To become a good carpenter or a good joiner, a young man must begin at the bottom, and first learn his A, B, C's, and the difficulties that beset him will disappear one after another as his lessons are learnt. It must always be borne in mind, however, that the young fellow who enters a shop, fully equipped with a knowledge of general mathematics and geometry, is in a much better position to solve the work problems that crop up daily, than the one who starts work without such equipment. If, however, the latter fellow be a boy possessed of courage and perseverance, there is no

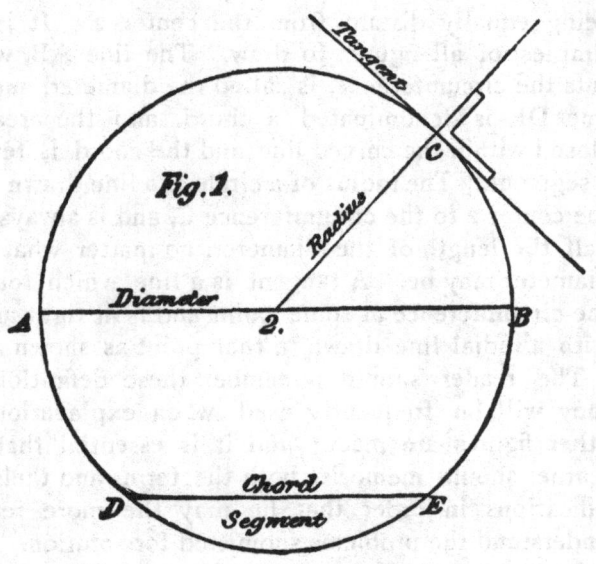

Fig.1.

reason why he should not "catch up"—even overtake—the boy with the initial advantages, for what is then learned will be more apt to be better understood, and more readily applied to the requirements of his work. To assist him in "catching up" with his more favored shopmate, I propose to submit for his benefit a brief description and explanation of what may be termed "Carpenter's Geometry," which will be quite sufficient if he learn it well, to enable him to execute any work that he may be called upon to perform; and I will do so as clearly and plainly as possible, and in as few words as the instructions can be framed so as to make them intelligible to the student.

The circle shown in Fig. 1 is drawn from the center 2, as shown, and may be said to be a plain figure within a continual curved line, every part of the line being equally distant from the center 2. It is the simplest of all figures to draw. The line AB, which cuts the circumference, is called the diameter, and the line DE is denominated a chord, and the area enclosed within the curved line and the chord is termed a segment. The radius of a circle is a line drawn from the center 2 to the circumference C, and is always one-half the length of the diameter, no matter what that diameter may be. A tangent is a line which touches the circumference at some point and is at right angles with a radial line drawn to that point as shown at C.

The reader should remember these definitions as they will be frequently used when explanations of other figures are made; and it is essential that the learner should memorize both the terms and their significations in order that he may the more readily understand the problems submitted for solution.

It frequently happens that the center of a circle is not visible but must be found in order to complete the circle or form some part of the circumference. The center of any circle may be found as follows: let BHC, Fig. 2, be a chord of the segment H; and BJA a chord enclosing the segment. Bisect or divide in equal parts, the chord BC, at H, and square down from this point to D. Do the same with the chord AJB, squaring over from J to D, then the point where JD and HD intersect, will be the center of the circle.

This is one of the most important problems for the carpenter in the whole range of geometry as it enables the workman to locate any center, and to draw curves he could not otherwise describe without this or other similar methods. It is by aid of this problem that through any three points not in a straight line, a

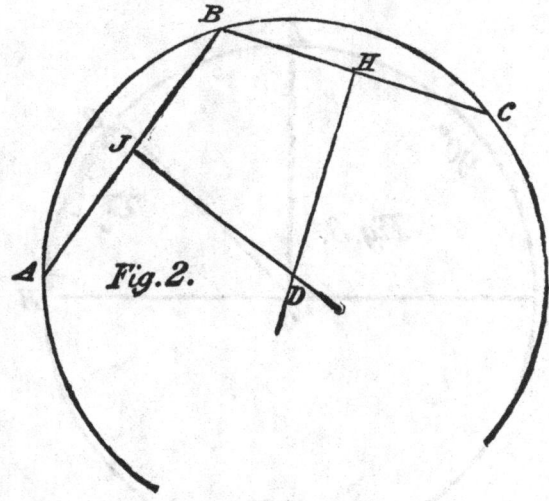

Fig.2.

circle can be drawn that will pass through each of the three points. Its usefulness will be shown further on as applied to laying out segmental or curved top window, door and other frames and sashes, and the learner should thoroughly master this problem before stepping further, as a full knowledge of it will assist him very materially in understanding other problems.

The circumference of every circle is measured by being supposed to be divided into 360 equal parts, called *degrees*; each degree containing 60 *minutes*, a

smaller division, and each minute into 60 *seconds*, a
still smaller division. Degrees, minutes, and seconds
are written thus: 45° 15′ 30″, which is read, forty-five
degrees, fifteen minutes, and thirty seconds. This, I
think, will be quite clear to the reader. Arcs are measured by the number of degrees which they contain: thus,
in Fig. 3, the arc AE, which contains 90°, is called a
quadrant, or the quarter of a circumference, because

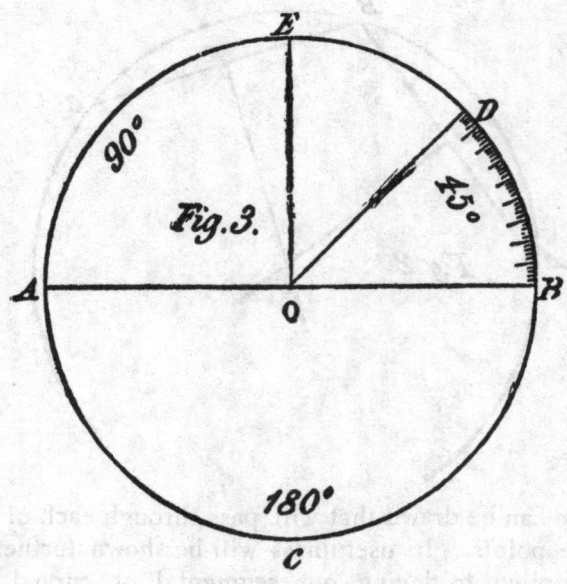

90° is one quarter of 360°, and the arc ABC which contains 180°, is a semi-circumference. Every angle is also
measured by degrees, the degrees being reckoned on an
arc included between its sides; described from the vertex of the angle as a center, as the point O, Fig. 3;
thus, AOE contains 90°; and the angle BOD, which is
half a right angle, is called an angle of 45°, which is

the number it contains, as will be seen by counting off the spaces as shown by the divisions on the curved line BD. These rules hold good, no matter what may be the diameter of the circle. If large, the divisions are large; if small, the divisions are small, but the manner of reckoning is always the same.

One of the qualities of the circle is, that when divided in two by a diameter, making two semicircles, any chord starting at the extremity of such a diameter, as at A or B, Fig. 4, and cutting the circumference at any point, as at C, D or E, a line drawn from this

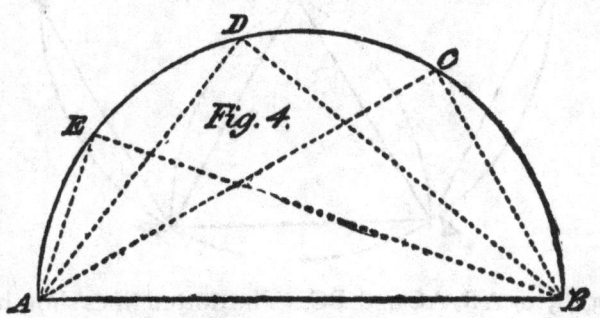

Fig. 4.

point to the other extremity of the diameter, will form a right angle—or be square with the first chord, as is shown by the dotted lines BCA, BDA, and BEA. This is something to be remembered, as the problem will be found useful on many occasions.

The diagram shown at Fig. 5 represents a hexagon within a circle. This is obtained by stepping around the circumference, with the radius of the circle on the compasses, six times, which divides the circumference into six equal parts; then draw lines to each point, which, when completed, will form a hexagon, a six-sided figure. By drawing lines from the points obtained in the circumference to the center, we get a

three-sided figure, which is called an equilateral triangle that is, a triangle having all its sides equal in

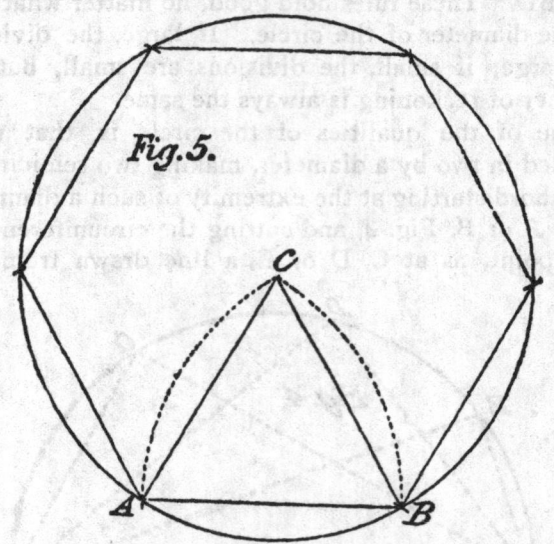

Fig. 5.

length; as AB, AC and BC. The dotted lines show how
an equilateral triangle may be produced on a straight
line if necessary.

The diagram shown
at Fig. 6 illustrates the
method of trisecting a
right angle or quadrant
into three equal parts.
Let A be a center, and
with the same radius
intersect at E, thus the
quadrant or right angle
is divided into three
equal parts.

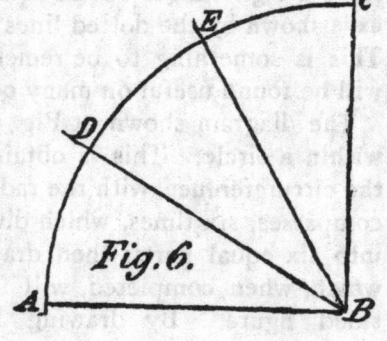

Fig. 6.

If we wish to get the length of a straight line that shall equal the circumference of a circle or part of circle or quadrant, we can do so by proceeding as follows: Suppose Fig. 7 to represent half of the circle, as at ABC; then draw the chord BC, divide it at P, join it at A; then four times PA is equal to the circumference of a circle whose diameter is AC, or equal to the curve CB.

To divide the quadrant AB into any number of equal parts, say thirteen, we simply lay on a rule and make the distance from A to R measure three and one-

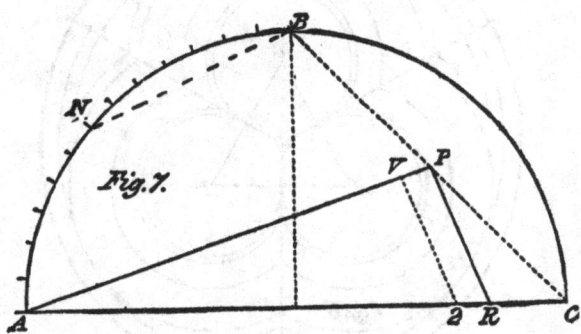

fourth inches, which are thirteen quarters or parts on the rule; make R2 equal one-fourth of an inch; join RP; draw from 2 parallel with RP, cutting at V; now take PV in the dividers and set off from A on the circle thirteen parts, which end at B, each part being equal to PV, and the problem is solved. The "stretchout" or length of any curved line in the circle can then be obtained by breaking it into segments by chords, as shown at BN.

I have shown in Fig. 5, how to construct an equilateral triangle by the use of the compasses. I give at

Fig 8 a practical example of how this figure, in connection with circles, may be employed in describing a
figure known as the trefoil, a figure made much use of
in the construction of church or other Gothic work and
for windows and carvings on doors and panelings.
Each corner of the triangle, as ABC, is a center from
which are described the curves shown within the outer
circles.   The latter curves are struck from the center

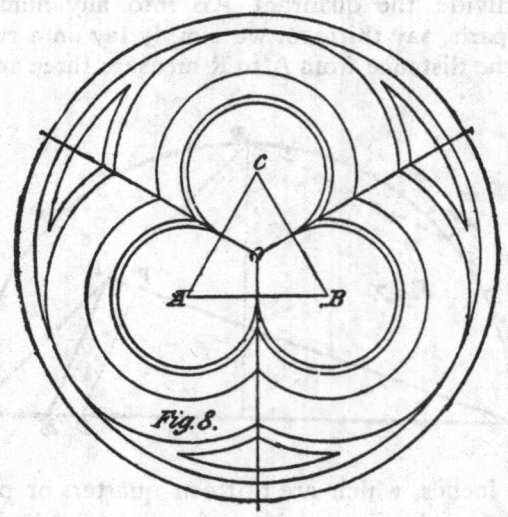

Fig. 8.

O, which is found by dividing the sides of the equilateral triangle and squaring down until the lines cross
at O.   The joint lines shown are the proper ones to
be made use of by the carpenter when executing his
work.   The construction of this figure is quite simple
and easy to understand, so that any one knowing how to
handle a rule and compass should be able to construct
it after a few minutes' thought.   This figure is the key
to most Gothic ornamentation, and is worth mastering.

There is another method of finding the length or "stretchout" of the circumference of a circle, which I show herewith at Fig. 9. Draw the semicircle SZT, and parallel to the diameter ST draw the tangent UZV; upon S and T as centers, with ST as radius, mark the arcs TR and SR; from R, the intersection of the arcs, draw RS and continue to U; also draw RT, and continue to V; then the line VU will nearly equal in

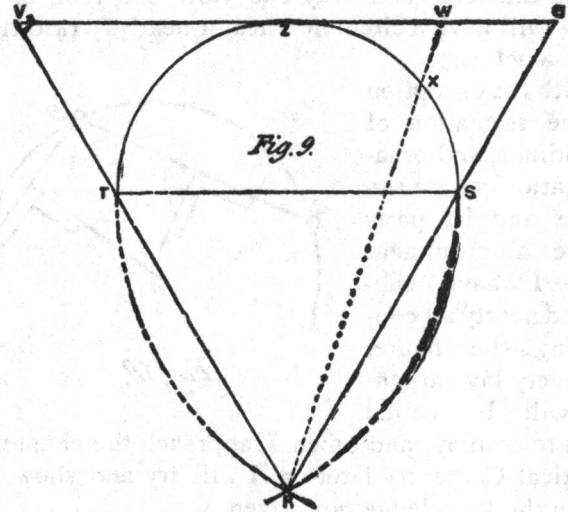

Fig. 9.

length the circumference of the semicircle. The length of any portion of a circle may be found as follows: Through X draw RW, then WU will be the "stretchout" or length of that portion of the circle marked SX. There are several other ways of determining by lines a near approach to the length of the circumference or a portion thereof; but, theoretically, the exact "stretchout" of a circumference has not been found by any of the known methods, either arith-

metically or geometrically, though for all practical
purposes the methods given are quite near enough.
No method, however, that is given geometrically is so
simple, so convenient and so accurate as the arith-
metical one, which I give herewith. If we multiply
the diameter of a circle by 3.1416, the product will
give the length of the circumference, very nearly.
These figures are based on the fact that a circle
whose diameter is 1—say one yard, one foot, or one
inch—will have a circumference of nearly 3.1416 times
the diameter.

With the exception
of the formation of
mouldings, and orna-
mentation where the
circle and its parts
t a k e a prominent
part, I have sub-
mitted nearly all con-
cerning the figure,
the everyday carpen-
ter will be called

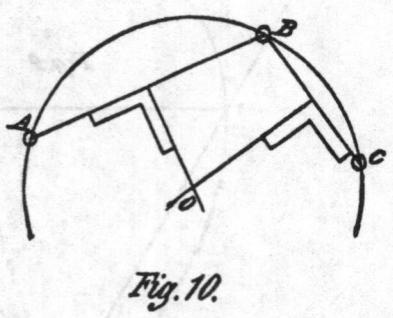

Fig. 10.

upon to employ, and when I approach the chapter on
Practical Carpentry later on, I will try and show how
to use the knowledge now given.

Before leaving the subject, however, it may be as
well to show how a curve, having any reasonable
radius, may be obtained—practically—if but three
points in the circumference are available; as referred
to in the explanation given of Fig. 5.   Let us suppose
there are three points given in the circumference of a
circle, as ABC, Fig. 10, then the center of such circle
can be found by connecting the points AB and BC
by straight lines as shown, and by dividing these lines

and squaring down as shown until the lines intersect at O as shown   This point O is the center of the circle.

It frequently happens that it is not possible to find a place to locate a center, because of the diameter being so great, as in segmental windows and doors of large dimensions.   To overcome this difficulty a method

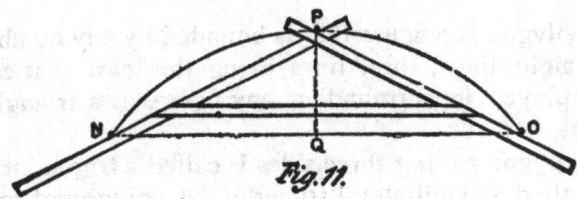

Fig. 11.

has been devised by which the curve may be correctly drawn by nailing three wooden strips together so as to form a triangle, as shown in Fig. 11.   Suppose NO to be the chord or width of frame, and QP the height of segment, measuring from the springing lines N and O; drive nails or pins at O and N, keep the triangle close against the nails, and place a pencil at P, then slide the triangle against the pins or nails while sliding, and the pencil will describe the necessary curve.   The arms of the triangle should be several inches longer than the line NO, so that when the pencil P arrives at N or O, the arms will still rest against the pins.

CHAPTER II

POLYGONS

A polygon is a figure that is bounded by any number of straight lines; three lines being the least that can be employed in surrounding any figure, as a triangle, Fig. 1.

A polygon having three sides is called a trigon; it is also called an equilateral triangle. A polygon of four **sides is call** a tetragon; it is also called a square and

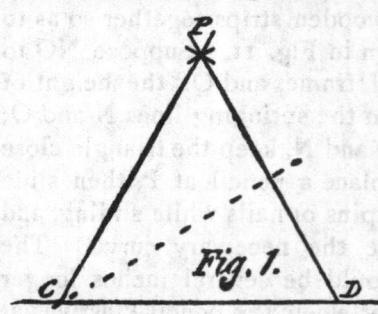

Fig. 1.

an equilateral rectangle. A polygon of five sides is a pentagon. A polygon of six sides is a hexagon. A polygon of seven sides is called a heptagon. A polygon of eight sides is called an octagon. A polygon of nine sides is called a nonagon. A polygon of ten sides is called a decagon. A polygon of eleven sides is called an undecagon. And a polygon of twelve sides is called a dodecagon.

There are regular and irregular polygons. Those having equal sides are regular; those having unequal sides are irregular. Polygons having more than twelve sides are known among carpenters by being denominated as a polygon having "so many sides," as a "polygon with fourteen sides," and so on.

Polygons are often made use of in carpenter work, particularly in the formation of bay-windows, oriels, towers, spires, and similar work; particularly is this the case with the hexagon and the octagon; but the most used is the equilateral rectangle, or square; therefore it is essential that the carpenter should know considerable regarding these figures, both as to their qualities and their construction.

The polygon having the least lines is the trigon, a three-sided figure. This is constructed as follows: Let CD, Fig. 1, be any given line, and the distance CD the length of the side required. Then with one leg of the compass on D as a center, and the other on C, describe the arc shown at P. Then with C as a center, describe another arc at P, cutting the first arc. From this point of intersection draw the lines PD and PC, and the figure is complete. To get the miter joint of this figure, divide one side into two equal parts, and from the point obtained draw a line through opposite angle as shown by the dotted line, and this line will be the line of joint at C, or for any of the other angles.

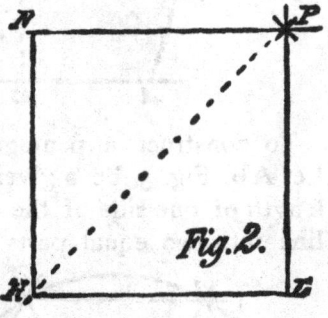

Fig. 2.

The square, or equilateral rectangle, Fig. 2, may be obtained by a number of methods, many of which will suggest themselves to the reader. I give one method that may prove suggestive. Suppose two sides of a square are given, LHN, the other sides are found by taking HL as radius, and with LN for centers make the intersection in P, draw LP and NP which completes the figure. The miter for the joints of a figure of this kind is an angle of 45°, or the regular miter. The dotted line shows the line of "cut" or miter.

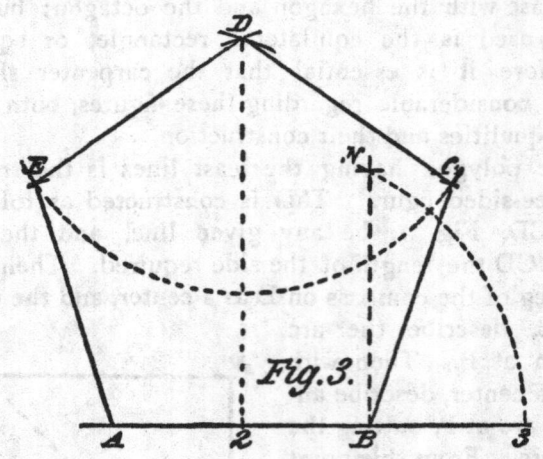

Fig. 3.

To construct a pentagon we proceed as follows: Let AB, Fig. 3, be a given line and spaced off to the length of one side of the figure required; divide this line into two equal parts. From B square up a line; make BN equal to AB, strike an arc 3N as shown by the dotted lines, with 2 as a center and N as a radius, cutting the given line at 3 Take A3 for radius; from A and B as centers, make the intersection in D; from D, with a

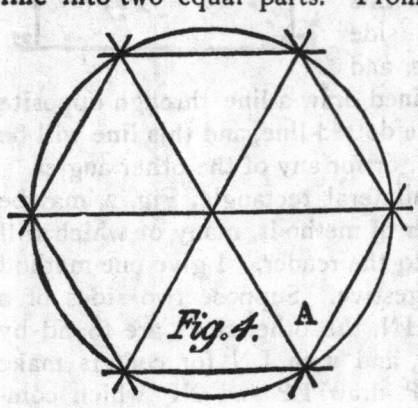

Fig. 4.

radius equal to AB, strike an arc; with the same radius and A and B as centers, intersect the arc in EC. By joining these points the pentagon is formed. The cut, or angle of joints, is found by raising a line from 2 and cutting D, as shown by the dotted line.

The hexagon, a six-sided figure shown at Fig. 4, is one of the simplest to construct. A quick method is described in Chapter I, when dealing with circles, but I show the method of construction in order to be certain that the student may be the better equipped to deal with the figure. Take the length of one side of the figure on compasses; make this length the radius of a circle, thus describe a circle as shown. Start from any point, as at A, and step around the circumference of the circle with the radius of it, and the points from which to draw the sides are found, as the radius of any circle will divide the circumference of that circle into six equal parts.

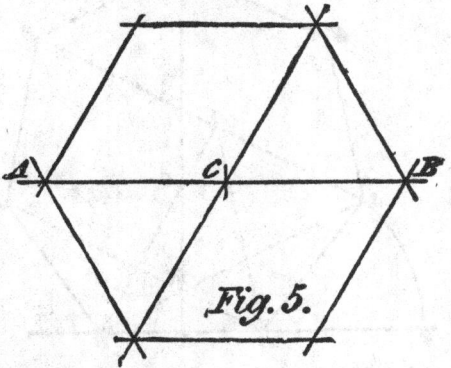

Fig. 5.

This figure may be drawn without first making a circle if necessary. Set off two equal parts, ABC, Fig. 5, making three centers; from each, with radius AC, make the intersection as shown, through which draw straight lines, and a hexagon is formed. The miter joint follows either of the straight lines passing through the center, the bevel indicating the proper angle.

The construction of a heptagon or seven-sided figure may be accomplished as follows: Let AB, Fig. 6, be a given line, and the distance AB the length of the side of the figure. Divide at K, square up from this point, then take AB for radius and B as a center; intersect the line from K at L; with same radius and A as center, draw the curve 2, 3; then take KL as radius, and from 2 as a center, intersect the circle at 3; draw from it to B, cutting at N, through which point draw from A; make AD equal B3; join A3 and BD; draw from 3 parallel with AD; draw from B through L, cutting at C; join it and A; draw from 3 parallel

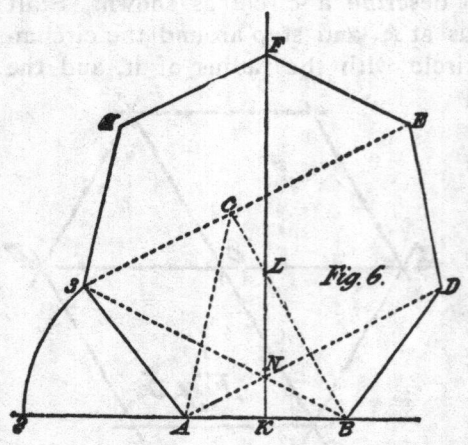

Fig. 6.

with AC; make 3H equal AB, and CE equal ND; join ED; draw from H parallel with 3C, cutting at F, join this line and E, which completes the heptagon. It is not often this figure is used in carpentry, though I have sometimes employed it in constructing bay windows and dormers, using the four sides, 3H, HF, FE, and ED This makes a bold front, and serves well in a conservatory or other similar place.

It is proper that the reader should know how to construct this figure, as it serves as an exercise, and illustrates a principle of drawing by parallels, a knowledge of which would be found invaluable to the ambitious young carpenter, who desires to become, not only a good workman, but a good draftsman as well.

The octagon or eight-sided figure claims rank next to the square and circle, in point of usefulness to the general carpenter, owing partly to its symmetry of form, and its simplicity of construction. There are a great number of methods of constructing this figure, but I will give only a few of the simplest, and the ones most likely to be readily understood by the ordinary workman.

One of the simplest methods of forming an octagon is shown at Fig. 7, where the corners of the square are used as centers, and to the center A of the square for radius. Parts of a circle are then drawn and continued until the boundary lines are cut. At the points found draw diagonal lines across the corner as shown, and the figure will be a complete octagon, having all its sides of equal length.

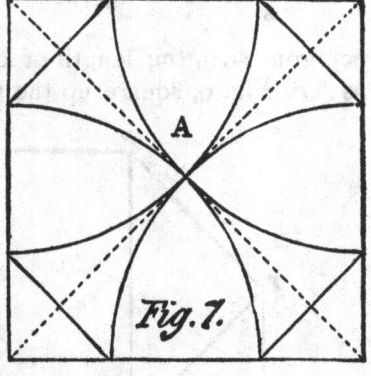

Fig. 7.

The method of obtaining the joint cut or miter for an octagon is shown at Fig. 8, where the angle ABC, is divided into two equal angles by the following process: From B, with any radius, strike an arc, giving A and C as centers, from which, with any radius, make an intersection, as shown, and through it from B, draw a line, and the proper angle for the cut is obtained, the dotted line being the angle sought. By this method of bisecting an angle, no matter how obtuse or acute it may be, the miter joint or cut may be obtained. This is a very useful problem, as it is often called into requisition for cutting mouldings in panels and other work, where the angles are not square, as in stair spandrils and raking wainscot.

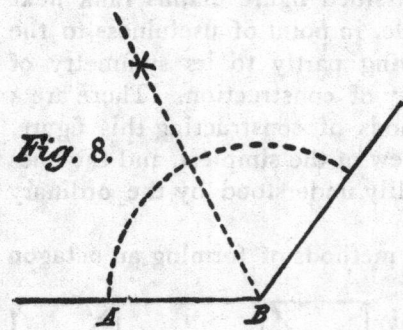

Fig. 8.

To construct an octagon when the length of one of its sides is given, as AB, Fig. 9, square up the two lines, AN, BF, then

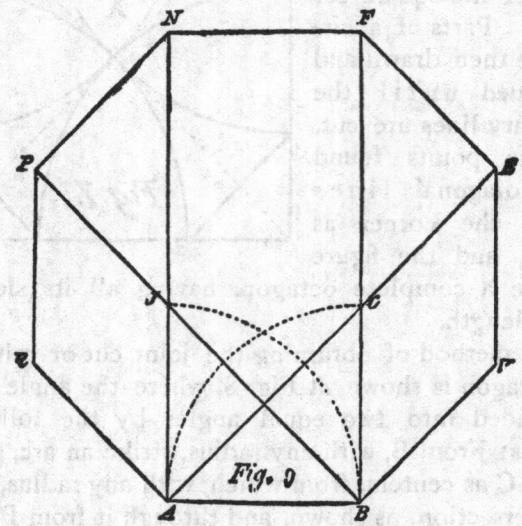

Fig. 9.

take AB as radius with A and B as centers, and draw the arcs, cutting the two lines at C and J;

draw from AB, through CJ, and again from A draw
parallel with BJ; then draw from B parallel with
AC; make BV and CF equal AB; join EV; make
CF equal CA; square over FN; join FE; draw NP
parallel with AC, then join PR, and the figure is
complete.

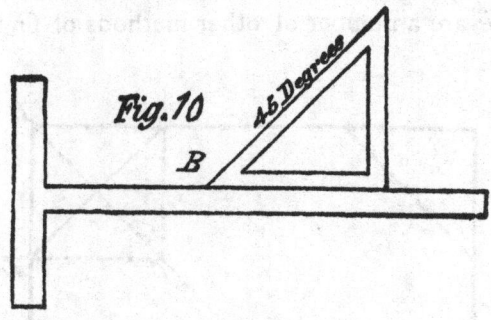

Fig. 10

As the sides of all regular octagons are at an angle
of 45° with each other, it follows that an octagon may
be readily constructed by making use of a set square
having its third side to correspond with an angle of
45°, for by extending the line AB, and laying the set
square on the line with one point at B, as shown in
Fig. 10, the line BV, Fig. 9, can be drawn, and when
made the same length as BV, the process can be
repeated to VE; and so on until all the points have
been connected.

Suppose we have a square stick of timber 12 x 12
inches, and any length, and we wish to make it an octagon; we will first be obliged to find the gauge points
so as to mark the stick, to snap a chalk line on it so as
to tell how much of the corners must be removed in
order to give to the stick eight sides of equal width.
We do this as follows: Make a drawing the size of a

section of the timber, that is, twelve inches square, then draw a line from corner to corner as AB, Fig. 11, and make AC equal in length to AD, which is twelve inches; square over from C to K; set your gauge to BK, and run your lines to this gauge, and remove the corners off to lines, and the stick will then be an octagon having eight equal sides.

There are a number of other methods of finding the

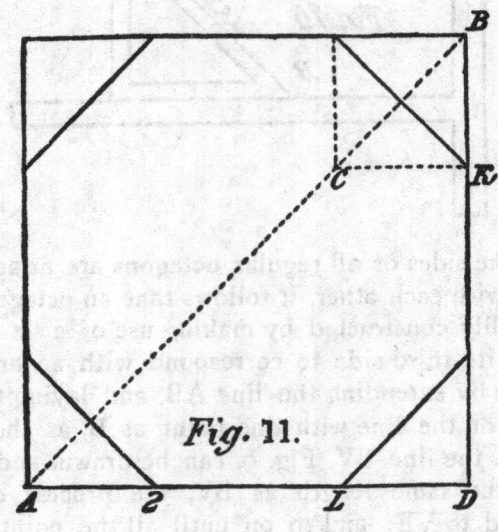

Fig. 11.

gauge points, some of which I may describe further on, but I think I have dwelt long enough on polygons to enable the reader to lay off all the examples given. The polygons not described are so seldom made use of in carpentry, that no authority that I am aware of describes them when writing for the practical workman; though in nearly all works on theoretical geom-

etry the figures are given with all their qualities. If
the solution of any of the problems offered in this
work requires a description and explanation of polygons with a greater number of sides than eight, such
explanation will be given.

CHAPTER III

SOME STRAIGHT LINE SOLUTIONS

The greatest number of difficult problems in carpentry are susceptible of solution by the use of straight lines and a proper application of the steel square, and

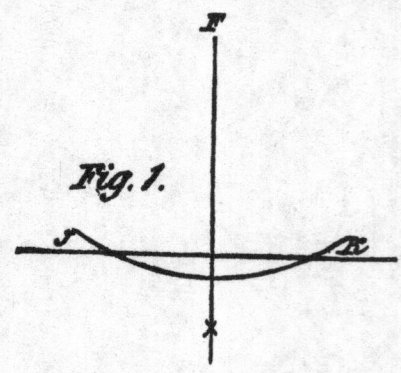

Fig. 1.

in this chapter I will endeavor to show the reader how some of the problems may be solved, though it is not intended to offer a treatise on the subject of the utility of the steel square, as that subject has been treated at length in other works, and another and exhaustive work is now in preparation; but it is thought no work on carpentry can be complete without, at least, showing some of the solutions that may be accomplished by the proper use of this wonderful instrument, and this will be done as we proceed.

One of the most useful problems is one that enables us to make a perpendicular line on any given straight line without the aid of a square. This is obtained as follows: Let JK, Fig. 1, be the given straight line, and make F any point in the square or perpendicular line required. From F with any radius, strike the are cutting in JK; with these points as centers, and any radius greater than half JK, make intersection as shown, and from this point draw a line to F, and this line is the perpendicular required. Foundations, and other works on a large scale are often "squared" or laid out by this method, or by another, which I will submit later.

In a previous illustration I showed how to bisect an angle by using the compasses and straight lines, so as to obtain the proper joints or miters for the angles. At Fig. 2, I show how this may be done by the aid of the steel square alone, as follows: The angle is obtuse, and may be that of an octagon or pentagon or other polygon. Mark any two points on the angle, as DN,

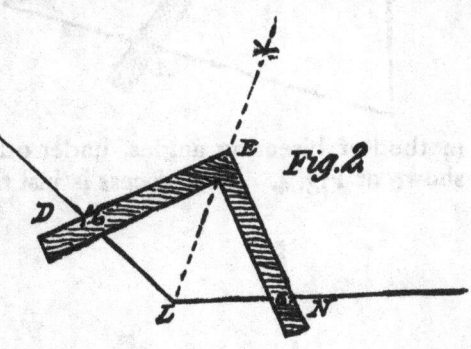

Fig. 2

equally distant from the point of angle L; apply the steel square as shown, keeping the distance EN and ED the same, then a line running through the angle L and the point of the square E will be the line sought.

To bisect an acute angle by the same method, proceed as follows: Mark any two points AC, Fig. 3, equally distant from B; apply the steel square as shown, keeping its sides on AC; then the distance on each side of the square being equal from the corner gives it for a point, through which draw a line from B, and the angle is divided. Both angles shown are divided by the same method, making the intersection in P the center of the triangle. The main thing to be considered in this solution is to have the distances A and C equal from the point B; also an equal distance from the point or toe of the square to the points of contact C and A on the boundary lines.

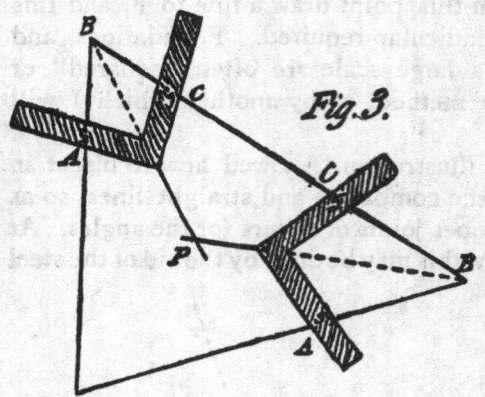

A repetition of the same method of bisecting angles, under other conditions, is shown at Fig. 4. The process is just the same, and the

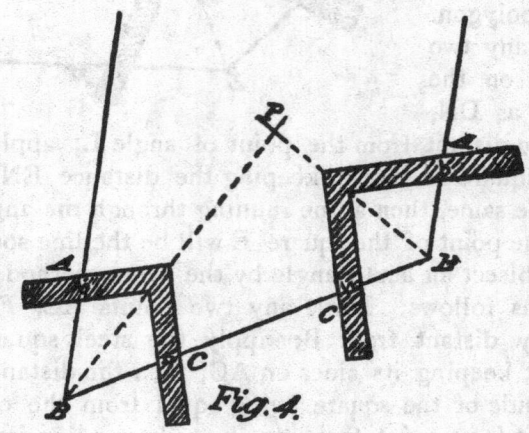

reference letters are also the same, so any further explanation is unnecessary.

To get a correct miter cut, or, in other words, an angle of 45°, on a board, make either of the points A or C, Fig. 5, the starting point for the miter, on the edge of the board, then apply the square as shown, keeping the figure 12″ at A or C, as the case may be, with the figure 12″ on the

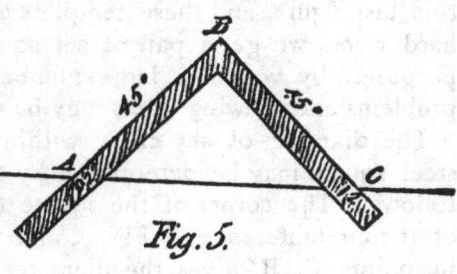

Fig. 5.

other blade of the square on the edge of the board as shown; then the slopes on the edge of the square from A to B and C to B, will form angles of 45° with the base line AC. This problem is useful from many points of view, and will often suggest itself to the workman in his daily labor.

To construct a figure showing on one side an angle of 30° and on the other an angle of 60°, by the use of

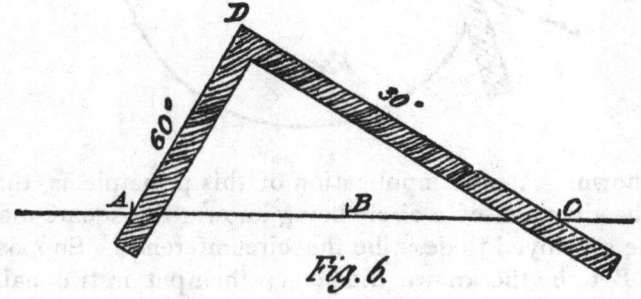

Fig. 6.

the steel square, we go to work as follows: Mark on the edge of a board two equal spaces as AB, BC, Fig. 6. apply the square, keeping its blade on AC and making

AD equal AB; then the angles 30° and 60° are
formed as shown. If we make a templet cut exactly
as shown in Fig. 5, also a templet cut as shown in
this last figure, and these templets are made of some
hard wood, we get a pair of set squares for drawing
purposes, by which a large number of geometrical
problems and drawing kinks may be wrought out.

The diameter of any circle within the range of the
steel square may be determined by the instrument as
follows: The corner of the square touching any part
of the circumference A, Fig. 7, and the blade cutting
in points C, B, gives the diameter of the circle as

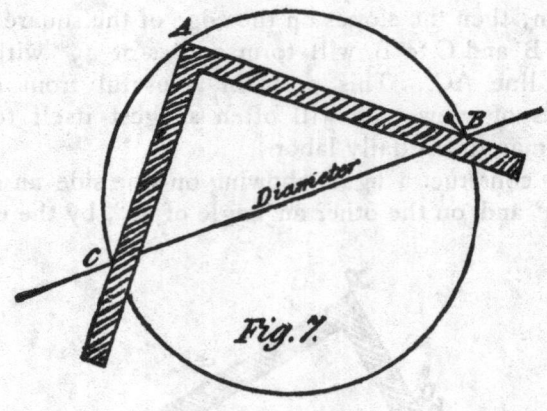

Fig. 7.

shown. Another application of this principle is, that
the diameter of a circle being known, the square may
be employed to describe the circumference. Suppose
CB to be the known diameter; then put in two nails
as shown, one at B and the other at C, apply the
square, keeping its edges firmly against the nails, con-
tinually sliding it around, then the point of the square
A will describe half the circumference. Apply the

square to the other side of the nails, and repeat the process, when the whole circle will be described. This problem may be applied to the solution of many others of a similar nature.

At Fig. 8, I show how an equilateral triangle may be obtained by the use of a square. Draw the line

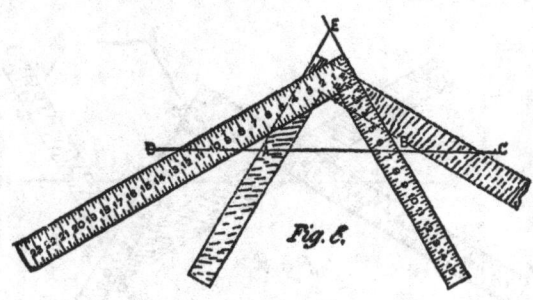

Fig. 8.

DC; take 12 on the blade and 7 on the tongue; mark on the tongue for one side of the figure. Make the distance from D to A equal to the desired length of one side of the figure. Reverse the square, placing it as shown by the dotted lines in the sketch, bringing 7 of the tongue against the point A. Scribe along the tongue, producing the line until it intersects the first line drawn in the point E, then AEB will be an equilateral triangle. A method of describing a hexagon by the square, is shown at Fig. 9, which is quite simple. Draw the line GH; lay off the required length of one side on this line, as DE. Place the square as before, with 12 of the blade and 7 of the tongue against the line GH; placing 7 of the tongue against the point D, scribe along the tongue for the side DC. Place the square as shown by the dotted lines; bringing 7 of the tongue against the point E, scribe the side EF. Continue in this way until the other half of the figure is drawn. All is shown by FABC.

The manner of bisecting angles has been shown in Figs. 2, 3 and 4 of the present chapter, so that it is not necessary to repeat the process at this time.

The method of describing an octagon by using the square, is shown at Fig. 10. Lay off a square

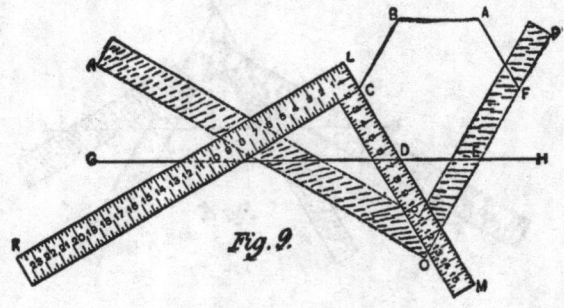

Fig. 9.

section with any length of sides, as AB. Bisect this side and place the square as shown on the side

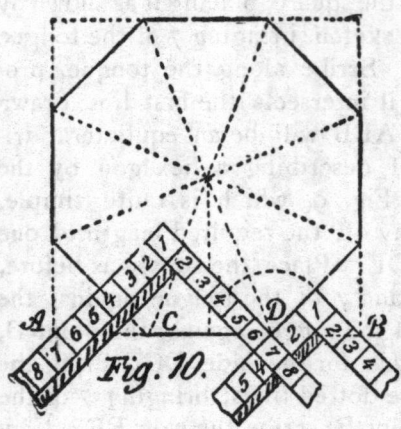

Fig. 10.

AB, with the length bisected on the blade and tongue; then the tongue cuts the side at the point to gauge for the piece to be removed. To find the size of square required for an octagonal prism, when the side is given: Let CD equal the given side; place the square on the line of the side, with one-half of the side on the blade and tongue; then the tongue cuts the line at the point B, which determines the size of the square, and the piece to be removed.

A near approxima-
tion to the length or
stretch-out of a cir-
cumference of a cir-
cle may be obtained
by the aid of the
steel square and a
straight line, as fol-
lows: Take three
diameters of the

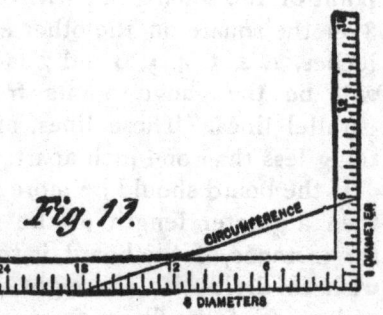

Fig. 11.

circle and measure up the side of the blade of the square, as shown at Fig. 11, and fifteen-sixteenths of one diameter on the tongue. From these two points

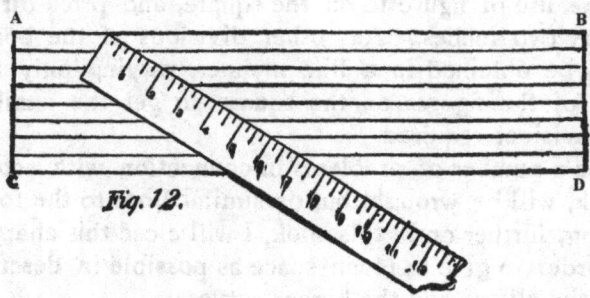

Fig. 12.

draw a diagonal, and the length of this diagonal will be the length or stretch-out of the circumference nearly.

If it is desired to divide a board or other substance into any given number of equal parts, without going through the process of calculation, it may readily be done by the aid of the square or even a pocket rule. Let AC, BD, Fig. 12, be the width of the board or other material, and this width is seven and one-quarter inches, and we wish to divide it into eight equal parts. Lay on the board diagonally, with furthermost point of the square fair with one edge, and the mark 8 on the square on the other edge; then prick off the inches, 1, 2, 3, 4, 5, 6 and 7 as shown, and these points will be the gauge points from which to draw the parallel lines. These lines, of course, will be something less than one inch apart.

If the board should be more than eight inches wide, then a greater length of the square may be used, as for instance, if the board is ten inches wide, and we wish to divide it into eight equal parts, we simply make use of the figure 12 on the square instead of 8, and prick off the spaces every one and a half inches on the square. If the board is more than 12 inches wide, and we require the same number of divisions, we make use of figure 16 on the square, and prick off at every two inches. Any other divisions of the board may be obtained in a like manner, varying only the use of the figures on the square to get the number of divisions required.

As a number of problems in connection with actual work, will be wrought out on similar lines to the foregoing, further on in this book, I will close this chapter in order to give as much space as possible in describing the ellipse and the higher curves.

CHAPTER IV

ELLIPSES, SPIRALS, AND OTHER CURVES

The ellipse, next to the circle, is the curve the carpenter will be confronted with more than any other, and while it is not intended to discuss all, or even a major part, of the properties and characteristics of this curve, I will endeavor to lay before the reader all in connection with it that he may be called upon to deal with.

According to geometricians, an ellipse is a conic section formed by cutting a cone through the curved surface, neither parallel to the base nor making a subcontrary section, so that the ellipse like the circle is a curve that returns within itself, and completely encloses a space. One of the principal and useful properties of the ellipse is, that the rectangle under the two segments of a diameter is as the square of the ordinate. In the circle, the same ratio obtains, but the rectangle under the two segments of the diameter becomes equal to the square of the ordinate.

It is not necessary that we enter into a learned description of the relations of the ellipse to the cone and the cylinder, as the ordinary carpenter may never have any practical use of such knowledge, though, if he have time and inclination, such knowledge would avail him much and tend to broaden his ideas. Suffice for us to show the various methods by which this curve may be obtained, and a few of its applications to actual work.

One of the simplest and most correct methods of describing an ellipse, is by the aid of two pins, a string and a lead-pencil, as shown at Fig. 1. Let FB be the major or longest axis, or diameter, and DC the minor or shorter axis or diameter, and E and K the two foci.

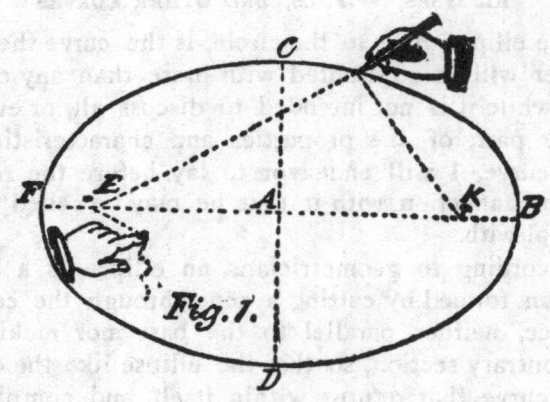

Fig. 1.

These two points are obtained by taking the half of the major axis AB or FA, on the compasses, and, standing one point at D, cut the points E and K on the line FB, and at these points insert the pins at E and K as shown. Take a string as shown by the dotted lines and tie to the pins at K, then stand the pencil at C and run the string round it and carry the string to the pin E, holding it tight and winding it once or twice around the pin, and then holding the string with the finger. Run the pencil around, keeping the loop of the string on the pencil and it will guide the latter in the formation of the curve as shown. When one-half of the ellipse is formed, the string may be used for the other half, commencing the curve at F or B, as the case may be. This is commonly called "a gardener's oval," because gardeners make use of it for forming ornamental beds for flowers, or in making curves for walks, etc., etc. This method of forming the curve, is based on the well-known property of the ellipse that the sum of any two lines drawn from the foci to their circumference is the same.

Another method of projecting an ellipse is shown at Fig. 2, by using a trammel. This is an instrument consisting of two principal parts, the fixed part

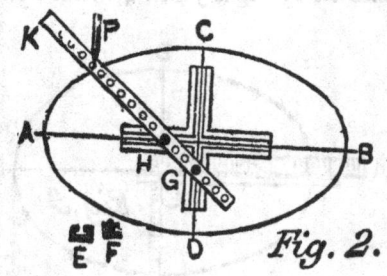

Fig. 2.

in the form of a cross as CD, AB, and the movable tracer HG. The fixed piece is made of two triangular bars or pieces of wood of equal thickness, joined together so as to be in the same plane. On one side of the frame when made, is a groove forming a right-angled cross; the groove is shown in the section at E. In this groove, two studs are fitted to slide easily, the studs having a section same as shown at F. These studs are to carry the tracer and guide it on proper lines. The tracer may have a sliding stud on the end to carry a lead-pencil, or it may have a number of small holes passed through it as shown in the cut, to carry the pencil. To draw an ellipse with this instrument, we measure off half the distance of the major axis from the pencil to the stud G, and half the minor axis from the pencil point to the stud H, then swing the tracer round, and the pencil will describe the ellipse required. The studs have little projections on their tops that fit easily into the holes in the tracer, but this may be done away with, and two brad awls or pins may be thrust through the tracer and into the studs, and then proceed with the work. With this instrument an ellipse may easily be described.

Another method, based on the trammel principle, is shown at Figs. 3 and 4, where the steel square is substi-

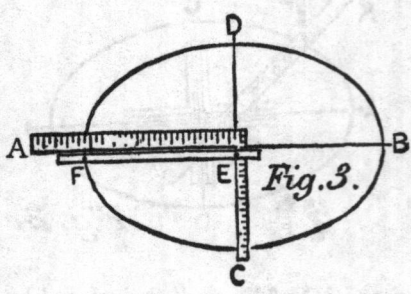

Fig.3.

tuted for the instrument shown in Fig 2. Draw the line AB, bisecting it at right angles, draw CD. Set off these lines the required dimensions of the ellipse to be drawn. Place an ordinary square as

shown. Lay the straightedge lengthwise of the figure, as shown in Fig. 3, and putting a pin at E against the square, place the pencil at F, at a point corresponding with the one of the figure. Next place the straight-

edge, as shown in Fig. 4, crosswise of the figure, and bring the pencil F to a point corresponding to one side of the figure, and set a pin at G. By keeping the two pins E and G against the square,

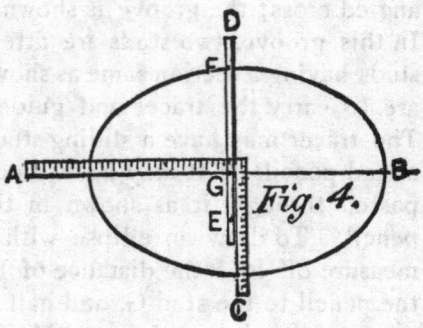

Fig. 4.

and moving the straightedge so as to carry the pencil from side to side, one-quarter of the figure will be struck. By placing the square in the same relative position in each of the other three-quarters, the other parts may be struck.

A method,—and one that is very useful for many purposes,—of drawing an ellipse approximately, is shown in Fig. 5. It is convenient and may be applied to hundreds of purposes, some of which will be illustrated as we proceed.

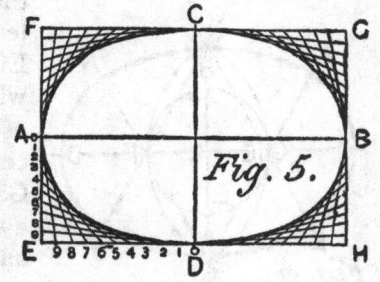

Fig. 5.

To apply this method, work as follows: First lay off the length of the required figure, as shown by AB, Fig. 5, and the width as shown by CD. Construct a parallelogram that shall have its sides tangent to the figure at the points of its length and width, all as shown by EFGH. Subdivide one-half of the end of the parallelogram into any convenient number of equal parts, as shown at AE, and one-half of its side in the same manner, as shown by ED. Connect these two sets of points by intersecting lines in the manner shown in the engraving. Repeat the operation for each of the other corners of the parallelogram. A line traced through the inner set of intersections will be a very close approximation to an ellipse.

There are a number of ways of describing figures that approximate ellipses by using the compasses, some of them being a near approach to a true ellipse, and it is well that the workman should acquaint himself with the methods of their construction. It is only necessary that a few examples be given in this work, as a knowledge of these shown will lead the way to the construction of others when required. The method exhibited in Fig. 6 is, perhaps, the most useful of any employed by workmen, than all other methods combined. To describe it, lay off the length CD, and at right angles to it and bisecting it lay off the width AB. On the larger diameter lay off a space equal to the shorter diameter or width, as shown by DE. Divide

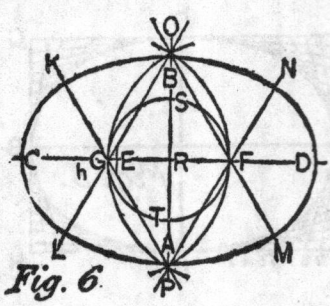

the remainder of the length or larger diameter EC into three equal parts; with two of these parts as a radius, and R as a center, strike the circle GSFT. Then, with F as a center and FG as radius, and G as center and GF as radius, strike the arcs as

Fig. 6

shown, intersecting each other and cutting the line drawn through the shorter diameter at O and P respectively From O, through the points G and F, draw OL and OM, and likewise from P through the same points draw PK and PN. With O as center and OA as radius, strike the arc LM, and with P as center and with like radius, or PB which is the same, strike the arc KN. With F and G as centers, and with FD and CG which are the same, for radii,

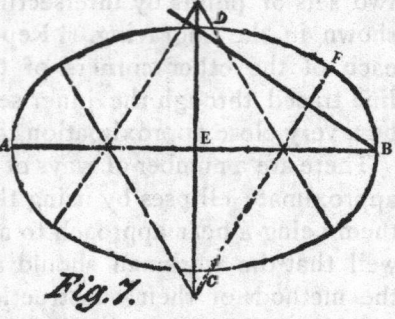

Fig. 7.

strike the arcs NM and KL respectively, thus completing the figure. Another method in which the centers for the longer arc are outside the curve lines, is shown at Fig 7. Let AB be the length and CD the breadth; join BD through the center of the line EB, and at

right angles to BD draw the line CF indefinitely; then at the points of intersection of the dotted lines will be found the points to describe the required ellipse.

A method of describing an ellipse by the intersection of lines is shown at Fig. 8, and which may be applied to any kind of an ellipse with longer or shorter axis. Let WX be the given major axis, and

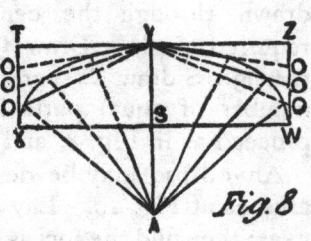

Fig. 8

YA the minor axis drawn at right angles to and at the center of each other.

Through Y parallel to WX draw ZT, parallel to AY, draw WZ and XT; divide WZ and XT into any number of equal parts, say four, and draw lines from the points

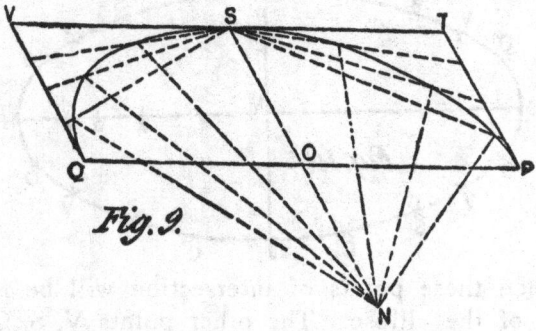

Fig. 9.

of division OOO, etc., to Y. Divide WS and XS each into the same number of equal parts as WZ and XT, and draw lines from A through these last points of division intersecting the lines drawn from OOO, etc., and at these intersections trace the semi-ellipse WYX. The other half of the ellipse may be described in the same manner.

To describe an ellipse from given diameters, by intersection of lines, even though the figure be on a rake: Let SN and QP, Fig. 9, be the given diameters, drawn through the centers of each other at any required angle. Draw QV and PT parallel to SN, through S draw TV parallel to QP. Divide into any number of equal parts PT, QV, PO, and OQ; then proceed as in Fig. 8, and the work is complete

An ellipse may be described by the intersection of arcs as at Fig. 10. Lay off HG and JK as the given axes; then find the foci as described in Fig. 1. Between L and L and the center M mark any number of points at pleasure as 1, 2, 3, 4. Upon L and L with H1 for radius describe arcs at O, O, O, O; upon L and with C1 for radius describe intersecting arcs at O, O, O, and

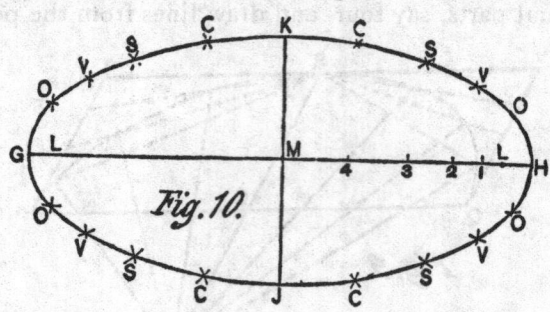

Fig. 10.

O; then these points of intersection will be in the curve of the ellipse. The other points V, S, C, are found in the same manner, as follows: For the point V take H2 for one radius, and G2 for the other; S is found by taking H3 for one radius, and G3 for the other; C is found in like manner, with H4 for one radius, and G4 for the last radius, using the foci for centers as at first. Trace a curve through the points H, O, V, S, C, K, etc., to complete the ellipse

It frequently happens that the carpenter has to make

the radial lines for the masons to get their arches in proper form, as well as making the centers for the same, and, as the obtaining of such lines for elliptical work is very tedious, I illustrate a device that may be employed that will obviate a great deal of labor in producing such lines.   The instrument and the method of using it is exhibited at Fig. 11 and marked Ee.   The semi-ellipse HI, or xx, may be described with a string or strings, the outer line being described by use of a string fastened to the foci F and D, with the extreme point at E; and the inner line, with the string being fastened at A and B, with the pencil point in the tightened string at O.   The sectional line LKJ shows the center of the arch, and the lines SSS are at

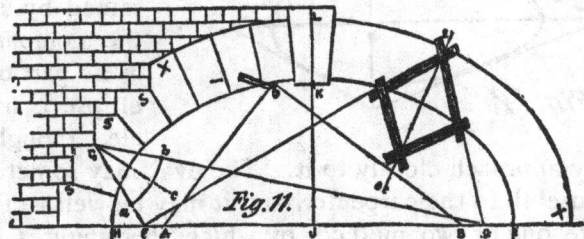

Fig. 11.

right angles with this vertical line.   The usual method of finding the normal by geometry is shown at GABC, but the more practical method of finding it is by the use of the instrument, where Ee shows the normal. I believe the device is of French origin, and I give a translation of a description and use of the instrument: "It is made of four pieces of lath or metal put together so as to form a perfect rectangle and having its joints loose, as shown in the diagram.   Considering that the most perfect elliptical curve is that described by a string from the foci (foyer) of the ellipse, draw the profiles of the extrados and intrados, as shown in Fig. 11, where your joints are to be, then take your string, draw it to the point marked as at E, adjust two sides of your instrument to correspond with the lines of the string, then, from the point marked, draw a line passing through the two angles, E and e, and the line Ee will be the normal or the radial line sought.''

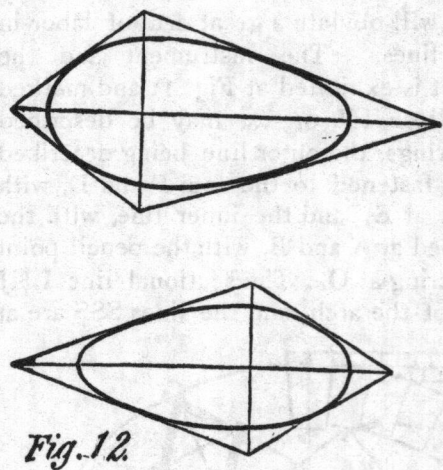

Fig. 12

The oval is not an ellipse, nor are any of the figures obtained by using the compasses, as no part of an ellipse is a circle, though it may approach closely to it. The oval may sometimes be useful to the carpenter, and it may be well to illustrate one or two methods by which these figures may be described.

Let us describe a diamond or lozenge-shaped figure, such as shown at Fig. 12, and then trace a curve inside of it as shown, touching the four sides of the figure, and a beautiful egg-shaped curve will be formed. For effect we may elongate the lozenge or shorten it at will, placing the short diameter at any point. This form of oval is much used by turners and lathe men generally, in the formation of pillars, balusters, newel-posts and turned ornamental work generally.

An egg-shaped oval may also be inscribed in a figure having two unequal but parallel sides, both of which are bisected by the same line, perpendicular to both as shown in Fig. 13. These few examples are quite sufficient to satisfy the requirements of the workman, as they give the key by which he may construct any oval he may ever be called upon to form.

I have dwelt rather lengthily on the subject of the ellipse because of its being rather difficult for the workman to deal with, and it is meet he should acquire a fair knowledge of the methods of constructing it. It is not my province to enter into all the details of the properties of this very intersecting figure, as the workman can find many of these in any good work on mensuration, if he should require more. I may say here, however, that geometricians so far have failed to discover

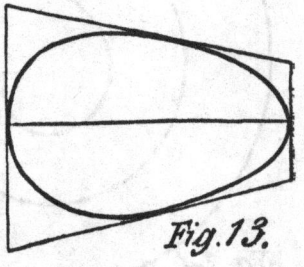

Fig. 13.

any scientific method of forming parallel ellipses, so that while the inside or outside lines of an ellipse can be obtained by any of the methods I have given, the parallel line must be obtained either by gauging the width of the material or space required, or must be obtained by "pricking off" with compasses or other aid. I thought it best to mention this as many a young man has spent hours in trying to solve the unsolvable problem when using the pins, pencil and string.

There are a number of other curves the carpenter will sometimes meet in daily work, chief among these being the scroll or spiral, so it will be well for him to have some little knowledge of its structure. A true spiral can be drawn by unwinding a piece of string that has been wrapped around a cone, and this is probably the method adopted by the ancients in the formation of the beautiful Ionic spirals they produced. A spiral drawn by this method is shown at Fig. 14. This was formed by using two lead-pencils which had been sharpened by one of those patent sharpeners and which gave them the shape seen in Fig. 15. A piece of string was then tied

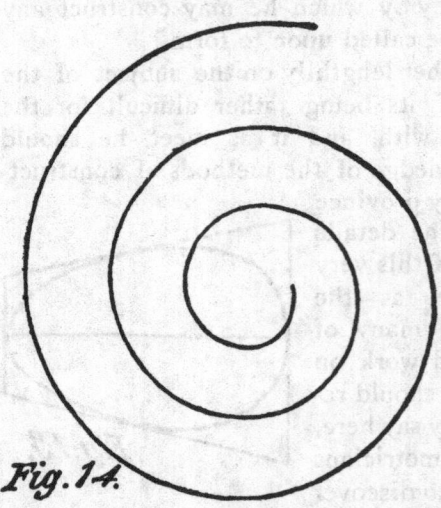

Fig. 14.

tightly around the pencil, and one end was wound round the conical end, so as to lie in notches made in one of the pencils; the point of a second pencil was pierced through the string at a convenient point near the first pencil, completing the arrangement shown in Fig. 15. To draw the spiral the pencils must be kept vertical, the point of the first being held firmly in the hole of the spiral, and the second pencil must then be carried around the first, the distance between the two increasing regularly, of course, as the string unwinds.

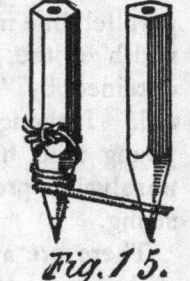

Fig. 15.

This is a rough-and-ready apparatus, but a true

spiral can be described by it in a very few minutes. By means of a larger cone, spirals of any size can, of course, be drawn, and that portion of the spiral can be used which conforms to the required height.

Another similar method is shown in Fig. 16, only in this case the string unwinds from a spool on a fixed center A, D, B. Make loop E in the end of the thread, in which place a pencil as shown. Hold the spool firmly and move the pencil around it, unwinding the thread. A curve will be described, as shown in the lines. It is evident that the proportions of the figure are determined by the size of the spool. Hence a larger or smaller spool is to be used, as circumstances require.

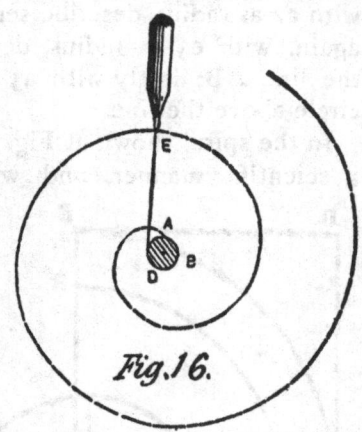

Fig. 16.

A simple method of forming a figure that corresponds to the spiral somewhat, is shown in Fig. 17. This is drawn from two centers only, a and e, and if the distance between these centers is not too great, a fairly smooth appearance will be given to the figure. The method

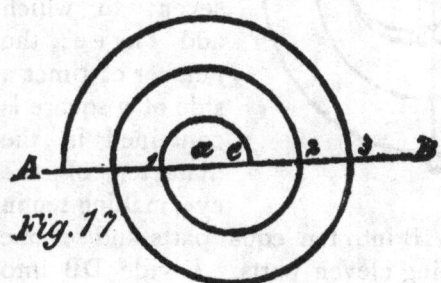

Fig. 17

of describing is simple. Take a1 as radius and
describe a semi-circle; then take e1 and describe
semi-circle 12 on the lower side of the line AB. Then
with a2 as radius describe semi-circle above the line;
again, with e3 as radius, describe semi-circle below
the line AB; lastly with a3 as radius describe semi-
circle above the line.

In the spiral shown at Fig. 18 we have one drawn in
a scientific manner, and which can be formed to

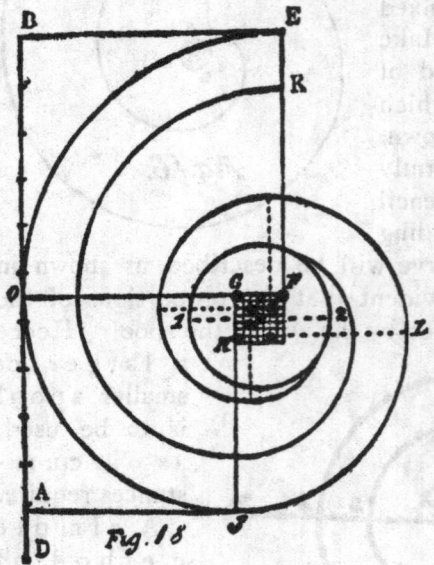

Fig. 18

dimensions. T o
draw it, proceed
as follows: Let
BA be the given
breadth, and the
number of revolu-
tions, say one and
three-fourths; now
multiply one and
three - fourths by
four, which equals
seven; to which
add t h r e e, the
number of times a
side of a square is
contained in the
diameter of the
eye, making ten in

all. Now divide AB into ten equal parts and set one
from A to D, making eleven parts. Divide DB into
two equal parts at O, then OB will be the radius of the
first quarter OF, FE; make the side of the square, as
shown at GF, equal to one of the eleven parts, and
divide the number of parts obtained by multiplying
the revolutions by four, which is seven; make the

diameter of the eye, 12, equal to three of the eleven parts. With F as a center and E as a radius make the quarter EO; then, with G as a center, and GO as a radius, mark the quar-ter OJ. Take the next center at H and HJL in the quarter; so keep on for centers, drop-ping one part each time as shown by the dotted angles. Let EK be any width de-sired, and carry it around on the same centers.

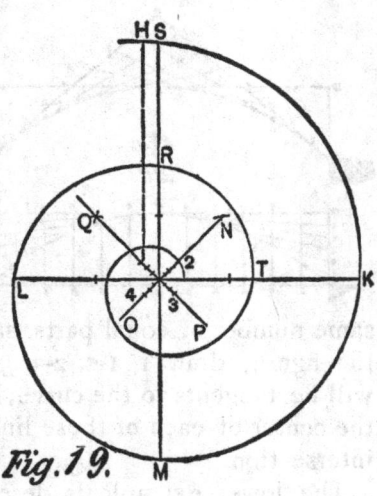

Fig. 19.

Another method of obtaining a spiral by arcs of circles is shown at Fig. 19, which may be confined to given dimensions. Proceed as follows: Draw SM and LK at right angles; at the intersection of these lines bisect the angles by the lines NO and QP; and on NO and QP from the intersection each way set off three equal parts as shown. On 1 as center and 1H as radius, describe the arc HK, on 2 describe the arc KM, on 3 describe the arc ML, on 4 describe the arc LR. The fifth center to describe the arc RT is under 1 on the line QP; and so proceed to complete the curve.

There are a few other curves that may occasionally prove useful to the workman, and I submit an example or two of each in order that, should occasion arise where such a curve or curves are required, they may be met with a certain amount of knowledge of the subject.

The first is the parabola, a curve sometimes used in bridge work or similar construction. Two examples of the curve are shown at Fig. 20, and the methods of

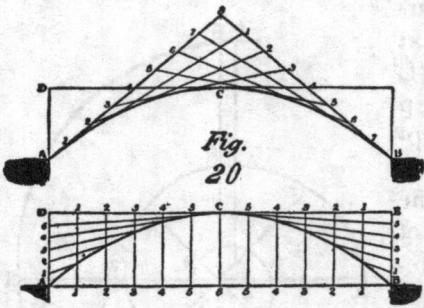

describing t h e m. The upper one is drawn as follows:

1. Draw C8 perpendicular to AB, and make it equal to AD.

Next, join A8 and B8, and divide both lines into the same number of equal parts, say 8; number them as in the figure; draw 1, 1-2, 2-3, 3, etc., then these lines will be tangents to the curve; trace the curve to touch the center of each of those lines between the points of intersection.

The lower example is described thus: 1. Divide AD and BE, into any number of equal parts; CD and CE into a similar number.

2. Draw 1, 1-2, 2, etc., parallel to AD, and from the points of division in AD and BE, draw lines to C. The points of intersection of the respective lines are points in the curve.

The curves found, as in these figures, are quicker at the crown than a true circular segment; but, where the rise of the arch is not more than one-tenth of the span, the variation cannot be perceived.

A raking example of this curve is shown in Fig. 21, and the method of describing it: Let AC be the ordinate or vertical line, and DB the axis, and B its vertex; produce the axis to E, and make BE equal to DB; join EC. EA, and divide them each into the same number of equal parts, and number the divisions as shown of the figures. Join the corresponding divisions by the lines 11, 22, etc., and their intersections will product the contour of the curve.

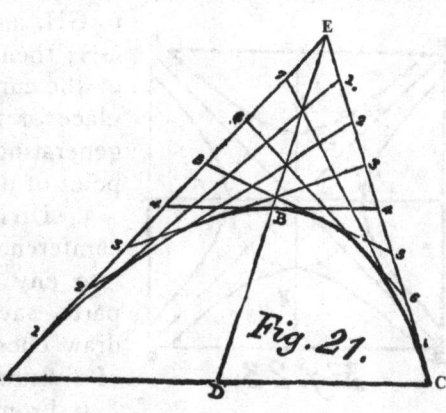

Fig. 21.

The hyperbola is somewhat similar in appearance to the parabola but it has properties peculiar to itself. It is a figure not much used in carpentry, but it may be well to refer to it briefly: Suppose there be two right equal cones, Fig. 22, having the same axis, and cut by a plane Mm, Nm, parallel to that axis, the sections MAN, mna, which result, are hyperbolas. In place of two cones opposite to each other, geometricians sometimes suppose four cones, which join on the lines EH, GB, Fig. 23, and of which axis form two right lines, Ff, F'f', crossing the center C in the same plane.

To describe a cycloid: The cycloid is the curve described by a point in the circumference of a circle rolling on a straight line, and is described as follows:

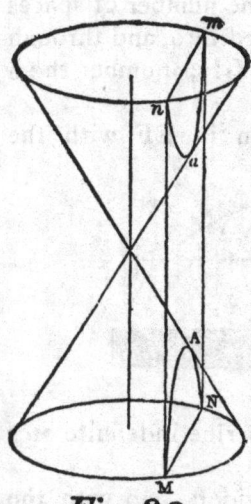

Fig. 22.

1. Let GH, Fig. 24, be the edge of a straight ruler, and C the center of the generating circle.

2. Through C draw the diameter AB perpendicular

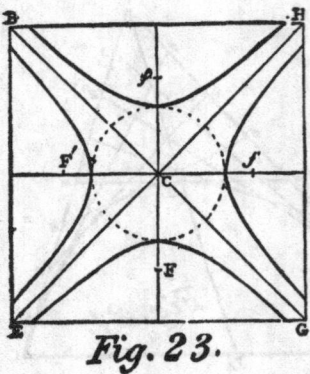

Fig. 23.

to GH, and EF parallel to GH; then AB is the height of the curve, and EF is the place of the center of the generating circle at every point of its progress.

3. Divide the semi-circumference from B to A into any number of equal parts, say 8, and from A draw chords to the points of division.

4. From C, with a space in the dividers equal to one of the divisions on the circle, step off on each side the same number of spaces as the semi-circumference is divided into, and through the points draw perpendiculars to GH; number them as in the diagram.

5. From the points of division in EF with the

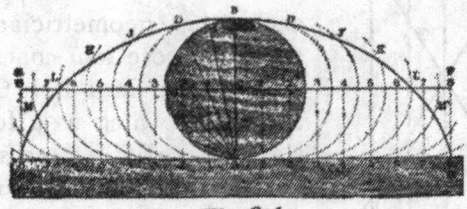

Fig. 24.

radius of the generating circle, describe indefinite arcs as shown by the dotted lines.

6. Take the chord A1 in the dividers, and with the foot at 1 and 1 on the line GH, cut the indefinite arcs

described from 1 and 1 respectively at D and D', then D and D' are points in the curve.

7 With the chord A2, from 2 and 2 in GH, cut the indefinite arcs in J and J', with the chord A3, from 3 and 3, cut the arcs in K and K' and apply the other chords in the same manner, cutting the arcs in LM, etc.

8. Through the points so found trace the curve.

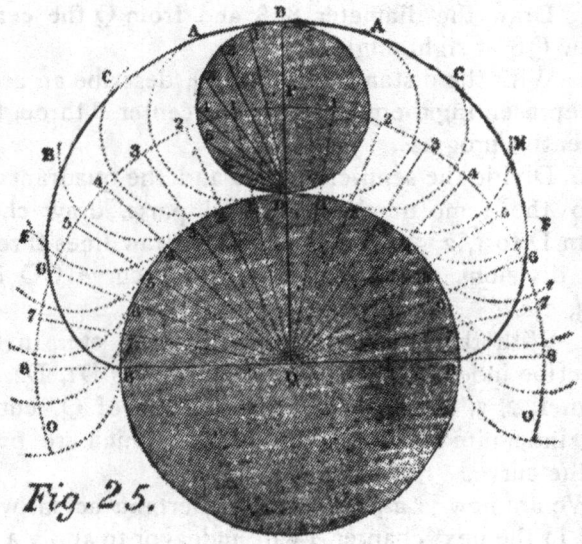

Fig. 25.

Each of the indefinite arcs in the diagram represents the circle at that point of its revolution, and the points D,J,K, etc., the position of the generating point B at each place. This curve is frequently used for the arches of bridges, its proportions are always constant, viz.: the span is equal to the circumference of the generating circle and the rise equal to the diameter. Cycloidal arches are frequently constructed which are

not true cycloids, but approach that curve in a greater
or less degree.

The epicycloidal curve is formed by the revolution
of a circle round a circle, either within or without its
circumference, and described by a point B, Fig. 25, in
the circumference of the revolving circle, and Q of the
stationary circle.

The method of finding the points in the curve is here
given:

1. Draw the diameter 8, 8 and from Q the center,
draw QB at right angles to 8, 8.

2. With the distance QP from Q, describe an arc O,
O representing the position of the center P throughout
its entire progress.

3. Divide the semi-circle BD and the quadrants D8
into the same number of equal parts, draw chords
from D to 1, 2, 3, etc., and from Q draw lines through
the divisions in D8 to intersect the curve OO in 1,
2, 3, etc.

4. With the radius of P from 1, 2, 3, etc., in OO,
describe indefinite arcs; apply the chords D1, D2, etc.
from 1, 2, 3, etc., in the circumference of Q, cutting
the indefinite arcs in A,C,E,F, etc., which are points
in the curve.

We are now in a position to undertake actual work,
and in the next chapter, I will endeavor to apply a part
of what has preceded to practical examples, such as
are required for every-day use.   Enough geometry has
been given to enable the workman, when he has mastered it all, to lay out any geometrical figure he may be
called upon to execute; and with, perhaps, the exception of circular and elliptical stairs and hand-railings,
which require a separate study, by what has been for-
mulated and what will follow, he should be able to execute almost any work in a scientific manner that may
be placed under his control.

PART II

PRACTICAL EXAMPLES
CHAPTER I

We are now in a position to undertake the solution of practical examples, and I will commence this department by offering a few practical solutions that will bring into use some of the work already known to the student, if he has followed closely what has been presented.

It is a part of the carpenter's duty to lay out and construct all the wooden centers required by the bricklayer and mason for turning arches over openings of all kinds; therefore, it is essential he should know as much concerning arches as will enable him to attack the problems with intelligence. I have said something of arches, in Part I but not sufficient to satisfy all the needs of the carpenter, so I supplement with the following on the same subject: Arches used in building are named according to their curves,—circular, elliptic, cycloid, parabolic, hyperbolic, etc. Arches are also known as three or four centered arches. Pointed arches are called lancet, equilateral and depressed. Voussoirs is the name given to the stones forming the arch; the central stone is called the keystone. The highest point in an arch is called the crown, the lowest the springing line, and the spaces between the crown and springing line on either side, the haunches or flanks. The under, or concave, surface of an arch is called the intrados or soffit, the upper or convex surface is called the extrados. The span of an arch is the width of the opening. The supports of an arch are called abutments, piers, or

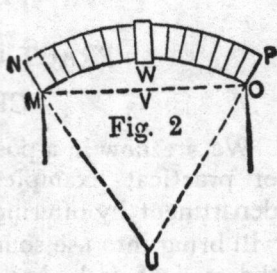

Fig. 2

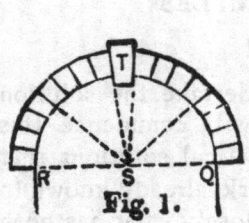

Fig. 1.

springing walls. This applies to the centers of wood, as well as to brick, stone or cement. The following six illustrations show the manner of getting the curves, as well as obtaining the radiating lines, which, as a rule, the carpenter will be asked to prepare for the mason. We take them in the following order:

Fig. 1. A Semi-circular Arch.—RQ is the span, and the line RQ is the springing line; S is the center from

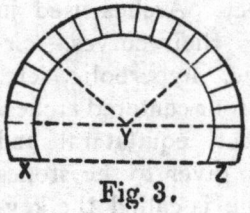

Fig. 3.

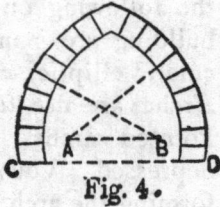

Fig. 4.

which the arch is described, and to which all joints of the voussoirs tend. T is the keystone of the arch.

Fig. 2. A Segment Arch.—U is the center from which the arch is described, and from U radiate all

the joints of the arch stones. The bed line of the arch OP or MN is called by mason builders a skewback. OM is the span, and VW is the height or versed sine of the segment arch.

Figs. 3 and 4. Moorish or Saracenic Arches, one of which is pointed. Fig. 3 is sometimes called the horseshoe arch. The springing lines DC and ZX of both arches are below the centers BA and Y.

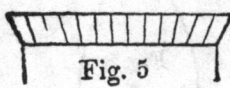

Fig. 5

Fig. 5. A Form of Lintol Called a Platband, built in this form as a substitute for a segment arch over the opening of doors or windows, generally of brick, wedge-shaped.

Fig. 6. The Elliptic Arch.—This arch is most perfect when described with the trammel, and in that case

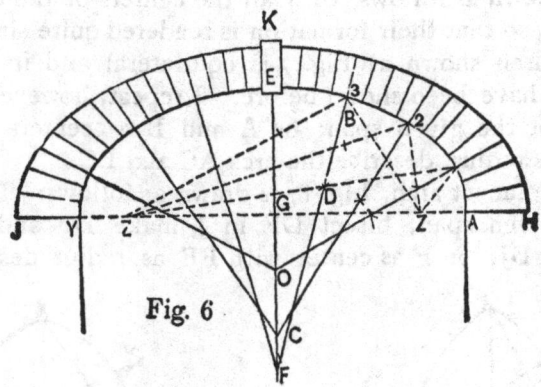

Fig. 6

the joints of the arch stones are found as follows: **Let** ZZ be the foci, and B a point on the intrados where **a** joint is required; from ZZ draw lines to B, bisect the angle at B by a line drawn through the intersecting arcs D produced for the joint to F. Joints at 1 and 2 are found in the same manner. The joints for the opposite side of the arch may be transferred as shown. The semi-axes of the ellipse, HG, GK, are in the same ratio as GE to GA. The voussoirs near the springing

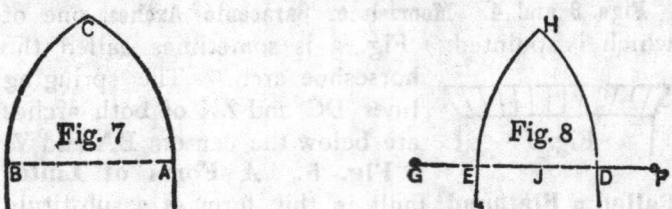

Fig. 7   Fig. 8

line of the arch are thus increased in size for greater strength. I gave a very good description of this latter arch in Part I, which see.

Another series of arches, known as Gothic arches, are shown as follows, with all the centers of the curve given, so that their formation is rendered quite simple. The arch shown at Fig. 7 is equilateral and its outlines have been shown before. I repeat, however, let AB be the given span; on A and B as centers with AB as radius, describe the arcs AC and BC.

The lancet arch, Fig. 8, is drawn as follows: DE is the given span; bisect DE in J, make DF and EG equal DJ; on F as center with FE as radius describe

Fig. 9   Fig. 10

the arc EH, and on G as center describe the arc DH. A lancet arch, not so acute as the previous one, is shown at Fig. 9. Let KL be the given span; bisect KL in M, make MP at right angles to KL and of the required height; connect LP, bisect LP by a line through the arcs R, Q produced to N; make MO equal MN; with N and O as centers, with NL for radius describe the arcs KP and LP. Fig. 10 shows a low or drop arch, and is obtained as follows: Let ST be the given span, bisect ST in W; let WX be the required height at right angles to TS; connect TX,

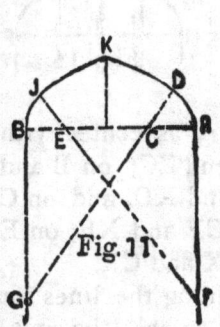

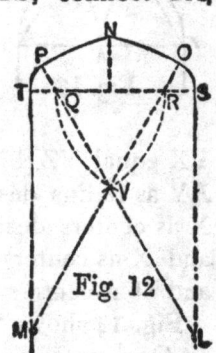

bisect TX by a line through the arcs YZ produced to V, make TU equal SV; on V and U as centers with VT as radius describe the arcs TX and SX. Another Gothic arch with a still less height is shown at Fig. 11. Suppose AB to be the given span; then divide AB into four equal parts; make AF and BG equal AB, connect FE and produce to D; with CA as radius, on C and E, describe the arcs AD and BK; on F and G as centers, describe the arcs JK and DK.

Another four-centered arch of less height is shown at Fig. 12. Let SI be the given span, divide into six equal parts; on R and Q as centers with RQ as radius, describe the arcs QV and RV, connect QV and RV and produce to L and M; on R and Q as centers with QT as radius describe the arcs TP and SO; on L and M as centers describe the arcs PN and ON.

To describe an equilateral Ogee arch, like Fig. 13, proceed as follows: Make YZ the given span; make

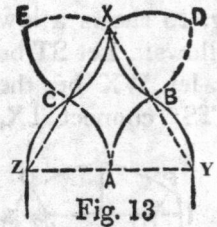

Fig. 13

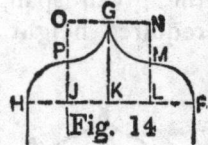

Fig. 14

YX equal YZ, bisect YZ in A; on A as center with AY as radius describe the arcs YB and ZC; on B and X as centers describe the arcs BD and XD, and on C and X as centers describe the arcs CE and XE, on E and D as centers describe the arcs BX and CX.

Fig. 14 shows the method of obtaining the lines for an Ogee arch, having a height equal to half the span. Suppose FH to be the span, divide into four equal parts, and at each of the points of division draw lines LN, KG and JO at right angles to FH; with LF for radius on L and J describe the quarter circles FM and HP; and with the same radius on O and N describe the quarter circles PG and MG.

These examples—all or any of them—can be made use of in a great number of instances. Half of the Ogee curve is often employed for veranda rafters, as for the roofs of bay-windows, for tower roofs and for bell bases, for oriel and bay-windows, and many other pieces of work the carpenter will be confronted with from time to time. They also have value as aids in forming mouldings and other ornamental work, as for example Fig. 15, which shows a moulding for a base or other like purpose. It is described as follows: Draw AB; divide it into five equal parts; make CD equal to four of these. Through D draw DF parallel with AB. From D, with DC as radius, draw the arc CE. Make EF equal to DE; divide EF into five parts; make the line above F equal to one of these; draw FG equal to six of these. From G, with radius DE, describe the arc; bisect GF, and lay the distance to H. It is the center of the curve, meeting the semi-circle described from M. Join NO, OS, and the moulding is complete.

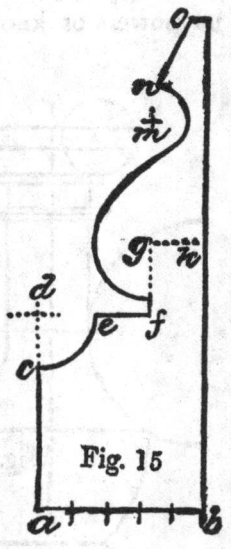

Fig. 15

The two illustrations shown at Figs. 16 and 17 will give the student an idea of the manner in which he can apply the knowledge he has now obtained, and it may not be out of place to say that with a little ingenuity he can form almost any sort of an ornament he wishes by using this knowledge. The two illustrations require no explanation as their formation is self evident. Newel posts, balusters, pedestals and other turned or wrought ornaments, may be designed easily if a little thought be brought to bear on the subject.

The steel square is a great aid in working out prob lems in carpentry, and I will endeavor to show, as briefly as possible, how the square can be applied to some difficult problems, and insure correct solutions.

It is unnecessary to give a full and complete descrip tion of the steel square. Every carpenter and joiner is supposed to be the possessor of one of these useful tools, and to have some knowledge of using it. It is not everyone, however, who thoroughly understands its powers or knows how to employ it in solving all

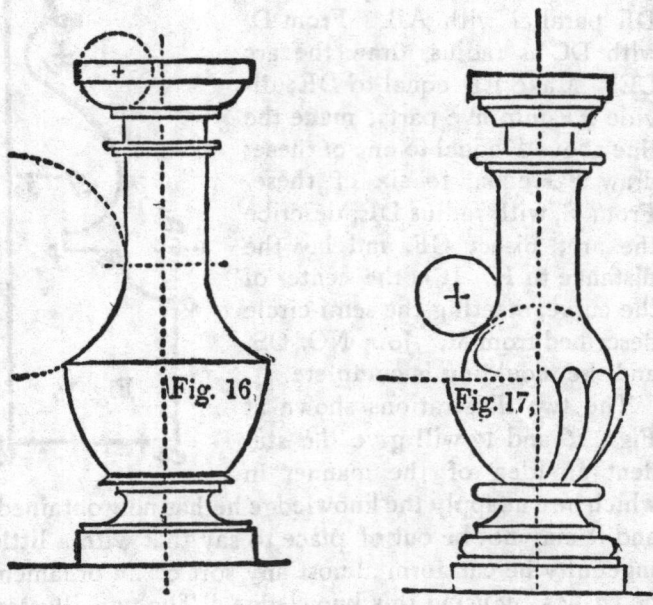

Fig. 16. Fig. 17,

the difficulties of framing, or to take advantage of its capabilities in laying out work. While it is not my intention to go deeply into this subject in this volume, as that would lengthen it out to unreasonable limits, so it must be left for a separate work, yet there are some simple things connected with the steel square, that I think every carpenter and joiner should know, no matter whether he intends to go deeper into the study of the steel square or not. One of these things is the learning to read the tool. Strange as it may appear, not over one in fifty of those who use the square are able to read it, or in other words, able to explain the meaning and uses of the figures stamped on its two sides. The following will assist the young fellows who want to master the subject.

The square consists of two arms, at right angles to each other, one of which is called the blade and which is two feet long, and generally two inches wide. The other arm is called the tongue, and may be any length from twelve to eighteen inches, and 1¼ to 2 inches in width. The best square has always a blade 2 inches wide. Squares made by firms of repute are generally perfect and require no adjusting or "squaring."

The lines and figures formed on squares of different make sometimes vary, both as to their position on the square and their mode of application, but a thorough understanding of the application of the scales and lines shown on any first-class tool, will enable the student to comprehend the use of the lines and figures exhibited on any good square.

It is supposed the reader understands the ordinary divisions and subdivisions of the foot and inch into twelfths, inches, halves, quarters, eighths and sixteenths, and that he also understands how to use that part of the square that is subdivided into twelfths of an inch. This being conceded, we now proceed to describe the various rules as shown on all good squares. Sometimes the inch is subdivided into thirty-seconds, in which the subdivision is very fine, but this scale will be found very convenient in the measurement of drawings which are made to a scale of half, quarter, one-eighth or one-sixteenth of an inch to a foot.

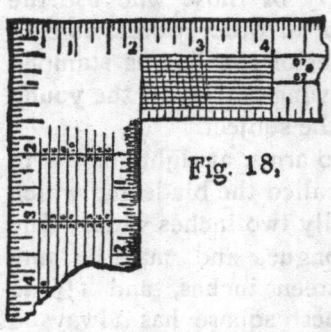

Fig. 18,

In the illustration Fig. 18, will be noticed a series of lines extending from the junction of the blade and tongue to the four-inch limit. From the figures 2 to 3 these lines are crossed by diagonal lines. This figure, reaching from 2 to 4, is called a diagonal scale, and is intended for taking off hundredths of an inch. The

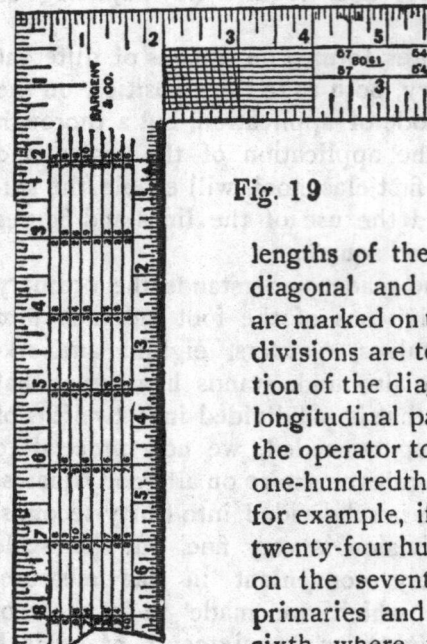

Fig. 19

lengths of the lines between the diagonal and the perpendicular are marked on the latter. Primary divisions are tenths, and the junction of the diagonal lines with the longitudinal parallel lines enables the operator to obtain divisions of one-hundredth part of an inch; as for example, if we wish to obtain twenty-four hundredths we operate on the seventh line, taking five primaries and the fraction of the sixth where the diagonal intersects the parallel line, as shown by the "dots" on the compasses, and this gives us the distance required.

The use of the scale is obvious, and needs no furtner explanation, as the dots or points are shown.

The lines of figures running across the blade of the square, as shown in Fig. 19, forms what is a very convenient rule for determining the amount of material in length or width of stuff. To use it proceed as follows: If we examine we will find under the figure 12, on the outer edge of the blade, where the length of the boards, plank or scantling to be measured is given, and the answer in feet and inches is found under the inches in width that the board, etc., measures. For example, take a board nine feet long and five inches wide, then under the figure 12, on the second line, will be found the figure 9, which is the length of the board; then run along this line to the figure directly under the five inches (the width of the board) and we find three feet nine inches, which is the correct answer in ' board measure.'' If the stuff is three inches thick it is trebled, etc., etc. If the stuff is longer than any figures shown on the square it can be measured as above and doubling the result. This rule is calculated, as its name indicates, for board measure, or for surfaces 1 inch in thickness. It may be advantageously used, however, upon timber by multiplying the result of the face measure of one side of a piece by its depth in inches. To illustrate, suppose it be required to measure a piece 25 feet long, 10x14 inches in size. For the length we will take 12 and 13 feet. For the width we will take 10 inches, and multiply the result by 14. By the rule a board 12 feet long and 10 inches wide contains 10 feet, and one 13 feet long and 10 inches wide, 10 feet 10 inches. Therefore, a board 25 feet long and 10 inches wide must contain 20 feet and

10 inches. In the timber above described, however, we have what is equivalent to 14 such boards, and therefore we multiply this result by 14, which gives 291 feet and 8 inches the board measure.

Along the tongue of the square following the diagonal scale is the brace rule, which is a very simple and very convenient method of determining the length of any brace of regular run. The length of any brace simply represents the hypothenuse of a right-angled triangle. To find the hypothenuse extract the square root of the sum of the squares of the perpendicular and horizontal runs. For instance, if 6 feet is the horizontal run and 8 feet the perpendicular, 6 squared equals 36, 8 squared equals 64; 36 plus 64 equals 100, the square root of which is 10. These are the rules generally used for squaring the frame of a building.

If the run is 42 inches. 42 squared is 1764, double that amount, both sides being equal, gives 3528, the square root of which is, in feet and inches, 4 feet 11.40 inches.

In cutting braces always allow in length from a sixteenth to an eighth of an inch more than the exact measurement calls for.

Directly under the half-inch marks on the outer edge of the back of the tongue, Fig. 19, will be noticed two figures, one above the other. These represent the run of the brace, or the length of two sides of a right-angled triangle; the figures immediately to the right represent the length of the brace or the hypothenuse. For instance, the figures $\frac{57}{57}$, and 80.61 show that the run on the post and beam is 57 inches, and the length of the brace is 80.61 inches.

Upon some squares will be found brace measurements given, where the run is not equal, as $\frac{18}{24}$.30. It will be noticed that the last set of figures are each just

three times those mentioned in the set that are usually used in squaring a building. So if the student or mechanic will fix in his mind the measurements of a few runs, with the length of braces, he can readily work almost any length required.

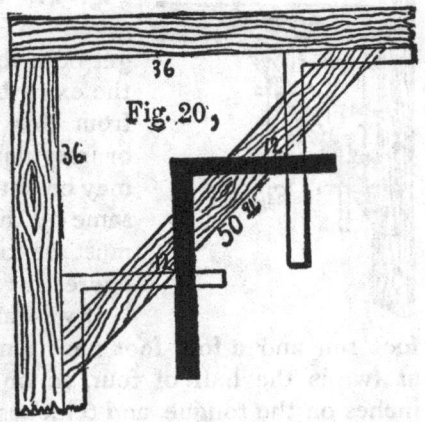

Fig. 20.

Take a run, for instance, of 9 inches on the beam and 12 inches on the post. The length of brace is 15 inches. In a run, therefore, of 12, 16, 20, or any number of times above the figures, the length of the brace will bear the same proportion to the run at the multiple used. Thus if you multiply all the figures by 3 you will have 36 and 48 inches for the run, and 60 inches for the brace, or to remember still more easily, 3, 4 and 5 feet.

There is still another and an easier method of obtaining the lengths of braces by aid of the square, also the bevels as may be seen in Fig. 20, where the run is 3 feet, or 36 inches, as marked. The length and bevels of the brace are found by applying the square three times in the position as shown; placing 12 and 12 on the edge of the timber each time. By this method both length and bevel are obtained with the least amount of labor. Braces having irregular runs may be oberated in the same manner. For instance, suppose we wish to set in a brace where the run is 4 feet and 3 feet; we simply take 9 inches on the tongue and 12 inches on the blade and apply **the** square four times, as shown **in** Fig. 21, where the brace is given in position. Here we get both the proper length and the exact bevels. It is evident from this that braces, regular or irregular, and of any length, may be obtained with bevels for same by this method, only care must be taken in adopting the figures for the purpose.

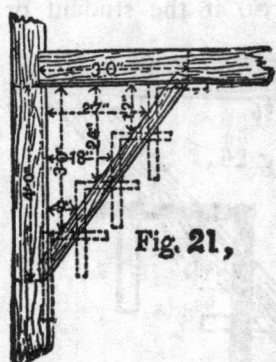

Fig. 21,

If we want a brace with a two-foot run and a four-foot run, it must be evident that as two is the half of four, so on the square take 12 inches on the tongue, and 6 inches on the blade, apply four times and we have the length and the bevels of a brace for this run.

For a three-by-four foot run take 12 inches on the tongue and 9 inches on the blade, and apply four times, because as 3 feet is ¾ of four feet, so 9 inches s ¾ of 12 inches.

While on the subject of braces I submit the following table for determining the length of braces for any run from six inches to fourteen feet. This table has been carefully prepared and may be depended upon as giving correct measurements. Where the runs are regular or equal the bevel will always be a miter or angle of 45°, providing always the angle which the brace is to occupy is a right angle—a "square." If the run is not equal, or the angle not a right angle, then the bevels or "cuts" will not be miters, and will have to be obtained either by taking figures on the square or by a scaled diagram.

TABLE

__	LENGTH OF RUN	LENGTH OF BRACE	LENGTH OF RUN	LENGTH OF BRACE
ft. in.	ft. in.	ft. in.	ft. in.	ft. in.
6 ×	6 =	8.48	4 3 × 4 3 =	6 0.12
6 ×	9 =	10.81	4 3 × 4 6 =	6 2.27
9 ×	9 =	1 0.72	4 3 × 4 9 =	6 4.49
1 0 ×	1 0 =	1 4.97	4 3 × 5 0 =	6 6.74
1 0 ×	1 3 =	1 7.20	4 6 × 4 6 =	6 4.36
1 3 ×	1 3 =	1 9.23	4 6 × 4 9 =	6 6.51
1 3 ×	1 6 =	1 11.43	4 6 × 5 0 =	6 8.72
1 6 ×	1 6 =	2 1.45	4 9 × 4 9 =	6 8.61
1 6 ×	1 9 =	2 3.65	4 9 × 5 0 =	6 10.75
1 9 ×	1 9 =	2 5.69	5 0 × 5 0 =	7 0.85
1 9 ×	2 0 =	2 7.89	5 3 × 5 3 =	7 5.09
2 0 ×	2 0 =	2 9.94	5 6 × 5 6 =	7 9.33
2 0 ×	2 3 =	3 0.12	5 9 × 5 9 =	8 1.58
2 0 ×	2 6 =	3 2.41	6 0 × 6 0 =	8 5.82
2 3 ×	2 6 =	3 4.36	6 3 × 6 3 =	8 10.06
2 6 ×	2 6 =	3 6.42	6 6 × 6 6 =	9 2.30
2 6 ×	2 9 =	3 8.59	6 9 × 6 9 =	9 6.55
2 9 ×	2 9 =	3 10.66	7 0 × 7 0 =	9 10.79
2 9 ×	3 0 =	4 0.83	7 3 × 7 3 =	10 3.03
3 0 ×	3 0 =	4 2.91	7 6 × 7 6 =	10 7.28
3 0 ×	3 3 =	4 5.02	7 9 × 7 9 =	10 11.52
3 0 ×	3 6 =	4 7.31	8 0 × 8 0 =	11 3.76
3 0 ×	3 9 =	4 9.62	8 3 × 8 3 =	11 8.00
3 3 ×	3 3 =	4 7.15	8 6 × 8 6 =	12 0.24
3 3 ×	3 6 =	4 9.31	8 9 × 8 9 =	12 4.49
3 3 ×	3 9 =	4 11.54	9 0 × 9 0 =	12 8.73
3 3 ×	4 0 =	5 1.84	9 6 × 9 6 =	13 5.22
3 6 ×	3 6 =	4 11.39	10 0 × 10 0 =	14 1.70
3 6 ×	3 9 =	5 1.55	10 6 × 10 6 =	14 10.19
3 6 ×	4 0 =	5 3.78	11 0 × 11 0 =	15 6.67
3 9 ×	3 9 =	5 3.63	11 6 × 11 6 =	16 3.16
3 9 ×	4 0 =	5 5.79	12 0 × 12 0 =	16 11.64
4 0 ×	4 0 =	5 7.88	12 6 × 12 6 =	17 8.13
4 0 ×	4 3 =	5 10.03	13 0 × 13 0 =	18 4.61
4 0 ×	4 6 =	6 0.25	13 6 × 13 6 =	19 1.10
4 0 ×	4 9 =	6 2.51	14 0 × 14 0 =	19 9.58
4 0 ×	5 0 =	6 4.83		

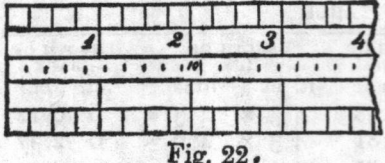

Fig. 22.

There is on the tongue of the square a scale called the "octagonal scale." This is generally on the opposite side to the scales shown on Fig. 19. Fig. 22 exhibits a portion of the tongue on which this scale is shown. It is the central division on which the number 10 is seen along with a number of divisions. It is used in this way: If you have a stick 10 inches square which you wish to dress up octagonal, make a center mark on each face, then with the compasses, take 10 of the spaces marked by the short cross-lines in the middle of the scale, and lay off this distance each side of the center lines, do the same at the other end of the stick, and strike a chalk line through these marks. Dress off the corners to the lines, and the stick will be octagonal. If the stick is not straight it must be gauged, and not marked with the chalk line. Always take a number of spaces equal to the square width of the octagon in inches. This scale can be used for large octagons by doubling or trebling the measurements.

On some squares, there are other scales, but I do not advise the use of squares that are surcharged with too many scales and figures, as they lead to confusion and loss of time.

It will now be in order to offer a few things that can be done with the steel square, in a shorter time than by applying any other methods. If we wish to get the

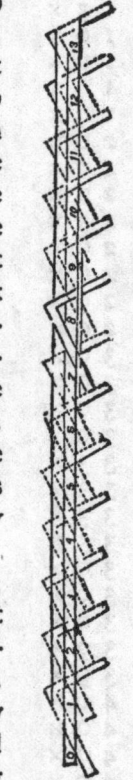

Fig. 23.

length and bevels for any common rafter it can be done on short notice by using the square as shown in Fig. 23. The pitch of the roof will, of course, govern the figures to be employed on the blade and tongue. For a quarter pitch, the figures must be 6 and 12. For half pitch, 12 and 12 must be used. For a steeper pitch, 12 and a larger figure must be used according to the pitch required. For the lower pitches, 8 and 12 gives a one-third pitch and 9 and 12 a still steeper pitch; and from this the workman can obtain any pitch he requires. If the span is 24 feet, the square must be applied 12 times, as 12 is half of 24. And so with any other span: The square must be applied half as many times as there are feet in the width. This is self-evident. The bevels and lengths of hip and valley rafters may be obtained in a similar manner, by first taking the length of the diagonal line between 12 and 12, on the square, which is 17 inches in round numbers. Use this figure on the blade, and the "rise" whatever that may be, on the tongue. Suppose we have a roof of one-third pitch, which has a span of 24 feet; then 8, which is one-third of 24, will be the height of the roof at the point or ridge, from the base of the roof on a line with the plates. For example, always use 8, which is one-third of 24, on tongue for altitude; 12, half the width of 24, on blade for base. This cuts common rafter. Next is the hip rafter. It must be understood that the diagonal of 12 and 12 is 17 in framing, as before stated, and the hip is the diagonal of a square added to the rise of roof; therefore we take 8 on tongue and 17 on blade; run the same number of times as common rafter. To cut jack rafters, divide the number of openings for common rafter. Suppose we have 5 jacks, with six openings, our common rafter 12 feet long, each jack would be 2 feet shorter, first 10 feet, second 8 feet, third 6 feet, and so on. The top down cut the same as cut of common rafter; foot also the same. To cut miter to fit hip: Take half the width of building on tongue and length of common rafter on blade; blade gives cut. Now find the diagonal of 8 and 12, which is $14\frac{7}{16}$, take 12 on tongue, $14\frac{7}{16}$ on blade; blade gives cut. The hip rafter must be beveled to suit; height of hip on tongue, length of hip on blade; tongue gives bevel. Then we take 8 on tongue, $8\frac{3}{4}$ on blade; tongue gives the bevel. Those figures will span all cuts in putting on cornice or sheathing. To cut bed moulds for gable to fit under cornice, take half width of building on

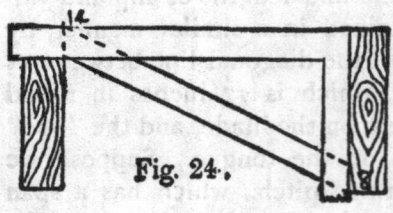

Fig. 24.

tongue, length of common rafter on blade; blade gives cut; machine mouldings will not member, but this gives a solid joint; and to member properly it is necessary to make moulding by hand, the diagonal plumb cut differences. To cut planceer to run up valley, take height of rafter on tongue, length of rafter on blade; tongue gives cut. The plumb cut takes the height of hip rafter on tongue, length of hip rafter on blade; tongue gives cut. These figures give the cuts for one-third pitch only, regardless of width of building. The construction of roofs generally will be taken up in another chapter.

A ready way of finding the length and cuts for cross-bridging is shown at Fig. 24. If the joists are 8 inches wide and 16 inches centers, there will be 14 inches

between. Place the square on 8 and 14, and cut on 8, and you have it. The only point to observe is that the 8 is on the lower side of the piece of bridging, while the 14 is on the upper, and not both on same side of timber, as in nearly all work. Bridging for any depth of joints, to any rea-

sonable distance of joists apart, may be obtained by this method. A quick way of finding the joists for laying out

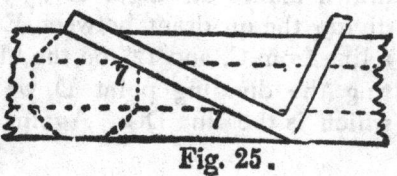

Fig. 25.

timber to be worked from the square to an octagon sec-tion is shown at Fig. 25. Lay your square diagonally across your timber and mark at 7 and 17, which gives corner of octagon. The figures 7 and 17, on either a square or two-foot pocket rule, when laid on a board or piece of timber as shown, always define the points where the octagonal angle or arris should be.

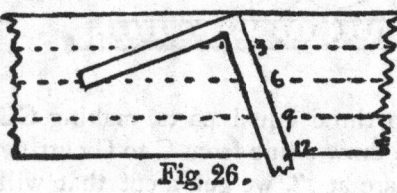

Fig. 26.

Fig. 26 shows a rapid method of dividing anything into several equal parts. If the board is 10½ inches wide, lay the square from

heel to 12, and mark at 3, 6 and 9, and you have it divided into four equal parts. Any width of board or any number of parts may be worked with accuracy under the same method.

A method for obtaining the "cuts" for octagon and hexagon joints is shown at Fig. 27. Lay off a quarter circle XA, with C as a center; then along the hori-zontal line AB the square is laid with 12" on the blade

at the center C, from which the quadrant was struck.
If we divide this quadrant into halves, we get the point
E, and a line drawn from 12″ on the blade of the
square and through the point E, we cut the tongue of
the square at 12″ and through to O, and the line thus
drawn makes an angle of 45°, a true miter. If we
divide the quadrant between E and X, and then draw
a line from C, and 12″ on the blade of the square, cutting the dividing point D, we get the octagon cut,
which is the line DC. Again, if we divide the space

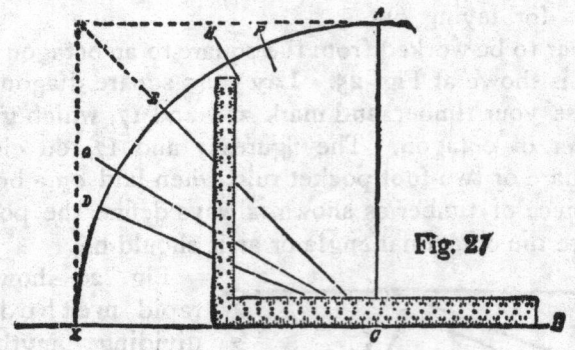

Fig. 27

between E and X into three equal parts, making GC
one of these parts, and draw a line from C to G cutting
the tongue of the square at 7″, we get a cut that will
give us a miter for a hexagon; therefore, we see from
this that if we set a steel square on any straight edge
or straight line, 12″ and 12″ on blade and tongue on
the line or edge, we get a true miter by marking along
the edge of the blade. For an octagon miter, we set
the blade on the line at 12″, and the tongue at 5″, and
we get the angle on the line of the blade—nearly; and,
for a hexagon cut, we place the blade at 12″ on the

line, and the tongue at 7″, and the line of the blade gives the angle of cut—nearly. The actual figure for octagon is 4¾⅓, but 5″ is close enough; and for a hexagon cut, the exact figures are 12″ and 6¼⅝, but 12″ and 7″ is as near as most workmen will require, unless the cut is a very long one.

The diagram shown at Fig. 28 illustrates a method of defining the pitches of roofs, and also gives the figures on the square for laying out the rafters for such pitches. By a very common usage among carpenters and builders, the pitch of a roof is described by indicating what fraction the rise is of the span. If, for example, the span is 24 feet (and here it should be remarked that the diagram shows only one-half the span), then 6 feet rise would be called quarter pitch, because 6 is one-quarter of 24. The rule, somewhat arbitrarily expressed, that is applicable

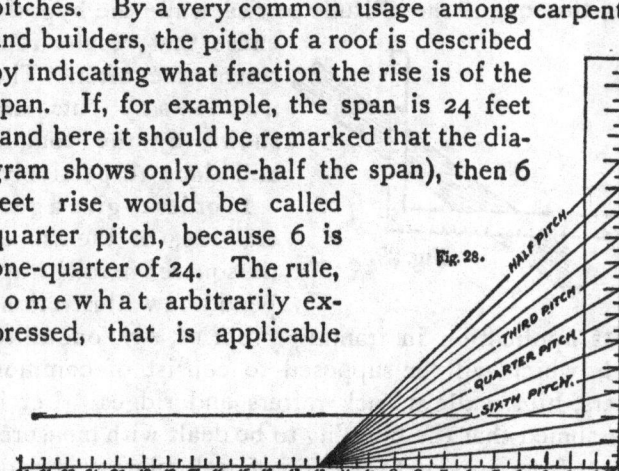

Fig. 28.

in such cases in roof framing where the roof is one-quarter pitch, is as follows: Use 12 of the blade, and 6 of the tongue. For other pitches use the figures appropriate thereto in the same general manner.

The diagram indicates the figures for sixth pitch, quarter pitch, third pitch and half pitch. The first three of these are in very common use, although the latter is somewhat exceptional.

It will take but a moment's reflection upon the part

of a practical man, with this diagram before him, to perceive that no changes are necessary in the rule where the span is more or less than 24 feet. The cuts are the same for quarter pitch irrespective of the actual dimensions of the building. The square in all such cases is used on the basis of similar triangles. The broad rule is simply this: To construct with the square such a triangle as will proportionately and correctly represent the full size, the blade becomes the base, the tongue the altitude or rise, while the hypoth-

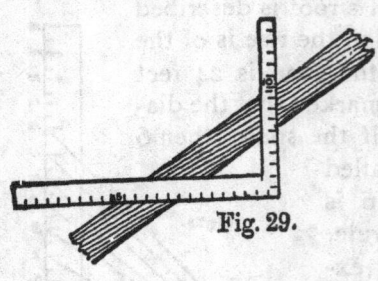

Fig. 29.

enuse that results represents the rafter. The necessary cuts are shown by the tongue and blade respectively.

In order to give a general idea of the use of the square I herewith append a few illustrations of its application in framing a roof of, say, one-third pitch, which will be supposed to consist of common rafters, hips, valleys, jack rafters and ridges. Let it be assumed that the building to be dealt with measures 30 feet from outside to outside of wall plates; the toe of the rafters to be fair with the outside of the wall plates, the pitch being one-third (that is the roof rises from the top of the wall plate to the top of the ridge, one-third of the width of the building, or 10 feet), the half width of the building being 15 feet. Thus, the figures for working on the square are obtained; if other figures are used, they must bear the same relative proportion to each other.

To get the required lengths of the stuff, measure across the corner of the square, from the 10-inch mark the tongue to the 15-inch mark on the blade, Fig. 29. This gives 18 feet as the length of the common rafter. To get the bottom bevel or cut to fit on the wall plate, lay the square flat on the side of the rafter. Start, say, at the right-hand end, with the blade of the square to the right, the point or angle of the square away from you, and the rafter, with its back (or what will be the top edge of it when it is fixed) towards you. Now place the 15-inch mark of the blade and the 10-inch mark of the tongue on the corner of the rafter—that is, towards you—still keeping the square laid flat, and mark along the side of the blade. This gives the bottom cut, and will fit the wall plate. Now move the square to the other

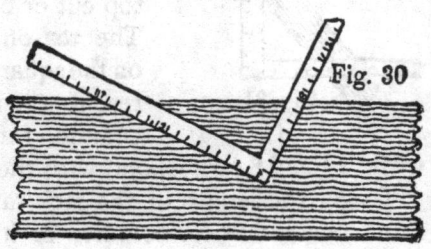

Fig. 30

end of the rafter, place it in the same position as before to the 18-foot mark on the rafter and to the 10-inch mark on the tongue, and the 15-inch mark on the blade; then mark alongside the tongue. This gives the top cut to fit against the ridge. To get the length of the hip rafter, take 15 inches on the blade and 15 inches on the tongue of the square, and measure across the corner. This gives $21\frac{3}{8}$ inches. Now take this figure on the blade and 10 inches on the tongue, then measuring across the corner gives the length of the hip rafter.

Another method is to take the 17-inch mark on the blade and the 8-inch mark on the tongue and begin as with the common rafter, as at Fig. 30. Mark along the side of the blade for the bottom cut. Move the square to the left as many times as there are feet in the half of the width of the building (in the present case, as we have seen, 15 feet is half the width), keeping the above mentioned figures 17 and 8 in line with the top edge of the hip rafter;

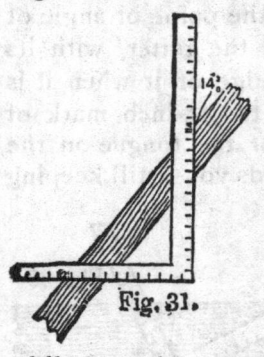

Fig. 31.

step it along just the same as when applying a pitch board on a stair-string, and after moving it along 15 steps, mark alongside the tongue. This gives the top cut or bevel and the length. The reason 17 and 8 are taken on the square is that 12 and 8 represent the rise and run of the common rafter to 1 foot on plan, while 17 and 8 correspond with the plan of the hips.

To get the length of the jack rafters, proceed in the same manner as for common or hip rafters; or alternately space the jacks and divide the length of the common rafter into the same number of spaces. This gives the length of each jack rafter.

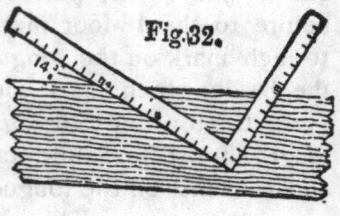

Fig. 32.

To get the bevel of the top edge of the jack rafter, Fig. 31, take the length, 14⅜ of the common rafter on the blade and the run of the common rafter on the tongue, apply the square to the jack rafter, and mark along the side of the blade; this gives the bevel or cut. The down bevel and the bevel at the bottom end are the same as for the common rafter

To get the bevel for the side of the purlin to fit

against the hip rafter, place the square flat against the side of the purlin, with 8 inches on the tongue and 14⅜ inches on the blade, Fig. 32. Mark alongside of the tongue. This gives the side cut or bevel. The 14⅜ inches is the length of the common rafter to the 1-foot run, and the 8 inches represent the rise.

For the edge bevel of purlin, lay the square flat against the edge of purlin with 12 inches on the tongue and 14½ inches on the blade, as at Fig. 33, and mark along the side of the tongue. This gives the bevel or cut for the edge of the purlin.

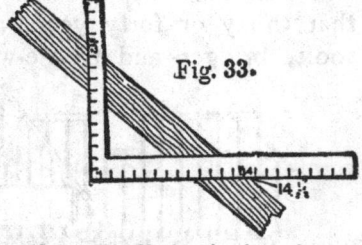

Fig. 33.

The rafter patterns must be cut half the thickness of ridge shorter; and half the thickness of the hip rafter allowed off the jack rafters.

These examples of what may be achieved by the aid of the square are only a few of the hundreds that can be solved by an intelligent use of that wonderful instrument, but it is impossible in a work of this kind to illustrate more than are here presented. The subject will be dealt with at length in a separate volume.

CHAPTER II

GENERAL FRAMING AND ROOFING

Heavy framing is now almost a dead science in this country unless it be in the far west or south, as steel and iron have displaced the heavy timber structures that thirty or forty years ago were so plentiful in roofs, bridges and trestle-work. As it will not be

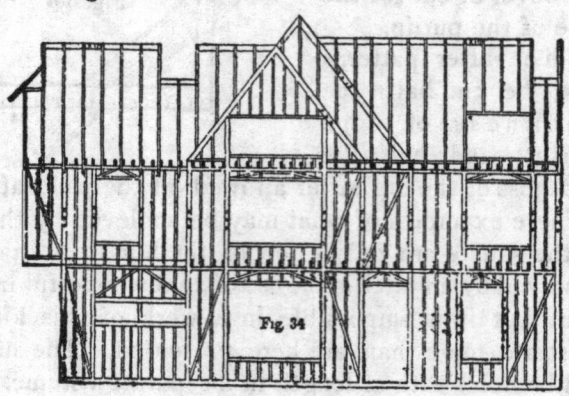

Fig. 34

necessary to go deeply into heavy-timber framing, therefore I will confine myself more particularly to the framing of ballon buildings generally.

A ballon frame consists chiefly of a frame-work of scantling. The scantling may be 2 x 4 inches, or any other size that may be determined. The scantlings are spiked to the sills, or are nailed to the sides of the joist which rests on the sills, or, as is sometimes the case, a rough floor may be nailed on the joists,

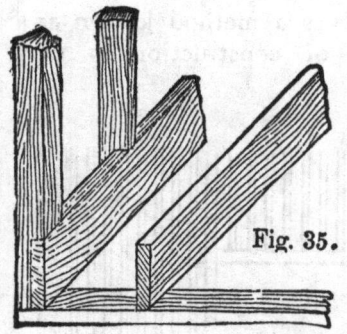

Fig. 35.

and on this, ribbon pieces of 2 x 4-inch stuff are spiked around to the outer edge of the foundation, and onto these ribbon pieces the scantling is placed and "toe-nailed" to them. The doors and windows are spaced off as shown in Fig. 34, which represents a ballon frame and roof in skeleton condition. These frames are generally boarded on both sides, always on the outside. Sometimes the boarding on the outside is nailed on diagonally, but more frequently horizontally, which, in my opinion, is the better way, providing always the boarding is dry and the joints laid close.

The joists are laid on "rolling," that is, there are no gains or tenons employed, unless in trimmers or similar work. The joists are simply "toe-nailed" onto sill plates, or

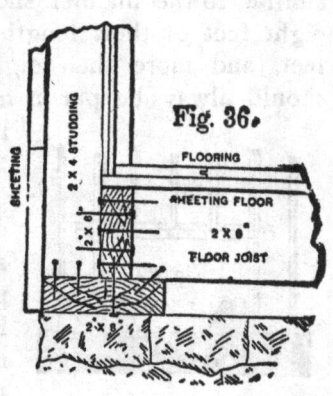

Fig. 36.

ribbon pieces, as shown in the illustration. Sometimes the joists are made to rest on the sills, as shown in Fig. 35, the sill being no more than a 2 x 4-inch scantling laid in mortar on the foundation, the outside joists forming a sill for the side studs. A better plan is

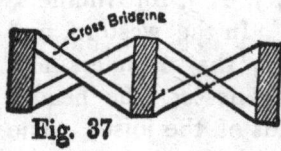

Fig. 37

shown in Fig. 36, which gives a method known as a "box-sill." The manner of construction is very simple.

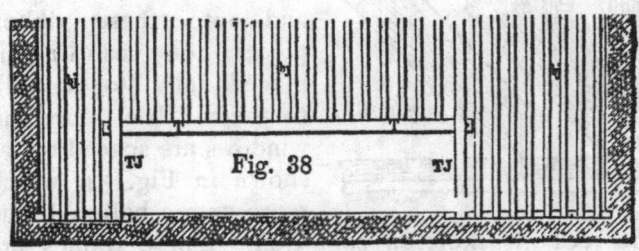

Fig. 38

All joists in a building of this kind must be bridged similar to the manner shown in Fig. 37, about every eight feet of their length; in spans less than sixteen feet, and more than eight feet, a row of bridging should always be put in midway in the span. Bridging should not be less than 1 to 1½ inches in section.

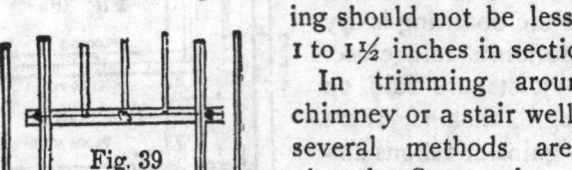

Fig. 39

In trimming around a chimney or a stair well-hole, several methods are employed. Sometimes the headers and trimmers are made from material twice as thick and the same depth as the ordinary joists, and the intermediate joists are tenoned into the header, as shown in Fig. 38. Here we have T, T, for header, and T, J, T, J, for trimmers, and b, j, for the ordinary joists. In the western, and also some of the central States, the trimmers and headers are made up of two thicknesses, the header being mortised to secure the ends of the joists. The two thicknesses are well nailed together. This method is exhibited at Fig. 39., which also shows one way to trim around a hearth; C shows the header with trimmer joists with tusk tenons, keyed solid in place.

Frequently it happens that a chimney rises in a building from its own foundation, disconnected from the walls, in which case the chimney shaft will require to be trimmed all around, as shown in

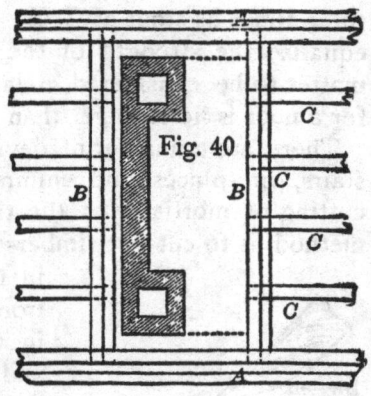

Fig. 40

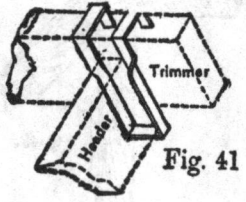

Fig. 41

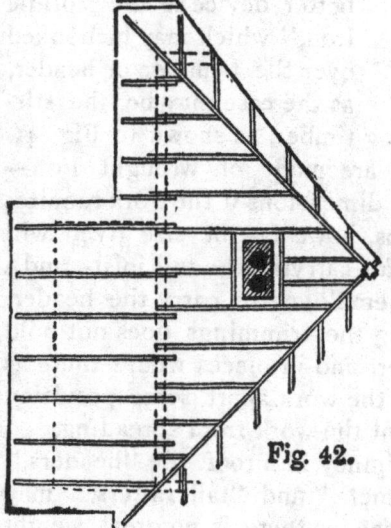

Fig. 42.

Fig. 40. In cases of this kind the trimmers A, A, should be made of stuff very much thicker than the joists, as they have to bear a double burden; B, B shows the heading, and C, C, C, C the tail joists. B, B, should have a thickness double that of C, C, etc., and A, A should at least be three times as stout as C, C. This will to some extent equalize the strength of the whole floor, which is a matter to be considered in laying down floor timbers, for a noor is no stronger than its weakest part.

There are a number of devices for trimming around stairs, fire-places and chimney-stacks by which the cutting or mortising of the timbers is avoided. One method is to cut the timbers the exact length, square

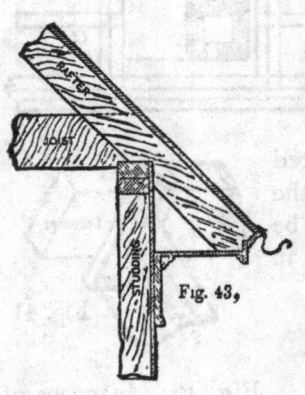

Fig. 43,

in the ends, and then insert iron dowels—two or more— in the ends of the joists, and then bore holes in the trimmers and headers to suit, and drive the whole solid together. The dowels are made from ¾-inch or 1-inch round iron. Another and a better device is the "bridle iron," which may be hooked over the trimmer or header, as the case may be, the stir-rup carrying the abutting timber, as shown in Fig. 41. These "bridle irons" are made of wrought iron— 2 x 2½ inches, or larger dimensions if the work requires such; for ordinary jobs, however, the size given will be found plenty heavy for carrying the tail joists, and a little heavier may be employed to carry the header. This style of connecting the trimmings does not hold the frame-work together, and in places where there is any tendency to thrust the work apart, some provision must be made to prevent the work from spreading.

In trimming for a chimney in a roof, the "headers," "stretchers" or "trimmers," and "tail rafters," may be simply nailed in place, as there is no great weight beyond snow and wind pressure to carry, therefore the same precautions for strength are not necessary. The sketch shown at Fig. 42 explains how the chimney openings in the roof may be trimmed, the parts being only spiked together. A shows a hip rafter against which the cripples on both sides are spiked. The chimney-stack is shown in the center of the roof—isolated—trimmed on the four sides. The sketch is

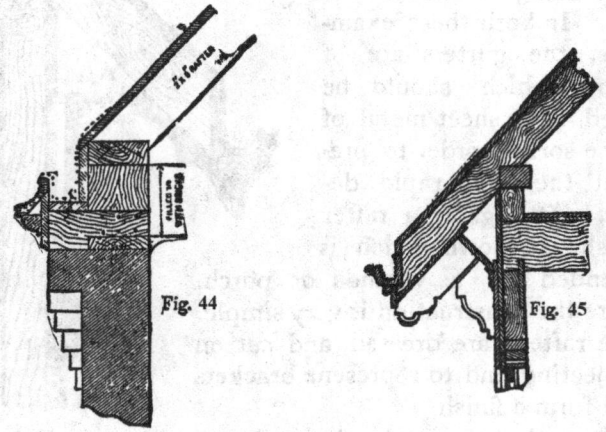

Fig. 44

Fig. 45

self-explanatory in a measure, and should be easily understood.

An example or two showing how the rafters may be connected with the plates at the eaves and finished for cornice and gutters, may not be out of place. A simple method is shown at Fig. 43, where the cornice is complete and consists of a few members only. The gutter is attached to the crown moulding, as shown.

Another method is shown at Fig. 44, this one being intended for a brick wall having sailing courses over cornice. The gutter is built in of wood, and in lined throughout with galvanized iron This makes a substantial job and may be used to good purpose on brick or stone warehouses, factories or similar buildings.

Another style of rafter finish is shown at Fig 45, which also shows scheme of cornice. A similar finish is shown at Fig. 46, the cornice being a little different. In both these examples, the gutters are of wood, which should be lined with sheet metal of some sort in order to prevent their too rapid decay. At Fig. 47 a rafter finish is shown which is intended for a veranda or porch. Here the construction is very simple. The rafters are dressed and cut on projecting end to represent brackets and form a finish

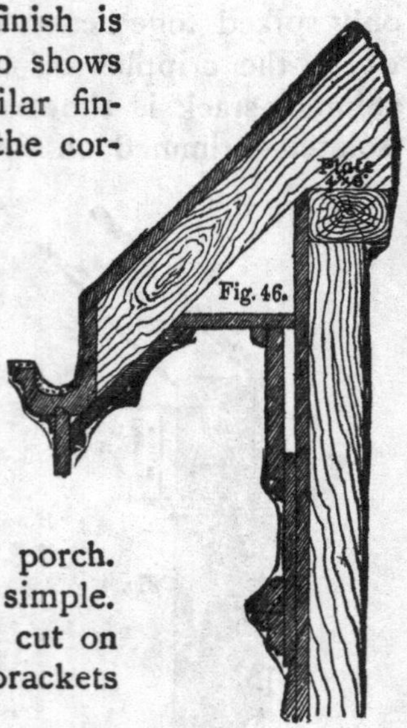

Fig. 46.

From these examples the workman will get sufficient ideas for working his rafters to suit almost any condition. Though there are many hundreds of styles which might be presented, the foregoing are ample for our purpose.

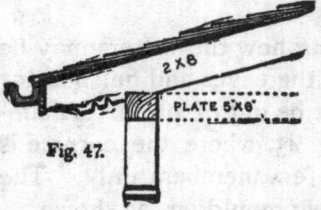

Fig. 47.

It will now be in order to take up the construction of roofs, and describe the methods by which such construction is obtained.

The method of obtaining the lengths and bevels of

rafters for ordinary roofs, such as that shown in Fig 48, has already been given in the chapter on the steel square. Something has also been said regarding hip and valley roofs; but not enough, I think, to satisfy the full requirements of the workman, so I will endeavor to give a clearer idea of the construction of these roofs by employing the graphic system, instead of depending altogether on the steel square, though I

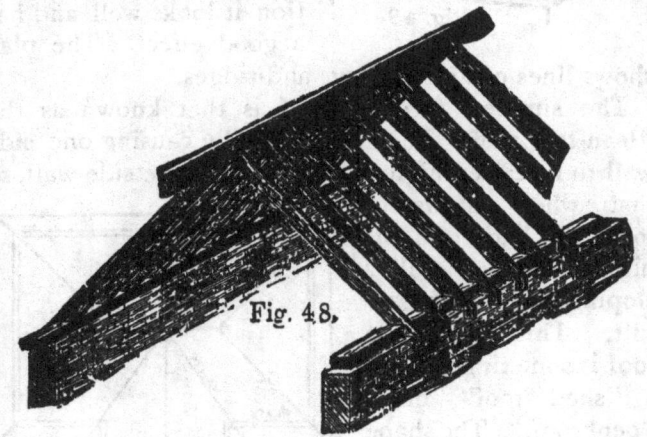

Fig. 48.

earnestly advise the workman to "stick to the square." It never makes a mistake, though the owner may in its application.

A "hip roof," pure and simple, has no gables, and is often called a "cottage roof," because of its being best adapted for cottages having only one, or one and a half, stories. The chief difficulty in its construction is getting the lengths and bevels of the hip or angle rafter and the jack or cripple rafter. To the expert workman, this is an easy matter, as he can readily obtain both lengths and bevels by aid of the square, or by lines such as I am about to produce.

The illustration shown at Fig. 49 shows the simplest form of a hip roof. Here the four hips or diagonal rafters meet in the center of the plan. Another style of hip roof, having a gable and a ridge in the center of the building, is shown at

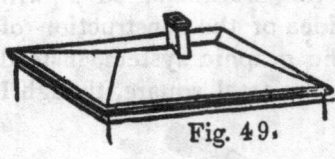

Fig. 49.

Fig. 50. This is quite a common style of roof, and under almost every condition it looks well and has a good effect. The plan shows lines of hips, valleys and ridges.

The simplest form of roof is that known as the "lean-to" roof. This is formed by causing one side wall to be raised higher than the opposite side wall, so that when rafters or joists are laid from the high to the low wall a sloping roof is the result. This style of a roof is sometimes called a "shed roof" or a "pent roof." The shape is shown at Fig. 51, the upper sketch showing an end view and the lower one a plan of the roof. The method of framing this roof, or adjusting the timbers

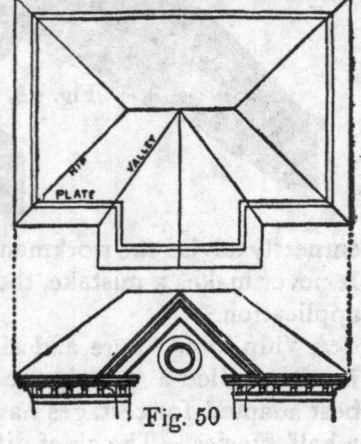

Fig. 50

for it, is quite obvious and needs no explanation. This style of roof is in general use where an annex or shed is built up against a superior building, hence its name of "lean-to," as it usually "leans" against the main building, the wall of which is utilized for the high part of the shed or annex, thus saving the cost of the most important wall of the structure.

Next to the "lean-to" or "shed roof" in simplicity comes the "saddle" or "double roof." This roof is shown at Fig. 52 by the end view on the top of the figure, and the plan at the bottom. It will be seen that this roof has a double slope, the planes forming the slopes are equally inclined to the horizon; the meeting of their highest sides makes an arris which is called the ridge of the roof; and the triangular spaces at the end of the walls are called gables.

It is but a few years ago when the mansard roof was very popular, and many of them can be found in the older parts of the country, having been erected between the early fifties and the eighties, but, for many reasons, they are now less used. Fig. 53 shows a roof of this kind. It is penetrated generally by dormers, as shown in the sketch, and the top is covered either by a "deck roof" or a very flat hip roof, as shown. Sometimes the sloping sides of these roofs are curved, which give them a graceful appearance, but adds materially to their cost.

Fig. 51.

Fig. 52.

Another style of roof is shown at Fig. 54. This is a gambrel roof, and was very much in evidence in prerevolutionary times, particularly among our Knickerbocker ancestors. In conjunction with appropriate dormers, this style of roof figures prominently in what is known as early "colonial style." It has some advantages over the mansard.   Besides these there are many other kinds of roofs, but it is not my purpose to enter largely into the matter of styles of roofs, but simply to arm the workman with such rules and prac-

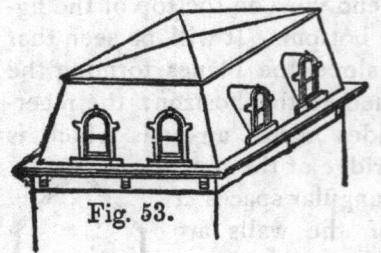

Fig. 53.

tical equipment that he will be able to tackle with success almost any kind of a roof that he may be called upon to construct.

When dealing with the steel square I explained how the lengths and bevels for common rafters could be obtained by the use of the steel square alone; also hips, purlins, valleys and jack rafters might be obtained by the use of the square, but, in order to fully equip the workman, I deem it necessary to present for his benefit a graphic method of obtaining the lengths, cuts and backing of

rafters and purlins required for a hip roof.

At Fig. 55, I show the plans of a simple hip roof having a ridge. The hips on the

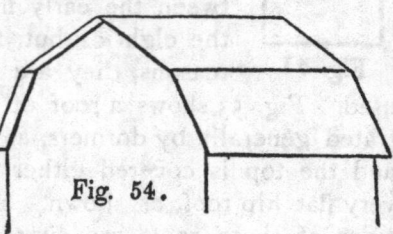

Fig. 54.

plan form an angle of 45°, or a miter, as it were. The plan being rectangular leaves the ridge the length of the difference between the length and the width of the building. Make *cd* on the ridge-line as shown, half the width of *ab*, and the angle *bda* will be a right angle. Then if we extend *bd* to *e*, making *de* the rise of the roof, *ae* will be the length of the hip rafter, and the angle at x will be the plumb cut at point of hip and the angle at a will be the cut at the foot of the rafter. The angle at v shows the backing of the hip. This bevel is obtained as follows: Make ag and ah equal distances—any distance will serve—then draw a line hg across the angle of the building, then with a center on ad at p, touching the line ae at s, describe a circle as shown by the dotted line, then draw the lines kh and

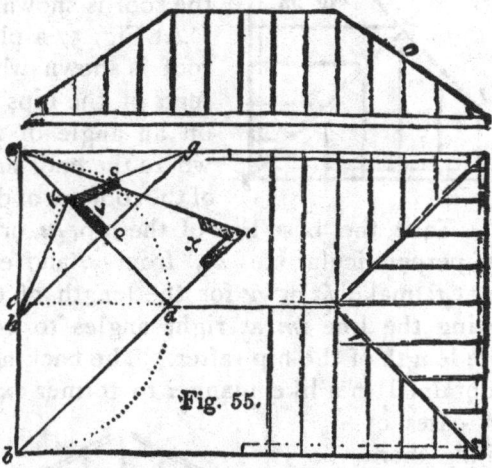

Fig. 55.

kg, and that angle, as shown by the bevel v, will be the backing or bevel for the top of the hip, beveling each way from a center line of the hip. This rule for backing a hip holds good in all kinds of hips, also for guttering a valley rafter, if the bevel is reversed. A hip roof where all the hips abut each other in the center is shown in Fig. 56. This style of roof is generally called a "pyramidal roof" because it has the appearance of a low flattened pyramid. The same rules governing Fig. 55 apply to this example. The bevels C and B show the backing of the hip, B showing the

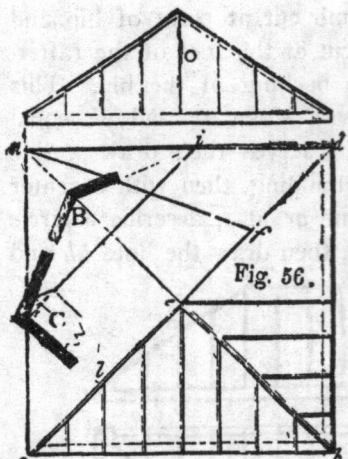

Fig. 56.

top from the center line *ae*; and C showing the bevel as placed against the side of the hip, which is always the better way to work the hip. A portion of the hip backed is shown at C. The rise of the roof is shown at O.

At Fig. 57 a plan of a roof is shown where the seats of the hips are not on an angle of 45° and where the ends and sides of the roof are of different pitches Take the base line of the hip, *ae* or *eg*, and make *ef* perpendicular to *ae*, from *e*, and equal to the rise at *f*; make *fa* or *fg* for the length of the hip, by drawing the line *lm* at right angles to *ae*. This gives the length of the hip rafter. The backing of the hip is obtained in a like manner to former examples, only, in cases of this kind, there are two bevels for the backing, one side of the hip being more acute than the other as shown at D and E. If the hips are to be mitered, as is sometimes the case in roofs of this kind, then

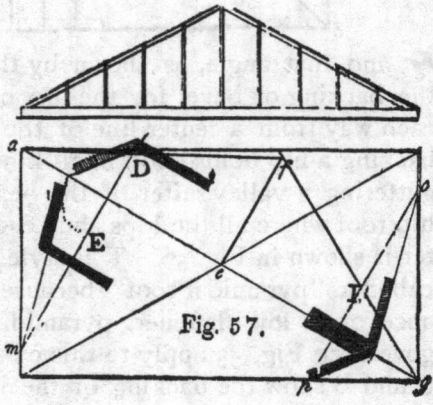

Fig. 57.

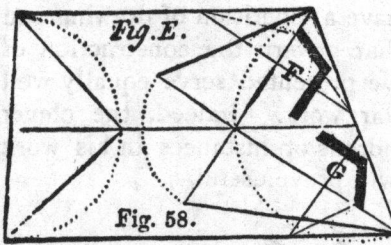

Fig. 58.

the back of the hip will assume the shape as shown by the two bevels at F. A hip roof having an irregular plan is shown at Fig. 58. This requires no explanation, as the hips and bevels are obtained in the same manner as in previous examples. The backing of the hips is shown at FG.

An octagon roof is shown at Fig. 59, with all the lines necessary for getting the lengths, bevels, and backing for the hips. The line *ax* shows the seat of the hip, *xe* the rise of roof, and *ae* the length of hip and plumb cut, and the bevel at E shows the backing of the hips.

These examples will be quite sufficient to enable the workman to understand the general theory of laying out hip roofs. I

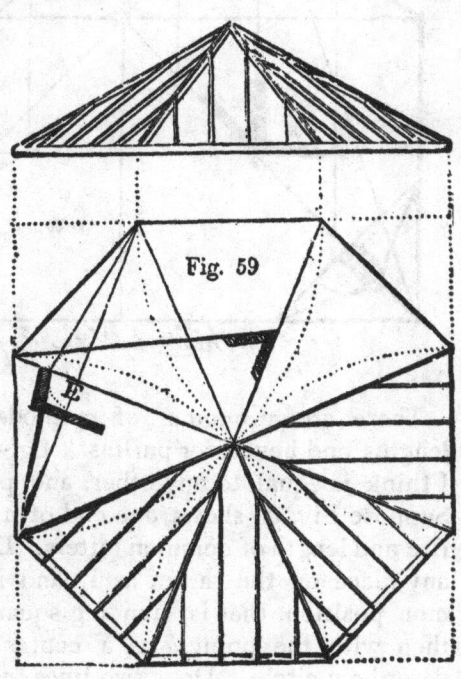

Fig. 59

may also state that to save a repetition of drawing and
explaining the rules that govern the construction of
hip roofs, such as I have presented serve equally well
for skylights or similar work. Indeed, the clever
workman will find hundreds of instances in his work
where the rules given will prove useful.

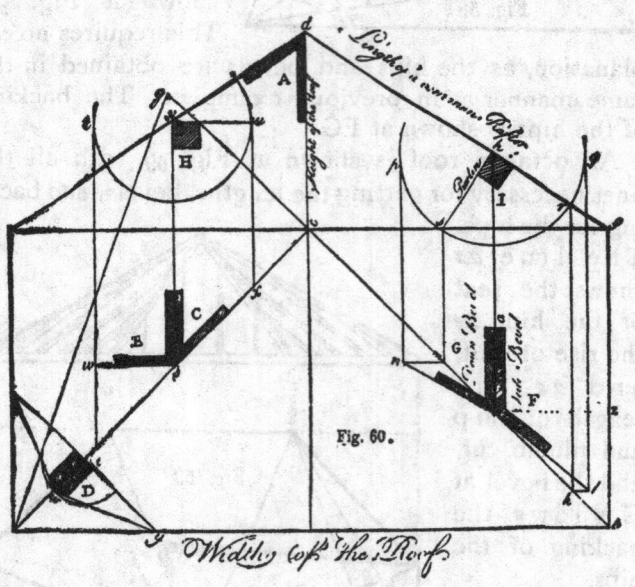

Fig. 60.

There are a number of methods for getting the
lengths and bevels for purlins. I give one here which
I think is equal to any other, and perhaps as simple.
Suppose Fig. 60 shows one end of a hip roof, also the
rise and length of common rafters. Let the purlin be in
any place on the rafter, as I, and in its most common position, that is, standing square with the rafter;
then with the point *b* as a center with any radius,
describe a circle. Draw two lines, *ql* and *pn*, to touch

the circle *p* and *q* parallel to *fb* and at the points *s* and *r*, where the two sides of the purlin intersect, draw two parallel lines to the former, to cut the diagonal in *m* and *k*; then G is the down bevel and F the side bevel of the purlin; these two bevels, when applied to the end of the purlin, and when cut by them, will exactly fit the side of the hip rafters.

To find the cuts of a purlin where two sides are parallel to horizon: The square at B and the bevel at C will show how to draw the end of the purlin in this easy case. The following is universal in all positions of the purlin: Let *ab* be the width of a square roof, make *bf* or *ae* one-half of the width, and make *cd* perpendicular in the middle of *ef*, the height of the roof or rise, which in this case is one-third; then draw *de* and *df*, which are each the length of the common rafter.

To find the bevel of a jack rafter against the hip, proceed as follows: Turn the stock of the side bevel at F from *a* around to the line *iz*, which will give the side bevel of the jack rafter The bevel at A, which is the top of the common rafter, is the down bevel of the jack rafter.

At D the method of getting the backing of a hip rafter is shown the same as explained in other figures.

There are other methods of obtaining bevels for purlins, but the one offered here will suffice for all practical purposes.

I gave a method of finding the back cuts for jack rafters by the steel square, in a previous chapter. I give another rule herewith for the steel square: Take the length of the common rafter on the blade and the run of the same rafter on the tongue, and the blade of the square will give the bevel for the cut on the back of the jack rafter. For example, suppose the rise to be 6 feet and the run 8 feet, the length of the common rafter will be 10 feet. Then take 10 feet on the blade of the square, and 8 feet on the tongue, and the blade will give the back bevel for the cut of the jack rafters.

To obtain the length of jack rafters is a very simple process, and may be obtained easily by a diagram, as shown in Fig. 61, which is a very common method:

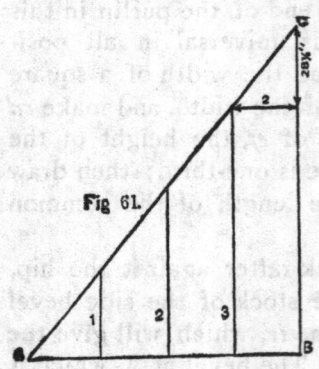

Fig 61.

First lay off half the width of the building to scale, as from A to B, the length of the common rafter B to C, and the length of the hip rafter from A to C. Space off the widths from jack rafter to jack rafter as shown by the lines 1, 2, 3, and measure them accurately. Then the lines 1, 2, and 3 will be the exact lengths of the jack rafters in those divisions Any number of jack rafters may be laid off this way, and the result will be the length of each rafter, no matter what may be the pitch of the roof or the distance the rafters are apart.

A table for determining the length of jack rafters is given below, which shows the lengths required for different spacing in three pitches:

One-quarter pitch roof:

They cut 13 5 inches shorter each time when spaced 12 inches

They cut 18 inches shorter each time when spaced 16 inches.

They cut 27 inches shorter each time when spaced 24 inches.

One-third pitch roof:

They cut 14.4 inches shorter each time when spaced 12 inches.

They cut 19.2 inches shorter each time when spaced 16 inches.

They cut 28.8 inches shorter each time when spaced 24 inches.

One-half pitch roof:

They cut 17 inches shorter each time when spaced 12 inches.

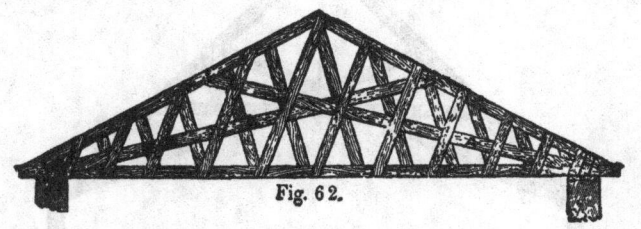

Fig. 62.

They cut 22.6 inches shorter each time when spaced 16 inches.

They cut 34 inches shorter each time when spaced 24 inches.

It is not my intention to enter deeply into a discussion of the proper methods of constructing roofs of all shapes, though a few hints and diagrams of octagonal, domical and other roofs and spires will doubtless be of service to the general workman. One of the most useful methods of trussing a roof is that known as a lattice "built-up" truss roof, similar to that shown at Fig. 62. The rafters, tie beams and the two main braces A, A, must be of one thickness—say, 2 x 4 or 2 x 6 inches, according to the length of the span— while the minor braces are made of 1-inch stuff and about 10 or 12 inches wide. These minor braces are well nailed to the tie beams, main braces and rafters. The main braces must be halved over each other at their juncture, and bolted. Sometimes the main braces are left only half the thickness of the rafters, then no halving will be necessary, but this method has the disadvantage of having the minor braces nailed to one side only. To obviate this, blocks may be nailed to the inside of the main braces to make up the thickness

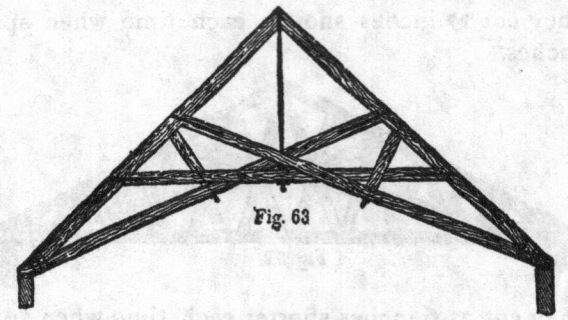

Fig. 63

required, as shown, and the minor braces can be nailed or bolted to the main brace.

The rafters and tie beams are held together at the foot of the rafter by an iron bolt, the rafter having a crow-foot joint at the bottom, which is let into the tie beam. The main braces also are framed into the rafter with a square toe-joint and held in place with an iron bolt, and the foot of the brace is crow-footed into the tie beam over the wall.

This truss is easily made, may be put together on the ground, and, as it is light, may be hoisted in place with blocks and tackle, with but little trouble. This truss can be made sufficiently strong to span a roof from 40 to 75 feet. Where the span inclines to the greater length, the tie beams and rafters may be made of built-up timbers, but in such a case the tie b e a m s should not be less than 6 x 10 inches, n o r the rafters less than 6 x 6 inches.

Another style of roof altogether is shown at Fig. 63. This is a self-supporting roof, but is somewhat expensive if intended for a building having a span of 30 feet or less. It is fairly w e l l adapted for halls or for country churches, where a high ceiling is required and the span anywhere from 30 to 50 feet over all. It would not be safe to risk a roof of this kind on a building having a span more than 50 feet. The main features of this roof are: (1) having

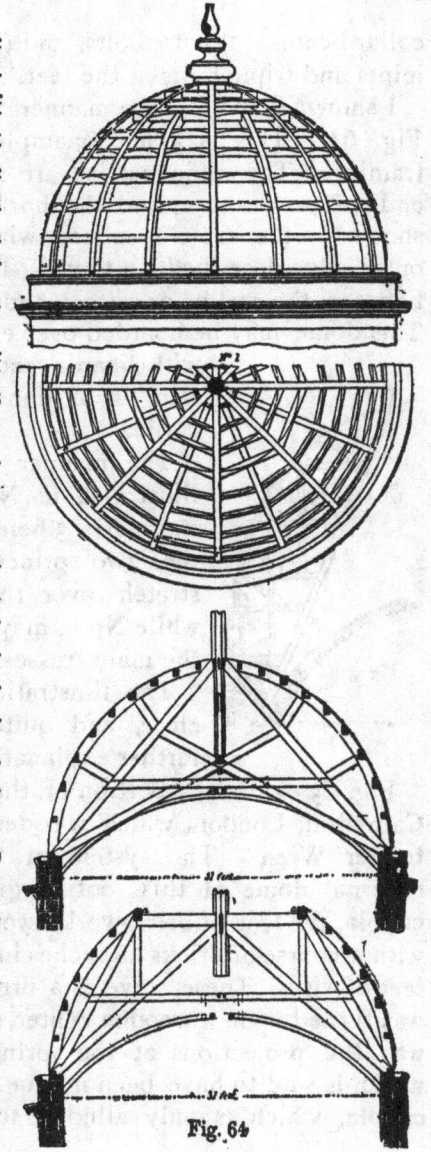

Fig. 64

collar beams, (2) truss bolts, and (3) iron straps at the joints and triple bolts at the feet.

I show a dome and the manner of its construction at Fig. 64. This is a fine example of French timber framing. The main carlins are shown at *a*, *b*, *c*, *d* and *e*, Nos. 1 and 2, and the horizontal ribs are also shown in the same numbers, with the curve of the outer edge described on them. These ribs are cut in between the carlins or rafters and beveled off to suit. This dome may be boarded over either horizontally or with boards made into "gores" and laid on in line with the rafters or carlins.

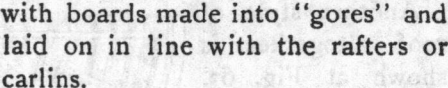

Fig. 65

The manner of framing is well illustrated in Nos. 3 and 4 in two ways, No. 3 being intended to form the two principal trusses which stretch over the whole diameter, while No. 4 may be built in between the main trusses.

The illustrations are simple and clear, and quite sufficient without further explanation.

Fig. 65 exhibits a portion of the dome of St. Paul's Cathedral, London, which was designed by Sir Christopher Wren The system of the framing of the external dome of this roof is given. The internal cupola, AA1, is of brick-work, two bricks in thickness, with a course of bricks 18 inches in length at every five feet of rise. These serve as a firm bond. This dome was turned upon a wooden center, whose only support was the projections at the springing of the dome, which is said to have been unique. Outside the brick cupola, which is only alluded to in order that the description may be the more intelligible, rises a brick-work cone B. A portion of this can be seen, by a spectator on the floor of the cathedral, through the central opening at A. The timbers which carry the external dome rest upon this conical brickwork. The horizontal hammer beams, C, D, E, F, are curiously tied to the corbels, G, H, I, K, by iron cramps, well bedded with lead into the corbels and bolted to the hammer beams. The stairs, or ladders, by which the ascent to the Golden Gallery or the summit

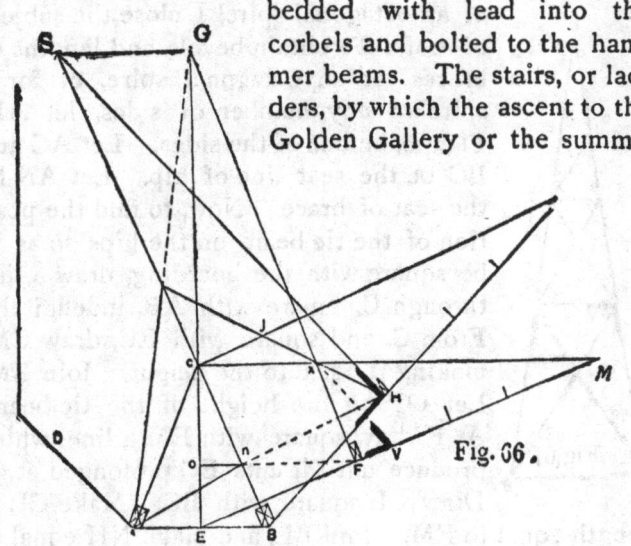

Fig. 66.

of the dome is made, pass among the roof trusses. The dome has a planking from the base upwards, and hence the principals are secured horizontally at a little distance from each other. The contour of this roof is that of a pointed dome or arch, the principals being segments of circles; but the central opening for the lantern, of course, hinders these arches from meeting at a point. The scantling of the curved principals is 10 x 11½ inches at the base, decreasing to 6 x 6 inches at the top. A lantern of Portland stone crowns the summit of the dome. The method of framing will be clearly seen in the diagram. It is in every respect an excellent specimen of roof construction, and is worthy of the genius and mathematical skill of a great workman.

With the rules offered herewith for the construction of an octagonal spire, I close the subject of roofs: To obtain bevels and lengths of braces for an octagonal spire, or for a spire of any number of sides, let AB, Fig. 66, be one of the sides. Let AC and BC be the seat line of hip. Let AN be the seat of brace. Now, to find the position of the tie beam on the hips so as to be square with the boarding, draw a line through C, square with AB, indefinitely. From C, and square with EC, draw CM, making it equal to the height. Join EM. Let OF be the height of the tie beam. At F draw square with EM a line, which produce until it cuts EC prolonged at G. Draw CL square with BC. Make CL in length equal to EM. Join BL, and make NH equal to OF. From G draw the line GS parallel with AB, cutting BC prolonged, at the point S; then the angle at H is the bevel on the hip for the tie beam. For a bevel to miter the tie beam, make FV equal ON. Join VX; then the bevel at V is the bevel on the face. For the down bevel see V, in Fig. 67. To find the length of brace, make AB, Fig. 67, equal to AB, Fig. 66. Make AL and BL equal to BL, Fig. 66. Make BP equal to BH. Join AP and BC, which will be the length of the brace. The bevels numbered 1, 3, 5 and 7 are all to be

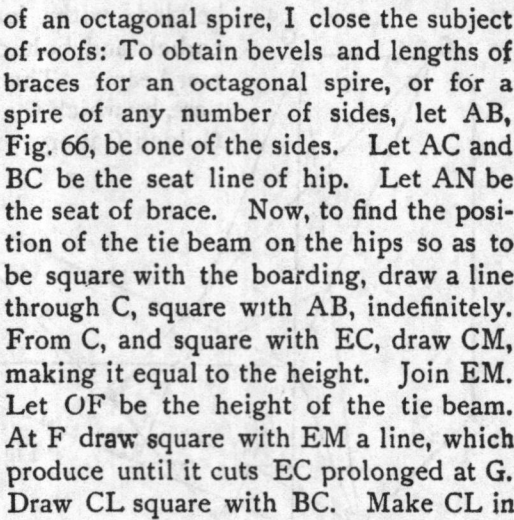

Fig. 67

used, as shown on the edge of the brace. No. 1 is to be used at the top above No. 5. For the bevel on the face to miter on the hip, draw AG, Fig. 66, cutting BS at J. Join JH. Next, in Fig. 68, make AP equal AP, Fig. 67, and make AJ equal to AJ, Fig. 66. Make PJ equal to JH, Fig. 66, and make PI equal to HI. Join AI; then the bevel marked No. 5 will be correct for the beam next to the hip, and the bevel marked No. 6 will be correct for the top. Bevel No. 2 in this figure will be correct for the beam next to the plate. The edge of the brace is to correspond with the boarding.

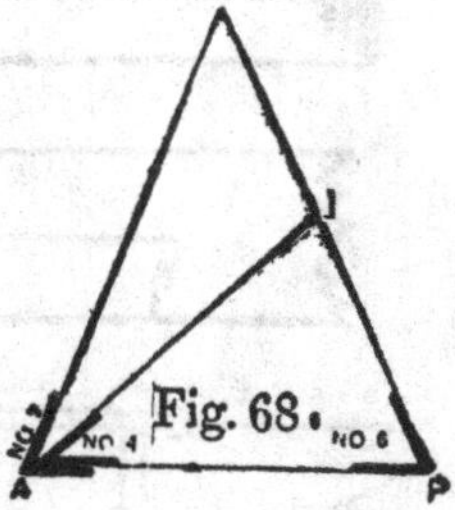

A few examples of scarfing timber are presented at Figs. 69, 70, 71
and 72. The example shown at
Fig. 69 exhibits a method by
which the two ends of the timber
are joined together with a step-
splice and spur or tenon on end, it
being drawn tight together by the
keys, as shown in the shaded part. Fig. 70 is a similar
joint though simpler, and therefore a better one; A, A
are generally joggles of hardwood, and not wedged
keys, but the latter are preferable, as they allow of
tightening up. The shearing used along BF should be
pine, and be not less than six and a half times BC;
and BC should be equal to at least twice the depth of
the key. The shear in the keys being at right angles
to the grain of the wood, a greater stress per square
inch of shearing area can be put upon them than
along BF, but their shearing area should be equal in
strength to the other parts of the joint; oak is the
best wood for them, as its shearing is from four to five
times that of pine.

Fig. 68.

Scarfed joints with bolts and indents, such as that shown at Fig. 71, are about the strongest of the kind. From this it will be seen that the strongest and most economical method in every way, in lengthening ties, is by adoption of the common scarf joint, as shown at Fig. 71, and finishing the scarf as there represented.

The carpenter meets with many conditions when timbers of various kinds have to be lengthened out

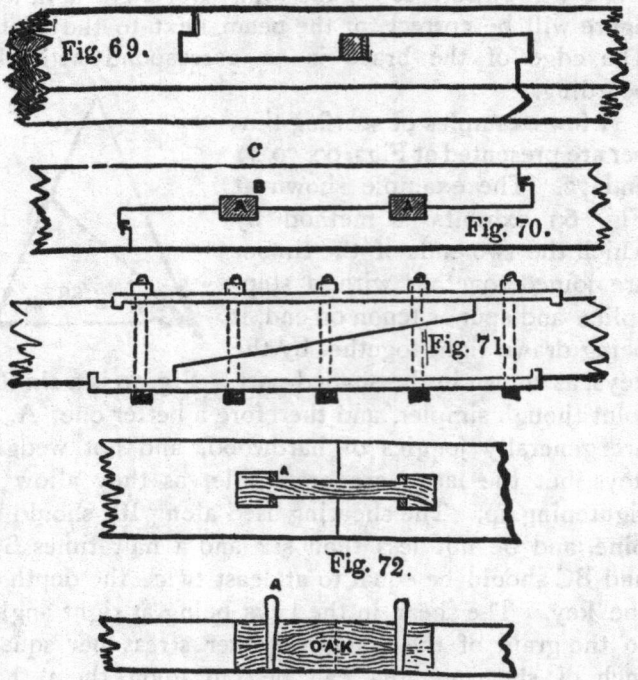

Fig. 69.

Fig. 70.

Fig. 71.

Fig. 72.

and spliced, as in the case of wall plates, etc., where there is not much tensile stress. In such cases the timbers may simply be halved together and secured with nails, spikes, bolts, screws or pins, or they may be halved or beveled as shown in Fig. 72, which, when loaded above, as in the case of wall plates built in the wall, or as stringers on which partitions are set, or joint beams on which the lower edges of the joists rest, will hold good together.

Treadgold gives the following rules, based upon the relative resistance to tension, crushing and shearing of different woods, for the proportion which the length or overlap of a scarf should bear to the depth of the tie:

	Without bolts	With bolts	With bolts and indents
Oak, ash, elm, etc. . .	6	3	2
Pine and similar woods .	12	6	4

There are many other kinds of scarfs that will occur to the workman, but it is thought the foregoing may be found useful on special occasions.

A few examples of odd joints in timber work will not be out of place. It sometimes happens that cross-beams are required to be fitted in between girders in position, as in

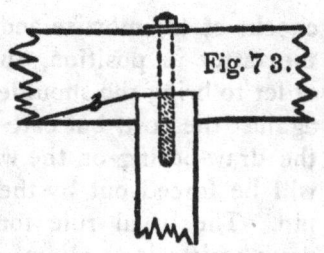

Fig. 73.

renewing a defective one, and when this has to be done, and a mortise and tenon joint is used, a chase has to be cut leading into the mortise, as shown in the horizontal section, Fig 73. By inserting the tenon at the other end of the beams into a mortise cut so as to allow of fitting it in at an angle, the tenon can be slid along the chase *b* into its proper position. It is better in this case to dispense with the long tenon, and, if necessary, to substitute a bolt, as shown in the sketch. A mortise of this kind is called a *chase mortise*, but an iron shoe made fast to the girder forms a better means of carrying the end of a cross-beam. The beams can be secured to the shoe with bolts or other fastenings.

To support the end of a horizontal beam or girt on the side of a post, the joint shown in Fig. 74 may be

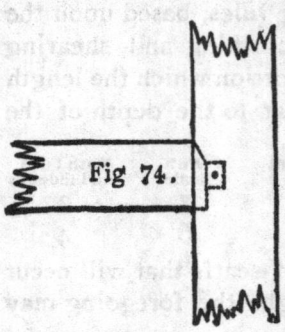

Fig 74.

used where the mortise for the long tenon is placed, to weaken the post as little as possible, and the tenon made about one-third the thickness of the beam on which it is cut. The amount of bearing the beam has on the post must greatly depend on the work it has to do. A hardwood pin can be passed through the cheeks of the mortise and the tenon as shown to keep the latter in position, the holes being *draw-bored* in order to bring the shoulders of the tenon tight home against the post, but care must be taken not to overdo the draw-boring or the wood at the end of the tenon will be forced out by the pin. The usual rule for draw-boring is to allow a quarter of an inch *draw* in soft woods and one-eighth of an inch for hard woods.

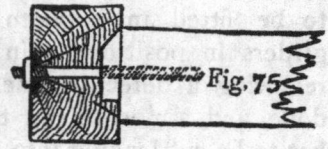

Fig. 75

These allowances may seem rather large, but it must be remembered that both holes in tenon and mortise will give a little, so also will the draw pin itself unless it is of iron, an uncommon circumstance.

Instead of a mortise and tenon, an iron strap or a screw bolt or nut may be used, similiar to that shown in Fig. 75.

The end of the beam may also be supported on a block which should be of hardwood, spiked or bolted

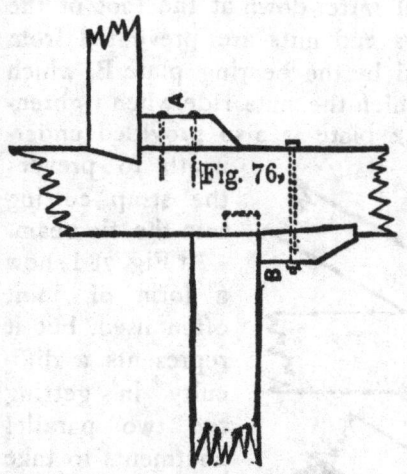

Fig. 76,

on to the side of the post, as at A and B, Fig. 76. The end of the beam may either be tenoned into the post as shown, or it may have a shoulder, with the end of the beam beveled, as shown at A.

Heavy roof timbers are rapidly giving place to steel, but there yet remain many cases where timbers will remain employed and the old method of framing continued. The use of iron straps and bolts in fastening timbers together or for trussing purposes will never perhaps become obsolete, therefore a knowledge of the proper use of these will always remain valuable.

Heel straps are used to secure the joints between inclined struts and horizontal beams, such as the joints between rafters and

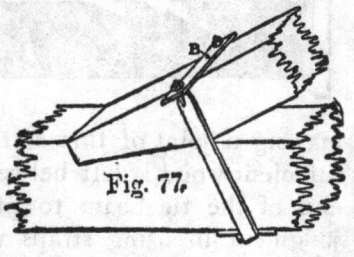

Fig. 77,

beams. They may be placed either so as merely to hold the beams close together at the joints, as in Fig. 77, or so as to directly resist the thrust of the inclined strut and prevent it from shearing off the portion of the horizontal beam against which it presses. Straps of the former kind are sometimes called *kicking-straps*. The example shown at Fig. 77 is a good form of strap for holding a principal rafter down at the foot of the tie beam. The screws and nuts are prevented from sinking into the wood by the bearing plate B, which acts as a washer on which the nuts ride when tightening is done. A check plate is also provided underneath to prevent the strap cutting into the tie beam.

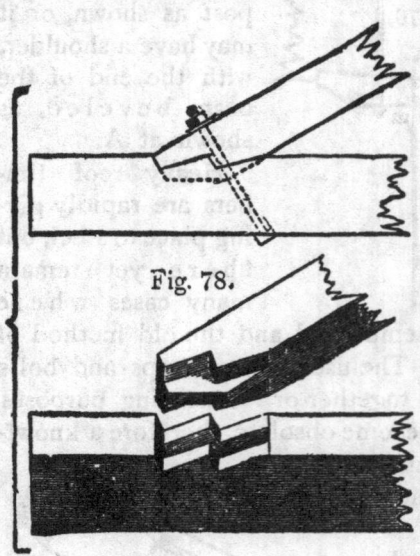

Fig. 78.

At Fig. 78 I show a form of joint often used, but it represents a difficulty in getting the two parallel abutments to take their fair share of the work, both from want of accuracy in workmanship as well as from the disturbing influence of shrinkage. In making a joint of this sort, care must be taken that sufficient wood is left between the abutments and the end of the tie beam to prevent shearing. A little judgment in using straps will often save both time and money and yet be sufficient for all purposes.

I show a few examples of strengthening and trussing joints, girders, and timbers at Fig 79. The diagrams need no explanation, as they are self-evident.

It would expand this book far beyond the dimensions

awarded me, to even touch on all matters pertaining to carpentry, including bridges, trestles, trussed girders and trusses generally, so I must content myself

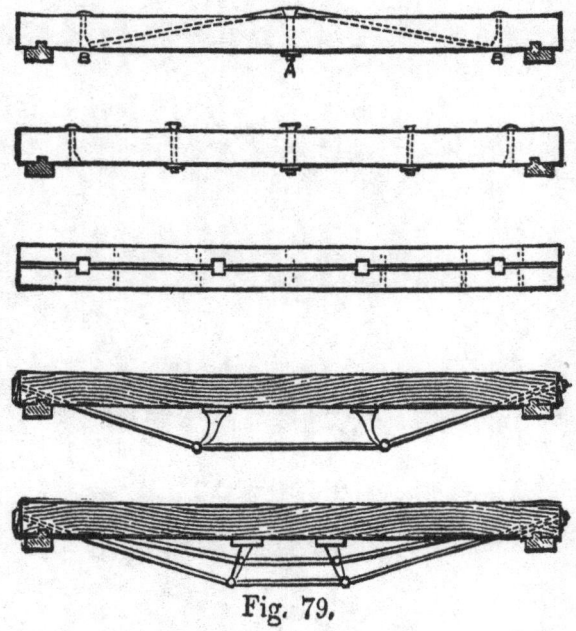

Fig. 79.

with what has already been given on the subject of carpentry, although, as the reader is aware, the subject is only surfaced.

PART III

JOINER'S WORK

CHAPTER I

KERFING, RAKING MOULDINGS, HOPPERS AND SPLAYS

This department could be extended indefinitely, as the problems in joinery are much more numerous than in carpentry, but as the limits of this book will not permit me to cover the whole range of the art, even if I were competent, I must be contented with dealing with those problems the workman will most likely be confronted with in his daily occupation.

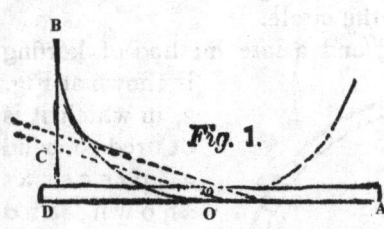

Fig. 1.

First of all, I give several methods of "kerfing," for few things puzzle the novice more than this little problem. Let us suppose any circle around which it is desired to bend a piece of stuff to be 2 inches larger on the outside than on the inside, or in other words, the veneer is to be 1 inch thick, then take out as many saw kerfs as will measure 2 inches. Thus, if a saw cuts a kerf one thirty-second of an inch in width, then it will take 64 kerfs in the half circle to allow for the veneer to bend around neatly. The piece being placed in position and bent, the kerfs will exactly close.

Another way is to saw one kerf near the center of the piece to be bent, then place it on the plan of the frame, as indicated in the sketch and bend it until the kerf closes. The distance, DC, Fig. 1, on the line DB, will be the space between the kerfs necessary to complete the bending.

In kerfing the workman should be careful to use the same saw throughout, and to cut exactly the same depth every time, and the spaces must be of equal distance. In diagram Fig. 1, DA shows the piece to be bent, and at O the thickness of the stuff is shown, also path of the inside and outside of the circle.

Another, and a safe method of kerfing is shown at Fig. 2, in which it is desired to bend a piece as shown, and which is intended to be secured at the ends. Up to A is the piece to be treated.

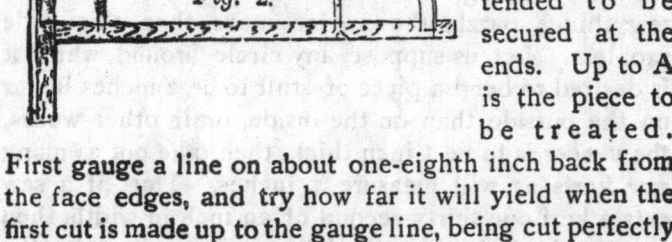

Fig. 2.

First gauge a line on about one-eighth inch back from the face edges, and try how far it will yield when the first cut is made up to the gauge line, being cut perfectly straight through from side to side, then place the work

on a flat board and try it gently until the kerf closes,
and it goes as far as is shown at A, which is the first
cut, B representing the second. Those are the distances the kerfs require to be placed apart to complete
the curve.   Try the work as it progresses.   This eases
the back of it and makes it much easier done when the
whole cuts are finished.   Now make certain that the
job will fold to the curve, then fill them all with hot
glue and proceed to fix.   The plan shown here is a
h a l f semi, and
may be in excess
of what is wanted,
but the principle
holds good.

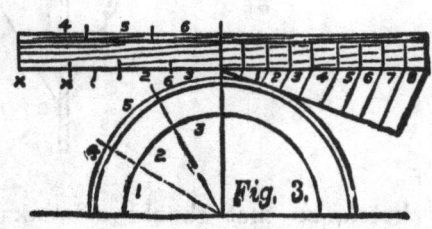

Fig. 3.

Another method
is shown at Fig. 3
f o r determining
the number and
distances apart of the saw kerfs required to bend a
board round a corner.   The board is first drawn in
position and a half of it divided into any number of
equal parts by radii, as 1, 2, 3, 4, 5, 6.   A straight
piece is then marked off to correspond with the divisions on the circular one.   By this it is seen that the
part XX must be cut away by saw kerfs in order to let
the board turn round.   It therefore depends upon the
thickness of the saw for the number of kerfs, and when
that is known the distances apart can be determined as
shown on the right in the figure.   Here eight kerfs are
assumed to be requisite.

To make a kerf for bending round an ellipse, such as
that shown at Fig. 4, proceed as shown, CC and OO
being the distances for the kerfs; 2 to 2 and 2 to 3 are the
lengths of the points EF, while BB is the length of the

points EE, making the whole head piece in one. In case it is necessary to joint D, leave the ends about 8 inches longer than is necessary, as shown by N in the

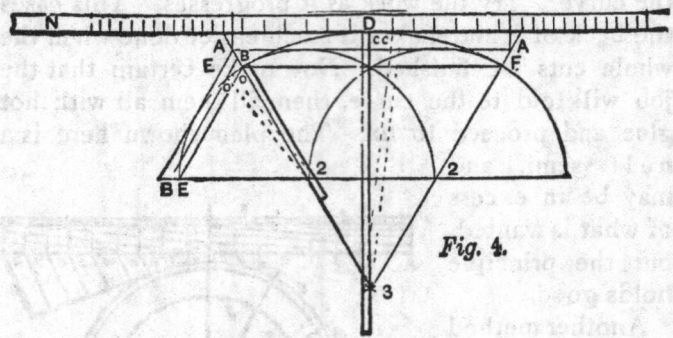

Fig. 4.

sketch, so that should a breakage occur this extra length may be utilized.

It is sometimes necessary to bend thick stuff around work that is on a rake, and when this is required, all that is necessary is to run in the kerfs the angle of the rake whatever that may be, as shown at Fig. 5. This rule holds good for all pitches or rakes. Fig. 6 shows a very common way of obtaining the distance to place the kerfs. The piece to be kerfed is shown at C; now make one at E; hold firm the lower part of C and bend

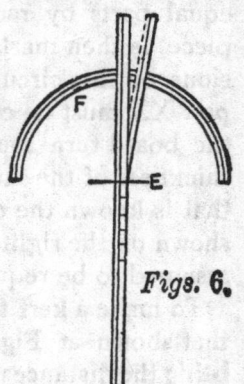

Figs. 6.

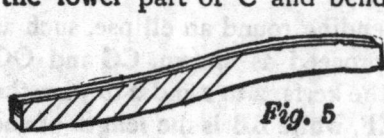

Fig. 5

the upper end on the circle F until the kerf is closed.
The line started at E and cutting the circumference of
the circle indicates at the circumference the distance
the saw kerfs will be apart. Set the dividers to this
space, and be-
ginning at the
center cut,
space the piece
to be kerfed
both ways.
Use the same
saw in all cuts
and let it be
clean and keen,
with all dust
well cleaned
out.

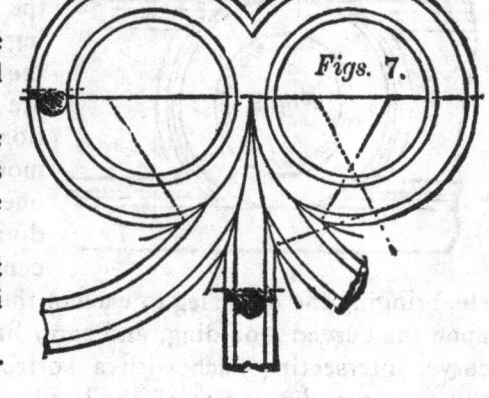

Figs. 7.

To miter
mouldings,
where straight lines must merge into lines having a
curvature as in Figs. 7 and 8: In all cases, where a
straight moulding is intersected with a curved moulding of the same profile at whatever angle, the miter is
necessarily other than a straight line. The miter line
is found by the intersec-
tion of lines from the
several points of the profile as they occur respectively in the straight and
the curved mouldings.
In order to find the miter
between two such mould-
irgs, first project lines
from all of the points of

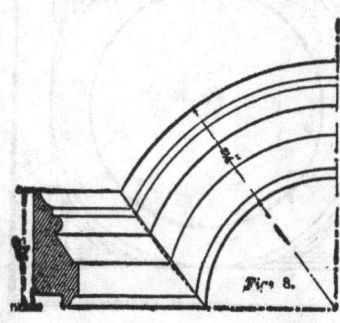

Fig. 8.

the profile indefinitely to the right, as shown in the elevation of the sketch. Now, upon the center line of the curved portion, or upon any line radiating from the center around which the curved moulding is to be

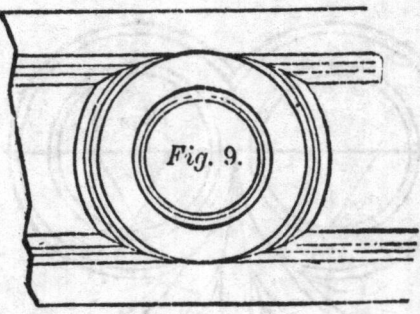

carried, set off the several points of the profile, spacing them exactly the same as they are in the elevation of the straight moulding. Place one leg of the dividers at t h e center of the circle, bringing the other leg to each of the several points upon the curved moulding, and carry lines around the curve, intersecting each with a horizontal line from the corresponding point of the level moulding. The dotted line drawn through the intersections at the miter shows w h a t must be the real miter line.

Another odd mitering of this class is shown in Fig. 9. In this it will be seen that the plain faces of the stiles and circular rail f o r m junctions, the mouldings all being mitered. The miters are curved in order

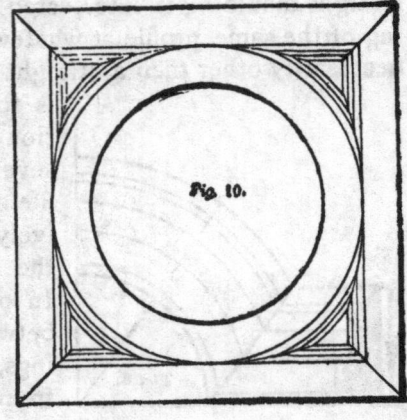

to have all the members of the mouldings merge in one another without overwood. Another example is shown at Fig. 10, where the circle and mouldings make a series of panels. These examples are quite sufficient to enable the workman to deal effectively with every problem of this kind.

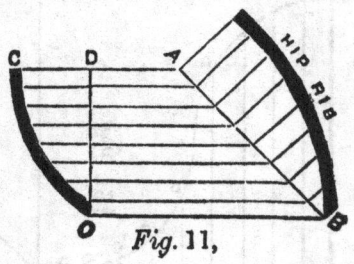

Fig. 11,

The workman sometimes finds it a little difficult to lay out a hip rafter for a veranda that has a curved roof. A very easy method of finding the curve of the hip is shown at Fig. 11. Let AB be the length of the angle or seat of hip, and CO the curve; raise perpendicular on AB, as shown, same as those on DO, and trace through the points obtained, and the thing is done.

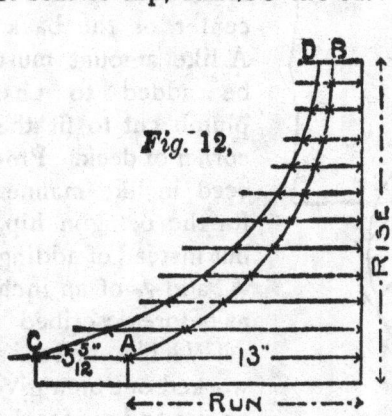

Fig. 12,

Another simple way of finding the hip for a single curve is shown at Fig. 12; AB represents the curve given the common rafter.

Now lay off any number of lines parallel with the seat from the rise, to and beyond the curve AB, as shown, and for each inch in length of these lines (between rise and curve), add $\frac{5}{12}$ of an inch to the same line to the left of the curve, and check. After all lines have thus been measured, run an off-hand curve through the checks, and the curve will represent the corresponding hip at the center of its back.

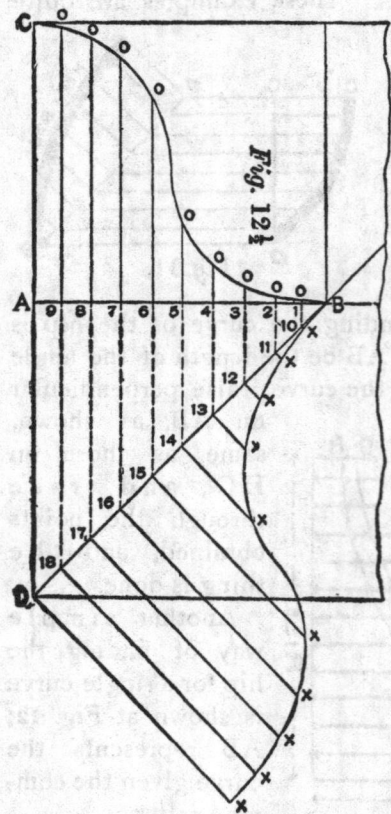

Fig. 12½

To find the bevel or backing of the hip to coincide with the plane of the common rafter, measure back on the parallel lines to the right of the curve one-half the thickness of the hip and d r a w another curve, which will be the lines on the side to trim to from the center of the back. A like amount must be added to t h e plumb cut to fit the corner of deck. Proceed in like manner for the octagon hip, but instead of adding $\frac{5}{18}$, add $\frac{4}{18}$ of an inch as before described.

[While this is worked out on a given rise and run for the rafter, the rule is applicable to any rise or run, as the workman will readily understand.]

A more elaborate system for obtaining the curve of a hip rafter, where the common rafters have an ogee or concave and convex shape, is shown at Fig. 12½. This

is a very old method, and is shown—with slight variations—in nearly all the old works on carpentry and
joinery.   Draw the seat of the common rafter, AB,
and rise, AC.   Then draw the curve of the common
rafter, CB.   Now divide the base line, AB, into any
number of equal spaces, as 1, 2, 3, 4, 5, etc., and draw
perpendicular lines to construct the curve CB, as 1 0,
2 0, 3 0, 4 0, etc.   Now draw the seat of the valley, or
hip rafter, as BD, and continue the
perpendicular lines referred to until
they meet BD, thus establishing the
points 10, 11, 12, 13, 14, etc.   From
these points draw lines at right
angles to BD, making 10 x equal in
length to 1 0, and 11 x equal to 2 0;

Figs. 13.

also 12 x equal to 3 0, and so on.   When this has been
done draw through the points indicated by **x** the
curve, which is the profile of the valley rafters.

Another method, based on the same principles as
Fig. 12½, is shown at Fig. 13.   Let ABCFED represent
the plan of the roof.   FCG represents the profile of the
wide side of common rafter.   First divide this common
rafter, GC, into any number of parts—in this case 6.

Transfer these points to the miter line EB, or, what is the same, the line in the plan representing the hip rafter From the points thus established at E, erect perpendiculars indefinitely. With the dividers take the distance from the points in the line FE, measuring to the points in the profile GC, and set the same off on corresponding lines, measuring from EB, thus establishing the points 1, 2, etc.; then a line traced through these points will be the required hip rafter.

For the common rafter, on the narrow side, continue the lines from EB parallel with the lines of the plan DE and AB. Draw AD at right angles to these lines. With the

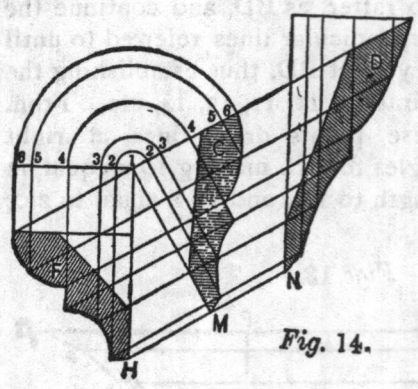

Fig. 14.

dividers, as before, measuring from FE to the points in GC, set off corresponding distances from AD, thus establishing the points shown between A and H. A line traced through the points thus obtained will be the line of the rafter on the narrow side.

These examples are quite sufficient to enable the workman to draw the exact form of any rafter no matter what the curve of its face may be, or whether it is for a veranda hip, or an angle bracket, for a cornice or niche.

Another class of angular curves the workman will meet with occasionally, is that when raking mouldings are used to work in level mouldings, as for

instance, a moulding down a gable that is to miter.
The figures shaded in Fig. 14 represent the moulding in its various phases and angles. Draw the outline of the common level moulding, as shown at F, in
the same position as if in its place on the building.
Draw lines through as many prominent points in the
profile as may be convenient, parallel with the line of
rake. From the same points in the moulding draw vertical lines, as shown by 1H, 2, 3, 4 and 5, etc. From
the point 1, square with the lines of the rake, draw 1M,

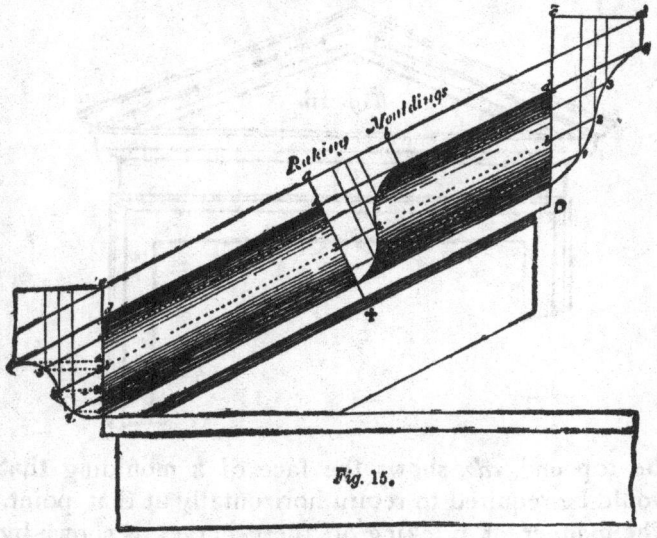

Fig. 15.

as shown, and from 1 as center, with the dividers
transfer the divisions 2, 3, 4, etc., as shown, and from
the points thus obtained, on the upper line of the rake
draw lines parallel to 1M. Where these lines intersect
with the lines of the rake will be points through which
the outline C may be traced.

In case there is a moulded head to put upon a raking

gable, the moulding D shown at the right hand must be worked out for the upper side. The manner in which this is done is self-evident upon examination of the drawing, and therefore needs no special description.

A good example of a raking moulding and its applications to actual work is shown in Fig. 15, on a different scale. The ogee moulding at the lower end is the regular moulding, while the middle line, ax, shows the shape of the raking moulding, and the curve on

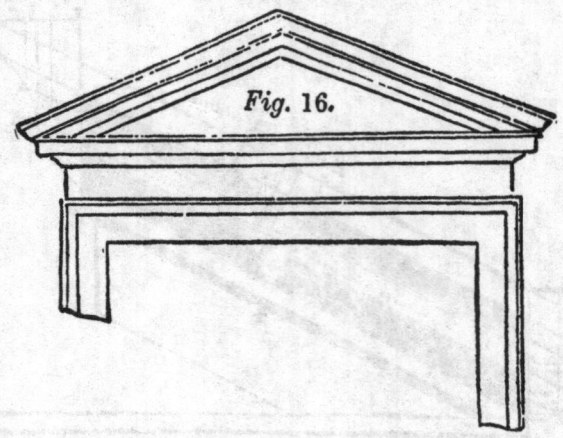

Fig. 16.

the top end, cdo, shows the face of a moulding that would be required to return horizontally at that point. The manner of pricking off these curves is shown by the letters and figures.

At Fig. 16 a finished piece of work is shown, where this manner of work will be required, on the returns.

Fig. 17 shows the same moulding applied to a curved window or door head. The manner of pricking the curve is given in Fig. 18.

At No. 2 draw any line, AD, to the center of the

pediment, meeting the upper edge of the upper fillet in D, and intersecting the lines AAA, *aaa*, *bbb ccc*,

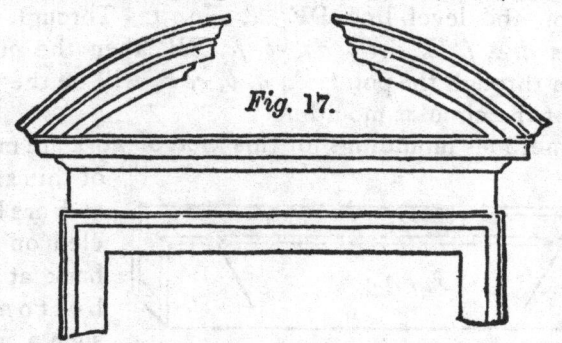

Fig. 17.

BBB in A, *a*, *b*, *c*, B, E. From these points draw lines *aa*, *bb*, *cc*, BB, EE, tangents to their respective arcs;

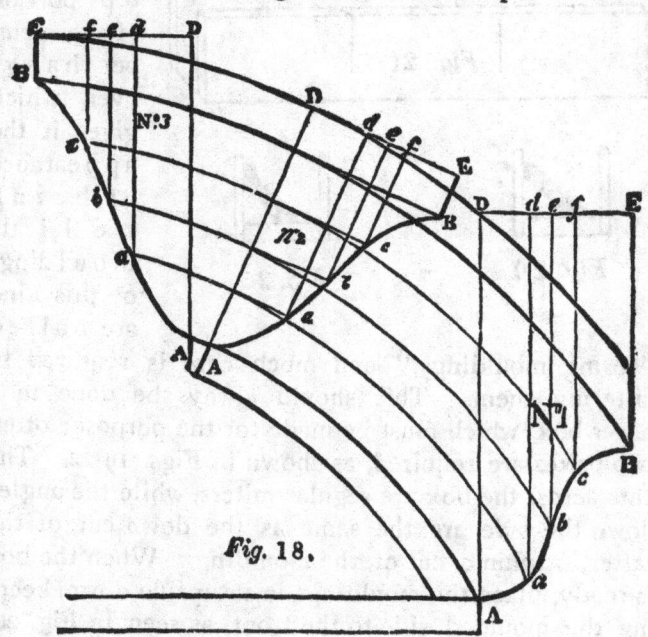

Fig. 18.

on the tangent line DE, from D, make D*d*, D*e*, D*f*, DE, respectively equal to the distances D*d*, D*e*, D*f*, DE on the level line DE, at No. 1. Through the points *d*, *e*, *f*, E, draw *da*, *eb*, *fc*, EB, then the curve drawn through the points A, *a*, *b*, *c*, B, will be the section of the circular moulding.

Sometimes mouldings for this kind of work are made of thin stuff, and are beveled on the back at the bottom in such a manner that the top portion of the member hangs over, which gives it the appearance of being solid. Mouldings of this kind are called

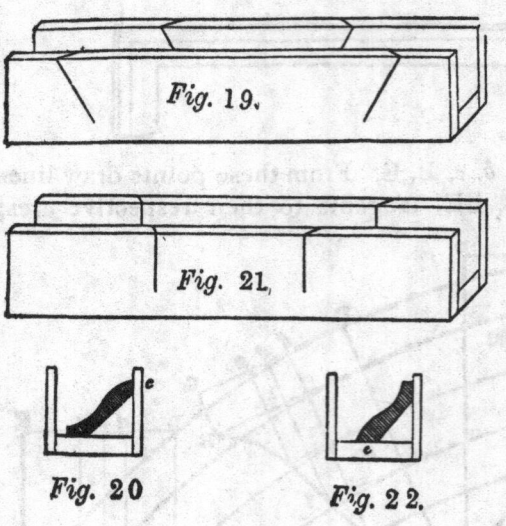

Fig. 19.

Fig. 21.

Fig. 20

Fig. 22.

"spring mouldings," and much care is required in mitering them. This should always be done in a miter box, which must be made for the purpose; often two boxes are required, as shown in Figs. 19-22. The cuts across the box are regular miters, while the angles down the side are the same as the down cut of the rafter, or plumb cut of the moulding. When the box is ready, place the mouldings in it upside down, keeping the moulded side to the front, as seen in Fig. 20

making sure that the level of the moulding at *c* fits close to the side of the box.

To miter the rake mouldings together at the top, the box shown in Fig. 21 is used. The angles on the top of the box are the same as the down bevel at the top of the rafter, the sides being sawed down square. Put the moulding in the box, as shown in Fig. 22, keeping the bevel at *c* flat on the bottom of the box, and having the moulded side to the front, and the miter for the top is cut, which completes the moulding for one side of the gable. The miter for the top of the moulding for the other side of the gable may then be cut.

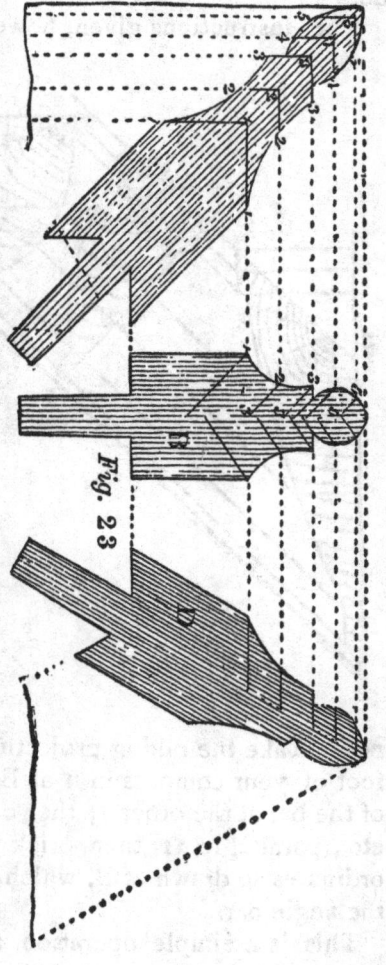

Fig. 23

When the rake moulding is made of the proper form these boxes are very convenient; but a great deal of the machine-made mouldings are not of the proper form to fit. In such cases the moulding should be made to suit, or they come bad; although many use the mouldings as they come from the factory, and trim the miters so as to make them do.

The instructions given, however, in Figs. 13, 14, 15 and 18 will enable the workman to make patterns for what he requires.

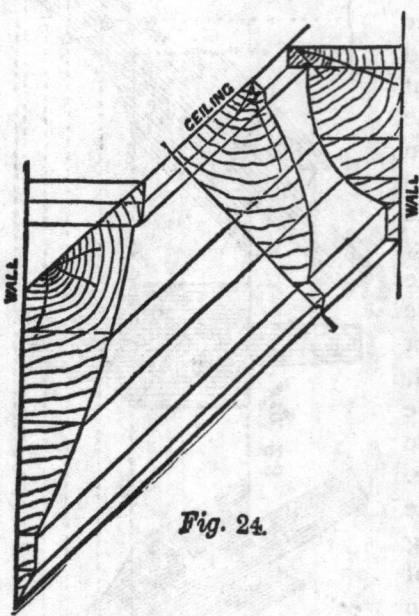

Fig. 24.

While the "angle bar" is not much in vogue at the present time, the methods by which it is obtained, may be applied to many purposes, so it is but proper the method should be embodied in this work. In Fig. 23, B is a common sash bar, and C is the angle bar of the same thickness. Take the raking projection, 11, in C, and set the foot of your compass in 1 at B, and cross the middle of the bar at the other 1; then draw the points 2, 2, 3, 3, etc., parallel to 11, then prick your bar at C from the ordinates so drawn at B, which, when traced, will give the angle bar.

This is a simple operation, and may be applied to

many other cases, and for enlarging or diminishing mouldings or other work.

The next figure, 24, gives the lines for a raking moulding, such as a cornice in a room with a sloping culling As may be seen from the diagram the three sections shcwn are drawn equal in thickness to miter at the angles of the room.

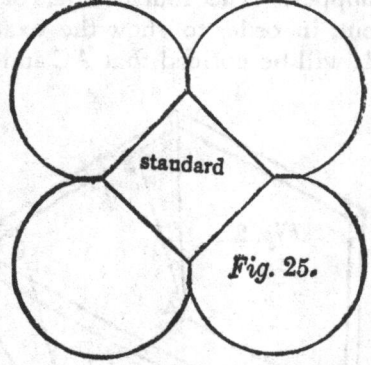

Fig. 25.

standard

The construction should be easily understood When a straight moulding is mitered with a curved one the line of miter is sometimes straight and sometimes curved, as seen at Fig. 18, and when the mouldings are all curved the miters are also straight and curved, as shown in previous examples.

If it is desired to make a cluster column of wood, it is first necessary to make a standard or core, which must have as many sides as there are to be faces of columns.

Fig. 26.

Fig. 25 shows how the work is done. This shows a cluster of four columns, which are nailed to a square standard or core. Fig. 26 shows the base of a clustered column. These are blocks turned in the lathe, requiring four of them for each base, which are cut and mitered as shown in Fig. 25. The cap, or capital, is, of course, cut in the same manner.

Laying out lines for hopper cuts is often puzzling, and on this account I will devote more space to this subject than to those requiring less explanations.

Fig. 27 shows an isometric view of three sides of a hopper. The fourth side, or end, is purposely left out, in order to show the exact build of the hopper. It will be noticed that AC and EO show the end of the

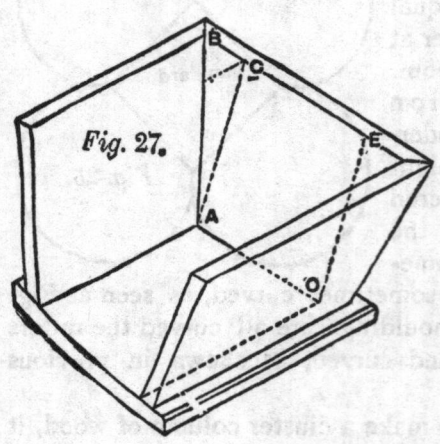

Fig. 27.

work as squared up from the bottom, and that BC shows the gain of the splay or flare. This gives the idea of what a hopper is, though the width of side and amount of flare may be any measurement that may be decided upon. The difficulty in this work is to get the proper lines for the miter and for a butt cut.

Let us suppose the flare of the sides and ends to be as shown at Fig. 28, though any flare or inclination will answer equally well. This diagram and the plan exhibit the method to be employed, where the sides and ends are to be mitered together. To obtain the bevel to apply for the side cut, use A′ as center, B′ as radius, and CDF′ parallel to BF. Project from B to D parallel to XY. Join AD, which gives the bevel required, as shown. If the top edge of the stuff is to be horizontal, as shown at B′G′, the bevel to apply to the edge will be simply as shown in plan by BG; but if the edge of the stuff is to be square to the side, as shown at B'C', Fig. 29, the bevel must be obtained as follows: Produce EB' to D', as indicated, Fig. 29. With B as center, describe the arc from C', which gives the point D.   Project down from D, making DF

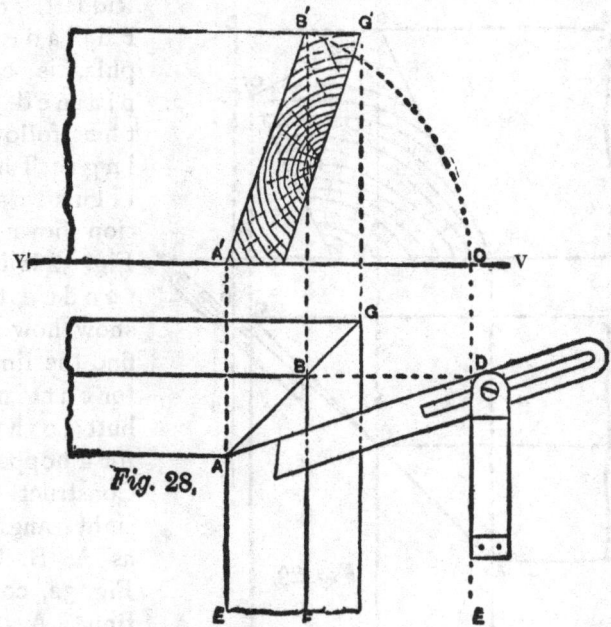

Fig. 28.

parallel to CC, as shown.   Project from C parallel to XY   This will give the point D.   Join BD, and this will give the bevel line required.   At A, Fig. 31, is shown the application of the bevel to the side of the stuff, and at B the application of the bevel to the edge of the stuff.   When the ends butt to the sides, as indicated at H, Fig. 30, the bevel, it will be noticed, is obtained in a similar manner to that shown at Fig. 28. It is not often that simply a butt joint is used between the ends and sides, but the ends are usually housed into the sides, as indicated by the dotted lines shown at H, Fig. 30.

Another system, which was first taught by the celebrated Peter Nicholson, and afterwards by Robert Riddell, of Philadelphia, is explained in the following: The illustration shown at Fig. 32 is intended to show how to find the lines for cutting butt joints for a hopper. Construct a right angle, as A, B, C, Fig. 32, continue. A, B past K. From K, B make

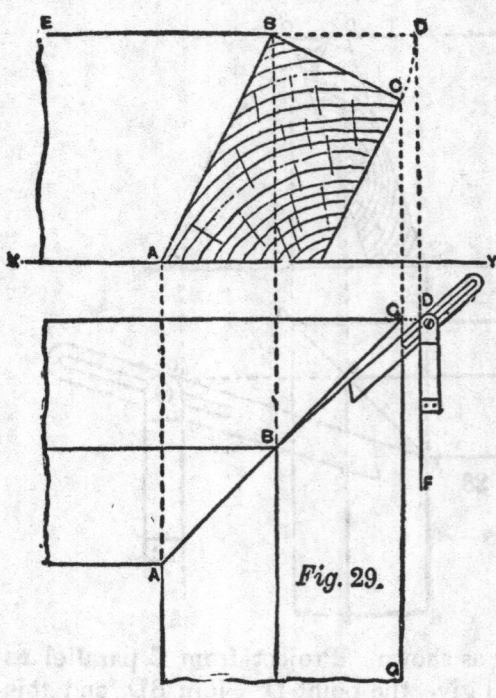

Fig. 29.

the inclination of the sides of the hopper, 2, 3.

Draw 3, 4 at right angles with 3, 2; take 3 as center and strike an arc touching the lower line, cutting in 4. Draw from 4, cutting the miter line in 5; from 5 square draw a line cutting in 6, join it and B; this gives bevel W, as the direction of cut on the surface of sides. To find the butt joint, take any two points, A, C, on the

right angle, equally distant from B, make the angle
B, K, L, equal that of 3, K, L, shown on the left; from
B draw through point L; now take C as a center, and
strike an arc, touching line BL.   From A draw a
line touching the arc at H, and cutting the extended
line through B
in N, thus fixing
N as a point.
Then by draw-
ing from C
through N, we
get the bevel
X for the butt
joint. Joints
on the ends of
timbers running
horizontally in
tapered framed
structures, when
the plan is
square and the
inclinations
equal, may be
found by this
method.

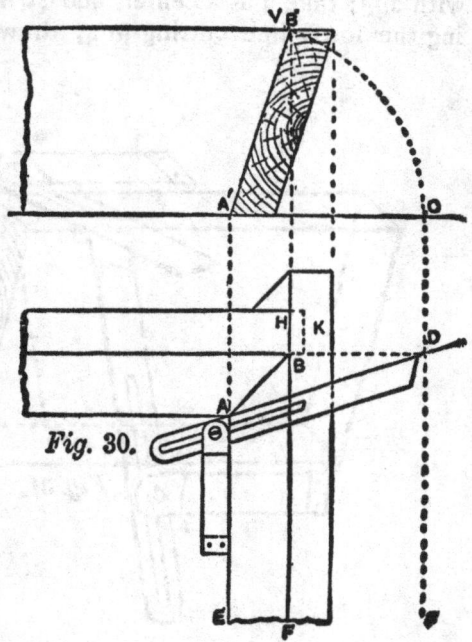

Fig. 30.

The backing
of a hip rafter may also be obtained by this method, as
shown at J, where the pitch line is used as at 2, 3,
which would be the inclination of the roof.

The solution just rendered is intended only for hoppers having right angles and equal pitches or splays,
as hoppers having acute or obtuse angles, must be
treated in a slightly different way.

Let us suppose a butt joint for a hopper having an

acute angle, such as shown at A, B, C, Fig. 33, and
with an inclination as shown at 2, 3. Take any two
points, A, C, equally distant from B. Join A, C,
bisect this line in P, draw through P, indefinitely.
Find a bevel for the side cut by drawing 3, 4, square
with 2, 3; take 3 as a center, and strike an arc, touching the lower line cutting in 4; draw from 4, cutting

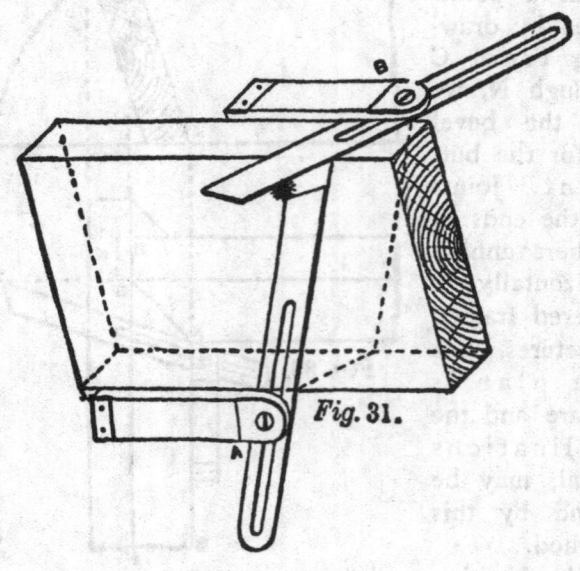

Fig. 31.

the miter line in 5, and from it square draw a line
cutting in 6. Join 6, B, this gives bevel W, for direction of cut on the surface of inclined sides.

The bevel for a butt joint is found by drawing C, 8,
square with A, B; make the angle 8, K, L, equal that
of 3, K, L, shown on the left. Draw from 8 through point
L; take C as a center and strike an arc touching the
line 8, L; draw from A, touching the arc at D, cutting

the line from P, in D, making it a point, then by drawing from C, through D, we get the bevel X for the butt joint.

As stated regarding the previous illustration, the backing for a hip in a roof having the pitch as shown at 2, 3, may be found at the bevel J. The same rule

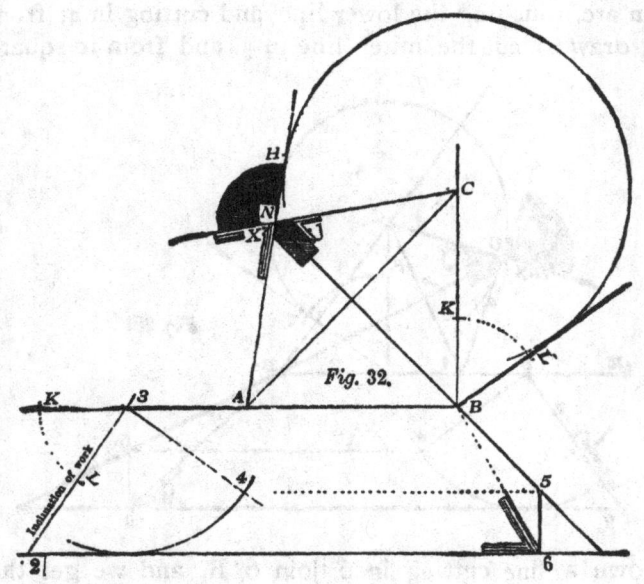

Fig. 32.

also applies to end joints on timbers placed in a horizontal double inclined frame, having an acute angle same as described.

Having described the methods for finding the butt joints in right-angled and acute-angled hoppers, it will be proper now to define a method for describing an obtuse-angled hopper having butt joints.

Let the inclination of the sides of the hopper be

exhibited at the line 2, 3, and the angle of the obtuse
corner of the hopper at A, B, C, then to find the joint,
take any two points, A, C, equally distant from B,
join these points, and divide the line at P. Draw
through P and B, indefinitely. At any distance below
the side A, B, draw the line 2, 6; make 3, 4, square
with the inclination. From 3, as a center, describe
an arc, touching the lower line and cutting in 4; from
4 draw to cut the miter line in 5, and from it square

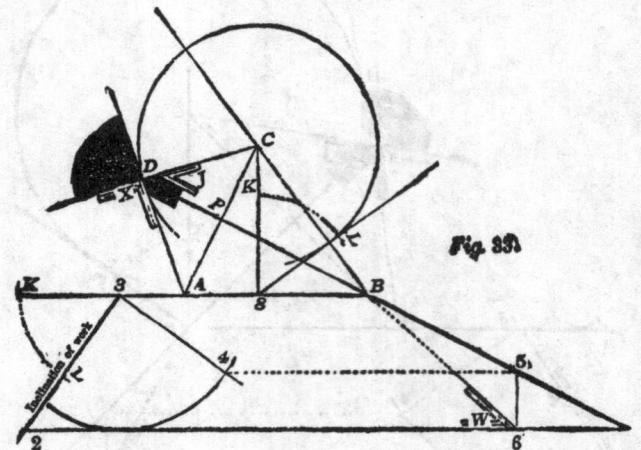

Fig. 33

down a line cutting in 6, join 6, B, and we get the
bevel W, for cut on surface sides.

The bevel for the butt joint is found by drawing C,
D, square with B, A, and making the angle D, K, L
equal to that of 3, K, L on the left. From C, as a
center, strike an arc, touching the line D, L; then
from A draw a line touching the arc H. This line
having cut through P, in N, fixes N as a point, so that
by drawing C through N an angle is determined, in
which is bevel X for the butt joint.

To obtain the evels or miters is a simple matter to one who has mastered the foregoing, as evidenced by the following:

Fig. 34 shows a right-angled hopper; its sides may stand on any inclination, as AB. The miter line,

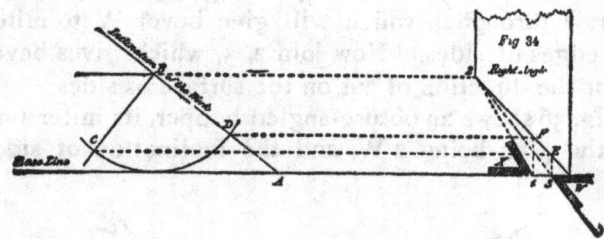

2, W, on the plan, being fixed, draw B, C square with the inclination.   Then from B, as center, strike an arc, touching the base line and cutting in CD.   From CD draw parallel with the base line, cutting the miters in F and E; and from these points square down the lines, cutting in 3 and 4.   From 2 draw through 3; this gives

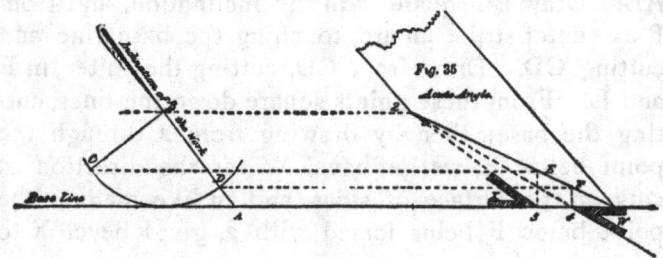

bevel W for the direction of cut on the surface sides. Now join 2, 4, this gives bevel X to miter the edges, which in all cases must be square, in order that bevels may be properly applied.

Fig. 35 shows a plan forming an acute-angled hopper, the miter line being 2, W. The sides of this plan are to stand on the inclination AB. Draw BC square with the inclination, and from B, as center, strike an arc, touching the base line and cutting in CD. Draw from CD, cutting the miter line at E and F; from these points square down the lines, cutting in 3 and 4. From 2 draw through 4, which will give bevel W to miter the edges of sides. Now join 2, 3, which gives bevel X for the direction of cut on the surface of sides.

Fig. 36 shows an obtuse-angled hopper, its miter line on the plan being 2 W, and the inclination of sides

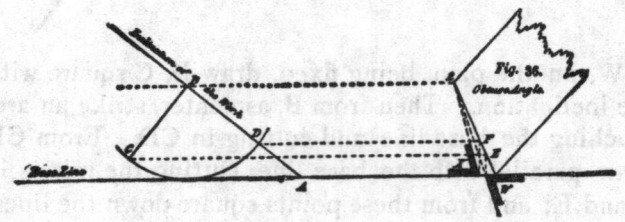

AB. Draw BC square with the inclination, and from B as center strike an arc, touching the base line and cutting CD. Draw from CD, cutting the miter in F and E. From these points square down the lines, cutting the base; then by drawing from 2 through the point below E, we get bevel W for the direction of cuts on the surface of sides, and in like manner the point below F being joined with 2, gives bevel X to miter the edges.

It will be noticed that the cuts for the three different angles are obtained on exactly the same principle, without the slightest variation, and so perfectly simple as to be understood by a glance at the drawing. The workman will notice that in each of the angles a

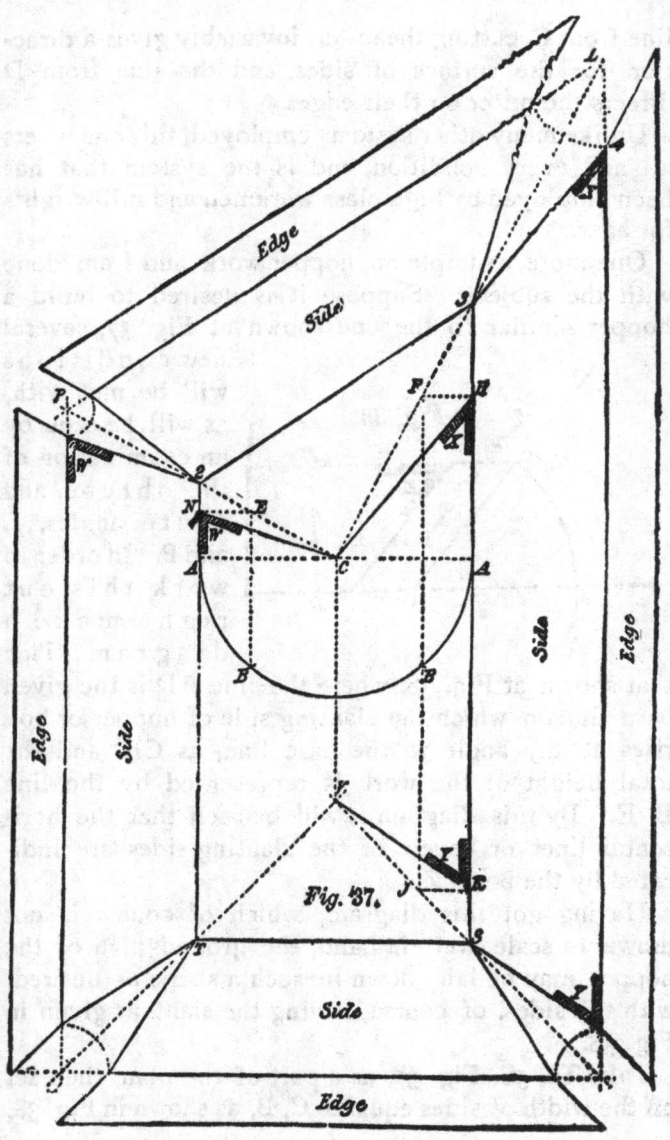

Fig. 37.

line from C, cutting the miter, invariably gives a direction for the surface of sides, and the line from D directs the miter on their edges.

Unlike many other systems employed, this one meets all and every condition, and is the system that has been employed by high class workmen and millwrights for ages.

One more example on hopper work and I am done with the subject: Suppose it is desired to build a hopper similar to the one shown at Fig. 37, several new conditions will be met with, as will be seen by an examination of the obtuse and acute angles, L and P. In order to work this out right make a diagram like

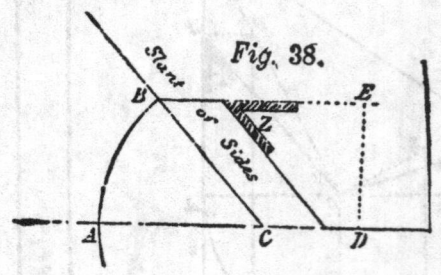

Fig. 38.

that shown at Fig. 38, where the line AD is the given base line on which the slanting side of hopper or box rises at any angle to the base line, as CB, and the total height of the work is represented by the line B, E. By this diagram it will be seen that the horizontal lines or bevels of the slanting sides are indicated by the bevel Z.

Having got this diagram, which of course is not drawn to scale, well in hand, the ground plan of the hopper may be laid down in such a shape as desired, with the sides, of course, having the slant as given in Fig 38.

Take T2, 3S, Fig. 37, as a part of the plan, then set off the width of sides equal to C, B, as shown in Fig. 38.

These are shown to intersect at P, L above; then draw lines from P, L through 2, 3, until they intersect at C, as the dotted lines show. Take C as a center, and with the radius A, describe the semi-circle A, A, and with the same radius transferred to C, Fig. 38, describe the arc A, B, as shown. Again, with the same radius, set off A, B, A, B on Fig. 37, cutting the semi-circle at B, as shown. Now draw through B, on the right, parallel with S, 3, cutting at J and F; square over F, H and J, K, and join H, C; this gives bevel X, as the cut for face of sides, which come together at the angle shown at 3. The miters on the edge of stuff are parallel with the dotted line, L, 3. This is the acute corner of the hopper, and as the edges are worked off to the bevel 2, as shown in Fig. 38, the miter must be correct.

Having mastered the details of the acute corner, the square corner at S will be next in order The first step is to join K, V, which gives the bevel Y, for the cut on the face of sides on the ends, which form the square corners. The method of obtaining these lines is the same as that explained for obtaining them for the acute-angled corner, as shown by the dotted lines, Fig. 35. As the angles, S, T, are both square, being right and left, the same operation answers both, that is, the bevel Y does for both corners.

Coming to the obtuse angle, P, 2, we draw a line B, E, on the left, parallel with A, 2, cutting at E, as shown by dotted line. Square over at E, cutting T, A, 2 at N; join N, C, which will give the bevel W, which is the angle of cut for face of sides. The miters on edges are found by drawing a line parallel with P, 2.

In this problem, like Fig. 34, every line necessary to the cutting of a hopper after the plan as shown by the boundary lines 2, 3, T, S, is complete and exhaustive, but it must be understood that in actual work the spreading out of the sides, as here exhibited, will not be necessary, as the angles will find themselves when the work is put together. When the plan of the base—which is the small end of the hopper in this case—is given, and the slant or inclination of the sides known, the rest may be easily obtained. In order to become thoroughly conversant with the problem, I would advise the workman to have the drawing made on cardboard, so as to cut out all the outer lines, including the open corners, which form the miters, leaving the whole piece loose. Then make slight cuts in the back of the cardboard, opposite the lines 2, 3, S, T, just deep enough to admit of the cardboard being bent upwards on the cut lines without breaking. Then run the knife along the lines, which indicates the edges of the hopper sides. This cut must be made on the face side of the drawing, so as to admit of the edges being turned downwards. After all cuts are made raise the sides until the corners come closely together, and let the edges fall level, or in such a position that the miters come closely together. If the lines have been drawn accurately and the cuts made on the lines in a proper manner, the work will adjust itself nicely, and the sides will have the exact inclination shown at Fig. 38, and a perfect model of the work will be the result.

This is a very interesting problem, and the working out of it, as suggested, cannot but afford both profit and pleasure to the young workman.

From what has preceded, it must be evident to the workman that the lines giving proper angles and bevels for the corner post of a hopper must of necessity give the proper lines for the corner post for a pyramidal building, such as a railway tank frame, or any similar structure. True, the position of the post is inverted, as in the hopper, its top falls outward, while in the timber structure the top inclines inward; but this makes no difference in the theory, all the operator has to bear in mind is that the hopper in this case is reversed —inverted Once the proper shape of the corner post has been obtained, all other bevels can readily be found, as the side cuts for joists and braces can be taken from them. A study of these two figures in this direction will lead the student up to a correct knowledge of tapered framing.

COVERING SOLIDS, CIRCULAR WORK, DOVETAILING AND
STAIRS

There are several ways to cover a circular tower roof.
Some are covered by bending the boarding around

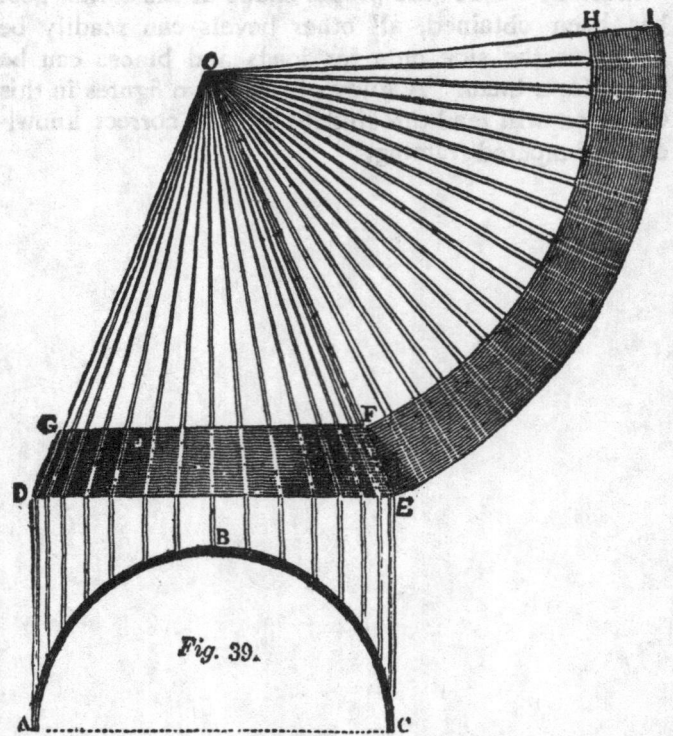

Fig. 39.

them, while others have the joints of the covering vertical, or inclined. In either case, the boarding has to
be cut to shape. In the first instance, where the joints

are horizontal, the covering must be curved on both edges.

At Fig. 39 I show a part plan, elevation, and development of a conical tower roof. ABC shows half the plan; DO and EO show the inclination and height of the tower, while EH and EI show the development of the lower course of covering. This is obtained by using O as a center, with OE as radius, and striking the curve EI, which is the lower edge of the board, and corresponds to DE in the elevation. From the same center O, with radius OF, describe the curve FH, which is the joint GF on the elevation. The board, EFHI, may be any convenient width, as may also the other boards used for covering, but whatever the width decided upon, that same width must be continued throughout that course. The remaining tiers of covering must be obtained in the same way. The joints are radial lines from the center O. Any convenient length of stuff over the distance of three ribs, or rafters, will answer. This solution is applicable to many kinds of work. The

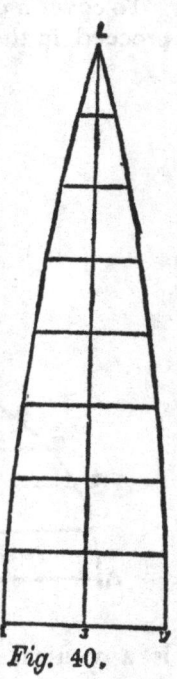

Fig. 40.

rafters in this case are simply straight scantlings; the bevels for feet and points may be obtained from the diagram. The shape of a "gore," when such is required is shown at Fig. 40, IJK showing the base, and L the top or apex. The method of getting it out will be easily understood by examining the diagram. When "gores" are used for covering it will be necessary to have cross-ribs na led in between the rafters, and these must be cut to the sweep of the circle, where they are nailed in, so that a rib placed in half way up will require only to be half the diameter of the base, and the other ribs must be cut accordingly.

To cover a domical roof with horizontal boarding we proceed in the manner shown in Fig. 41, where ABC

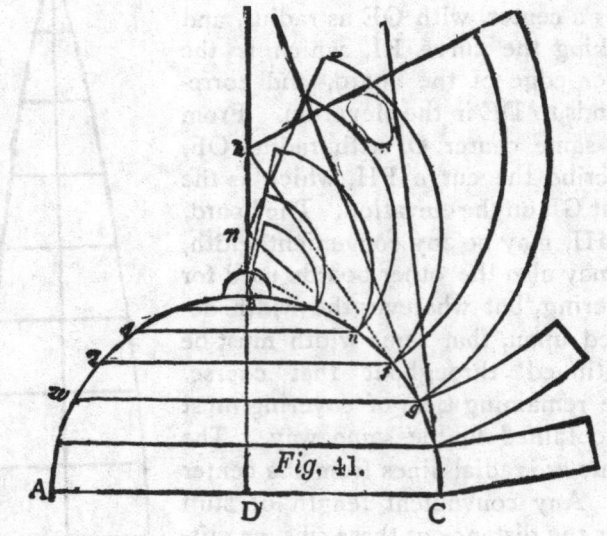

Fig. 41.

is a v rtical section through the axis of a circular dome, and it is required to cover this dome horizontal y. Bisect the base in the point D, and draw DBE perpendicular to AC, cutting the circumference in B. Now divide the arc, BC, into equal parts, so that each part will be rather less than the width of a board, and join the points of division by straight ' mes, which will form an inscribed polygon of so many ⧫ es; and through these points draw lines parallel to the base AC, meeting the opposite sides of the circumference. The trapezoids formed by the sides of the polygon and the horizontal lines may then be regarded as the sections of so many frustrums of cones; whence results the following mode of procedure: Produce, until they meet the line DE, the lines FG, etc., forming the sides of the polygon. Then to describe a board which corresponds to the surface of one of the zones, as FG, of which the trapezoid is a section from

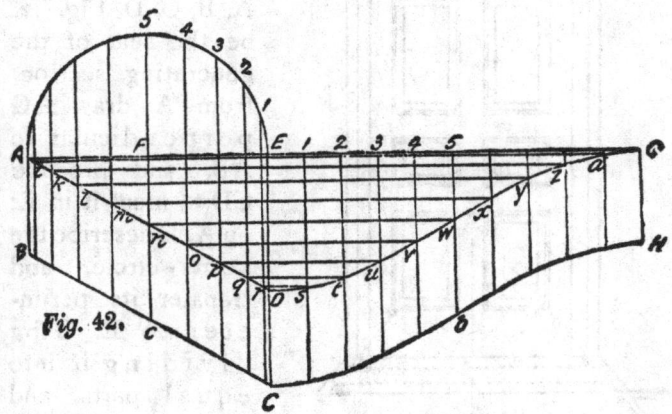

Fig. 42.

the point E, where the line FG produced meets DE, with the radii EF, EG describe two arcs and cut off the end of the board K on the line of a radius EK. The other boards are described in the same manner.

There are many other solids, some of which it is possible the workman may be called upon to cover, but as space will not admit of us discussing them all, we will illustrate one example, which includes within itself the principles by which almost any other solid may be dealt with. Let us suppose a tower, having a domical roof, rising from another roof having an inclination as shown at BC, Fig. 42, and we wish to board

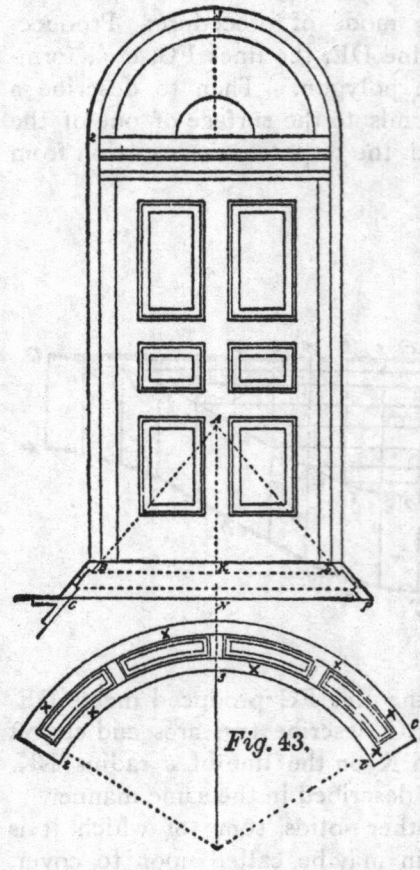

Fig. 43.

it with the joints of the boards on the same inclination as that of the roof through which the tower rises. To accomplish this, let A, B, C, D, Fig. 42, be the seat of the generating section; from A draw AG perpendicular to AB, and produce CD to meet it in E; on A, E describe the semi-circle, and transfer its perimeter to E, G by dividing it into equal parts, and setting off corresponding divisions on E, G. Through the divisions of the semi-circle draw lines at right angles to AE, producing them to meet the lines A, D and B, C in *i, k, l, m,* etc. Through the divisions on E, G, draw lines perpendicular to them then through the intersections of the ordinates of the semi-circle, with the line AD draw the lines *i, a, k, z, l, y*, etc., parallel to AG, and where these intersect the perpendiculars from EG, in points *a, z, y, x, w, v, u*, etc., trace a curved line, GD, and draw parallel to it the curved line HC; then will DC, HG be the development of the covering required.

Almost any description of dome, cone, ogee or other solid may be developed, or so dealt with under the principle as shown in the foregoing, that the workman, it is hoped, will experience but little difficulty in laying out lines for cutting material to cover any form of curved roof he may be confronted with.

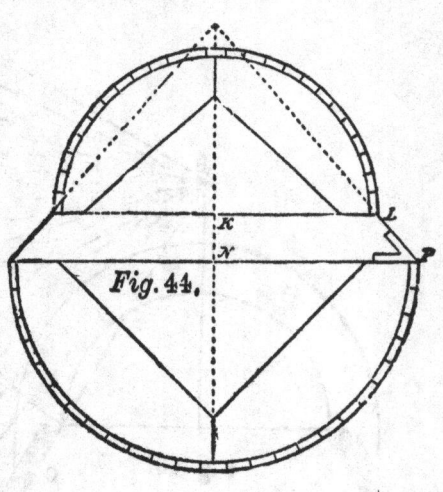

Fig. 44.

Another class of covering is that of making soffits for splayed doors or windows having circular or segmental heads, such as shown in Fig. 43, which exhibits a door with a circular head and splayed jambs. The head or soffit is also splayed and is paneled as shown. In order to obtain the curved soffit, to show the same splay or angle, from the vertical lines of the door, proceed as follows: Lay out the width of the doorway, showing the splay of the jambs, as at C, B and L. P; extend the angle lines, as shown by the dotted lines, to A, which gives A, B as the radius of the inside curve, and A, C as radius of the outside curve. These radii correspond to the radii A, B and A, C in Fig. 43; the figure showing the flat plan of the pan-eled soffit complete. To find the development, Fig. 43, get the stretch-out of the quarter circle 2 and 3, shown in the elevation at the top of the doorway, and

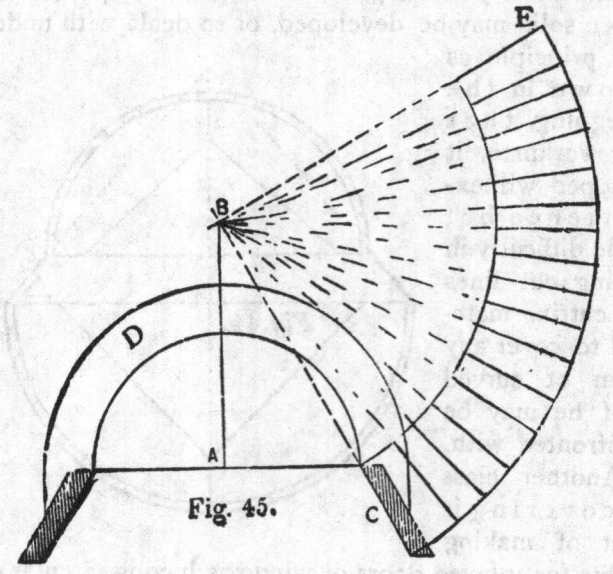

Fig. 45.

make 2, 3 and 3B, Fig. 43, equal to it, and the rest of the work is very simple.

If the soffit is to be laid off into panels, as shown at Fig. 44, it is best to prepare a veneer, having its edges curved similar to those of Fig. 43, making the veneer of some flexible wood, such as basswood, elm or the like, that will easily bend over a form, such as is shown at Fig. 44. The shape of this form is a portion of a cone, the circle L being less in diameter than the circle P. The whole is covered with staves, which, of course, will be tapered to meet the situation. The veneer, x, x, etc., Fig. 43, may then be bent over the form and finished to suit the conditions. If the mouldings used in the panel work are bolection mouldings, they cannot be planted in place until after the veneer is taken off the form.

This method of dealing with splayed work is applicable to windows as well as doors, to circular pews in

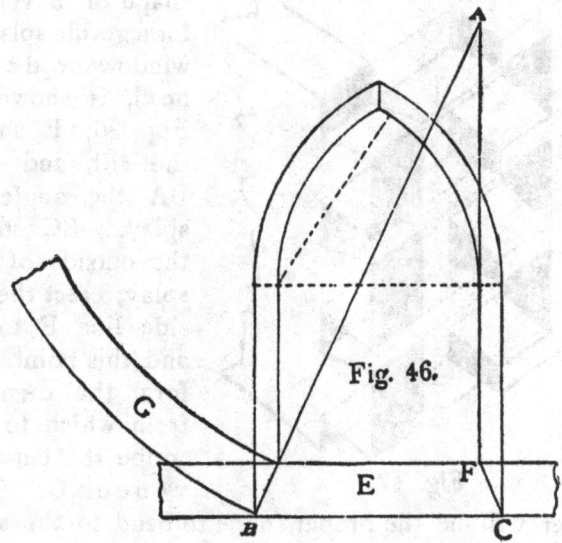

Fig. 46.

churches and many other places where splayed work is required.

A simple method of finding the veneer for a soffit of the form shown in Fig. 43 is shown at Fig. 45. The splay is seen at C, from which a line is drawn on the angle of the splay to B through which the vertical line A passes. B forms the center from which the veneer is described. A is the center of the circular head, for both inside and outside curves, as shown at D. The radial lines centering at B show how to kerf the stuff when necessary for bending. The line E is at right angles with the line CB, and the veneer CE is the proper length to run half way around the soffit. The joints are radial lines just as shown.

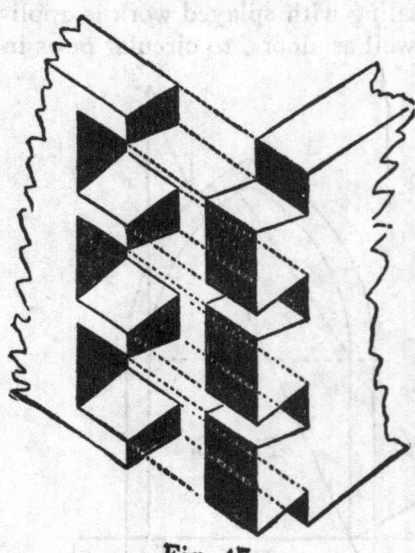

Fig. 47.

A method for obtaining the correct shape of a veneer for a gothic splayed window or door-head, is shown at Fig. 46; E shows the sill, and line BA the angle of splay. BC shows the outside of the splay; erect the inside line F to A, and this point will form the center from which to describe the curve or veneer G. This veneer will be the proper shape to bend in the soffit on either side of the window head.

The art of dovetailing is almost obsolete among carpenters, as most of this kind of work is now done by cabinet-makers, or by a few special workmen in the factories. It will be well, however, to preserve the art, and every young workman should not rest until he can do a good job of work in dovetailing; he will not find it a difficult operation.

There are three kinds of dovetailing, i.e., the common dovetail, Fig. 47; the lapped dovetail, Fig. 48, and the secret, or mitered dovetail, Fig. 49. These may be subdivided into other kinds of dovetailing, but there will be but little difference.

The common dovetail is the strongest, but shows the ends of the dovetails on both faces of the angles,

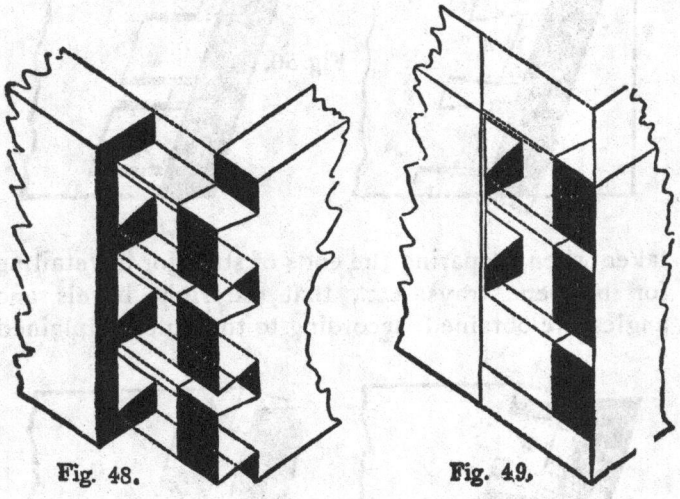

Fig. 48.   Fig. 49.

and is, therefore, only used in such places as that of a drawer, where the external angle is not seen.

The lapped dovetail, where the ends of the dovetails show on one side of the angle only, is used in such places as the front of a drawer, the side being only seen when opened.

In the miter or secret dovetail, the dovetails are not seen at all. It is the weakest of the three kinds.

At Figs. 50 and 51 I show two methods of dovetailing hoppers, trays and other splayed work. The reference letters A and B show that when the work is together A will stand directly over B. Care must be

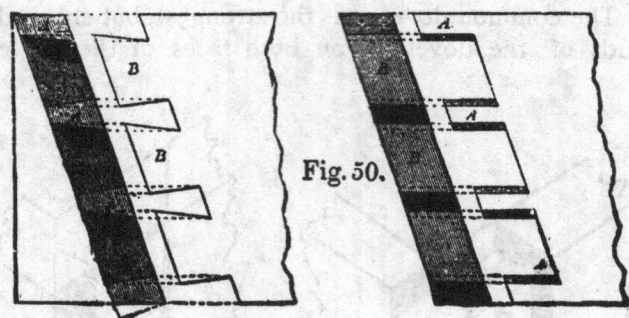

Fig. 50.

taken when preparing the ends of stuff for dovetailing for hoppers, trays, etc., that the right bevels and angles are obtained, according to the rules explained

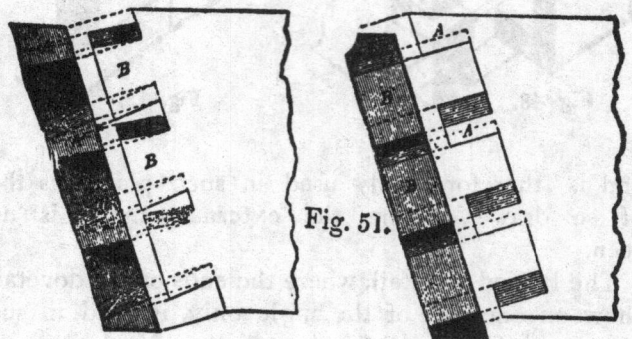

Fig. 51.

for finding the cuts and bevels for hoppers and work of a similar kind, in the examples given previously. All stuff for hopper work intending to be dovetailed must be prepared with butt joints before the dovetails are laid out. Joints of this kind may be made common, lapped or mitered. In making the latter much skill and labor will be required.

Stair building and handrailing combined is a science in itself, and one that taxes the best skill in the market, and it will be impossible for me to do more than touch the subject, and that in such a manner as to enable the workman to lay out an ordinary straight flight of stairs. For further instructions in stair building I would refer my readers to some one or two of the many works on the subject that can be obtained from any dealer in mechanical or scientific books.

The first thing the stair builder has to ascertain is the dimension of the space the stairs are to occupy; then he must get the height, or the risers, and the width of the treads, and, as architects generally draw the plan of the stairs, showing the space they are to occupy and the number of treads, the stair builder has only to measure the height from floor to floor and divide by the number of risers and the distance from first to last riser, and divide by the number of treads. (This refers only to straight stairs.) Let us take an example: Say that we have ten feet of height and fifteen feet ten inches of run, and we have nineteen treads; thus fifteen feet ten inches divided by nineteen gives us ten inches for the width of the tread, and we have ten feet rise divided by twenty (observe here that there is always one more riser than tread), which gives us six inches for the height of the riser. The pitch-board must now be made, and as all the work has to be set out from it, care must be taken to make it exactly right. Take a piece of board, same as shown in Fig. 52, about half an inch thick, dress it and square the side and end, A, B, C; set off the height of the rise from A to B, and the width of the tread from B to C; now cut the line AC, and the pitch-board is complete, as shown in Fig. 53. This may be done by the steel square as shown at Fig. 54. To get the width of string-boards draw the line AB, Fig. 53; add to the length of this line about half an inch more at A, the margin to be allowed, and the total will be the width of string-boards. Thus, say that we allow three inches

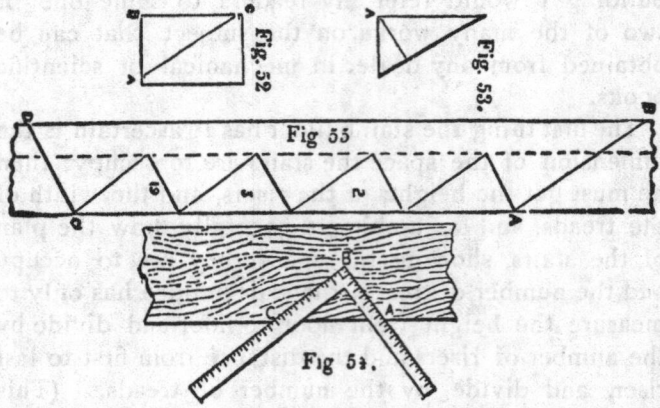

for margin, one-half inch to be left on the under side of string-board, will make the width of string-boards in this case about nine inches. Now get a plank, say one and a half inches, of any thickness that may be agreed upon, the length may be obtained by multiplying the longest side of the pitch-boards, AC, Fig. 52, by the number of risers; but as this is the only class of stairs that the length of string-boards can be obtained in this way I would recommend the beginner to practice the sure plan of taking the pitch-board and applying it as at 1, 2, 3, 19, Fig. 55. Drawing all the steps this way will prevent a mistake that sometimes occurs, viz. the string-boards being cut too short. Cut the foot at the line AB, and the top, as at CD. This will give about one and a half inches more than the extreme length. Now cut out the treads and risers; the width of stair is, say, three feet, and we have one and a half inches on each side for string-boards. Allow three-eights of an inch for housing on each side. This will make the length of tread and risers two and one-fourth inches less than the full width of stairs; and as the treads must project their own thickness over rise, which is, say, one and a half inches, the full size of tread will be two feet by eleven and one-half inches, and of the risers two feet nine and three-fourths inches by six inches; and observe that the first riser will be the thickness of the tread less than the others; it will be only four and one-half inches wide. The reason of this riser being less than the others is because it has a tread thickness extra.

I will now leave the beginner to prepare all his work. Dress the risers on one face and one edge; dress the treads on one face and both edges, making them all of equal width; gauge the ends and the face edge to the required thickness, and round off the nosings; dress the string-boards to one face and edge to match each other.

A plan of a stair having 13 risers and three winders below is shown at Fig. 56. This shows how the whole stair may be laid out. It is inclosed between two walls.

The beginner in stair-work had better resort to the old method of using a story-rod for getting the number of risers. Take a rod and mark on it the exact height from top of lower floor to top of next floor, then divide up and mark off the number of risers required. There is always one more riser than tread in every flight of stairs. The first riser must be cut the thickness of the tread less than the others.

When there are winders, special treatment will be

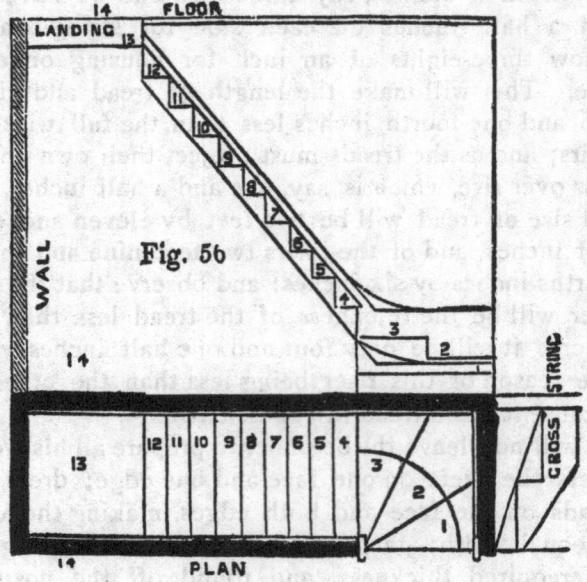

Fig. 56

required, as shown in Fig. 56, for the treads, but the riser must always be the same width for each separate flight.

When the stair is straight and without winders, a rod may be used for laying off the steps. The width of the steps, or treads, will be governed somewhat by the space allotted for the run of the stairs.

There is a certain proportion existing between the tread and riser of a stair, that should be kept to as close as possible when laying out the work Architects say that the exact measurement for a tread and riser should be sixteen inches, or thereabouts. That is, if a riser is made six inches, the tread should be ten inches wide, and so on. I give a table herewith, showing the rule generally made use of by stair builders for determining the widths of risers and treads:

Treads Inches	Risers Inches	Treads Inches	Risers Inches
5	9	12	5½
6	8½	13	5
7	8	14	4½
8	7½	15	4
9	7	16	3½
10	6½	17	3
11	6	18	2½

It is seldom, however that the proportion of the

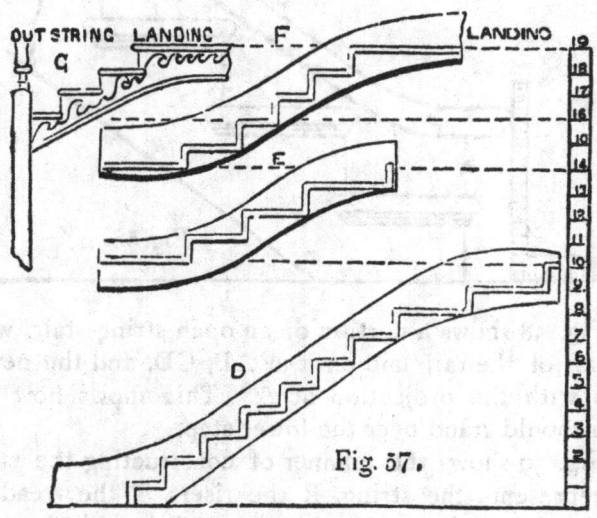

Fig. 57.

riser and step is exactly a matter of choice—the room

allotted to the stairs usually determines this proportion; but the above will be found a useful standard, to which it is desirable to approximate.

In better class buildings the number of steps is considered in the plan, which it is the business of the architect to arrange, and in such cases the height of the story-rod is simply divided to the number required.

An elevation of a stair with winders is shown at Fig. 57, where the story-rod is in evidence with the number of risers figured off.

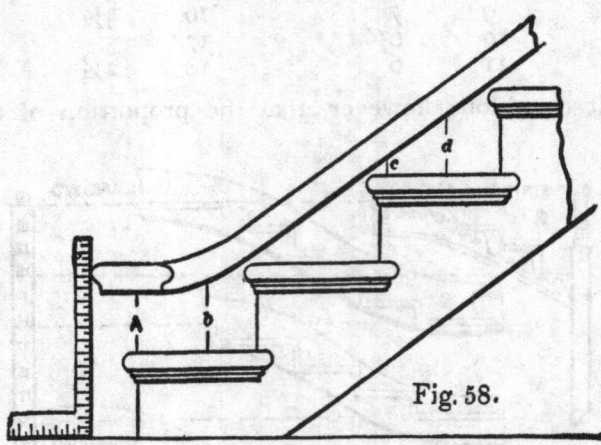

Fig. 58.

Fig. 58 shows a portion of an open string stair, with a part of the rail laid on it at AB, CD, and the newel cap with the projection at A. This shows how the cap should stand over the lower step.

Fig. 59 shows the manner of constructing the step; S represents the string, R the risers, T the tread, O the nosing and cove moulding, and B is a block glued or otherwise fastened to both riser and tread to render

them strong and firm. It will be seen the riser is let
into the tread, and has a shoulder on the inside. The
bottom of the riser is nailed to the back of the next
lower tread, which binds the whole lower part together. The
nosing of the
stair is gen-
erally re-
turned at the
open end of
the tread,
and this cov-
ers the end
wood of the
tread and the
joints of the
balusters, as
shown at
Fig 60.

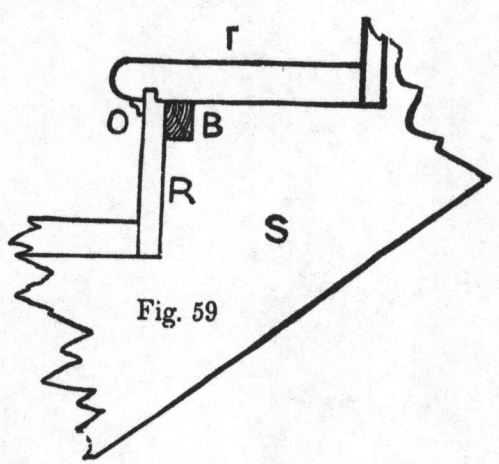

Fig. 59

When a stair is bracketed, as shown at B, Fig. 60,
the point of the riser on its string end should be left

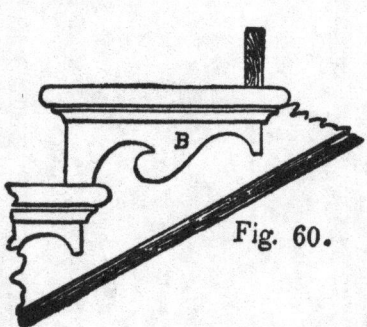

Fig. 60.

standing past the string
the thickness of the
bracket, and the end of
the bracket miters
against it, thus avoid-
ing the necessity of
showing end wood or
joint The cove should
finish inside the length
of the bracket, and the
nosing should fin-
ish just outside the
length of the bracket. When brackets are employed

they should continue along the cylinder and all around the well hole trimmers, though they may be varied to suit conditions when continuously running on a straight horizontal facia.

CHAPTER III

I am well aware that workmen are always on the lookout for details of work, and welcome everything in this line that is new. While styles and shapes change from year to year, like fashion in women's dress, the principles of construction never change, and styles of finish in woodwork that may be in vogue to-day, may be old-fashioned and discarded next year, therefore it may not be wise to load these pages with many examples of finish as made use of to-day. A few examples, however, may not be out of place, so I close this section by offering a few pages of such details as I feel assured will be found useful for a long time to come.

Fig. 1 is a full page illustration of three examples of stairs and newels in modern styles. The upper one is a colonial stairway with a square newel, as shown at A. A baluster is also shown, so that the whole may be copied if required. The second example shows two newels and balusters, and paneled string and spandril AB, also section of paneled work on end of short flight. The third shows a plain open stair, with baluster and newel, the latter starting from first step.

At Fig. 2, which is also a full page, seven of the latest designs for doors are shown. Those marked

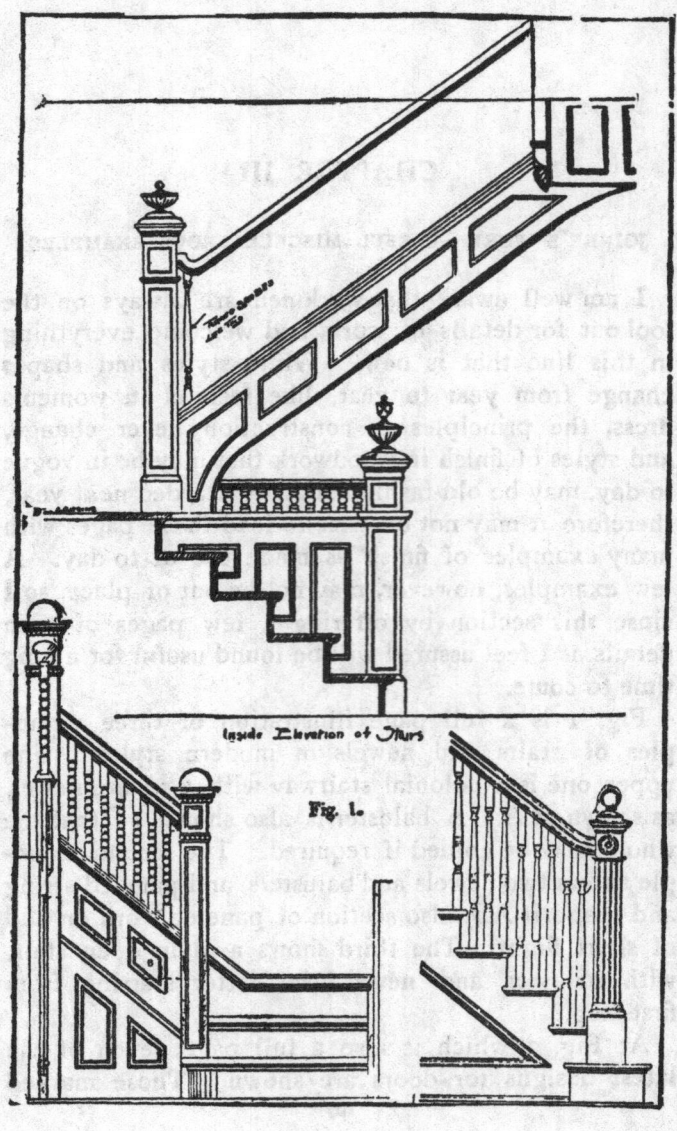

Inside Elevation of Stairs

Fig. 1.

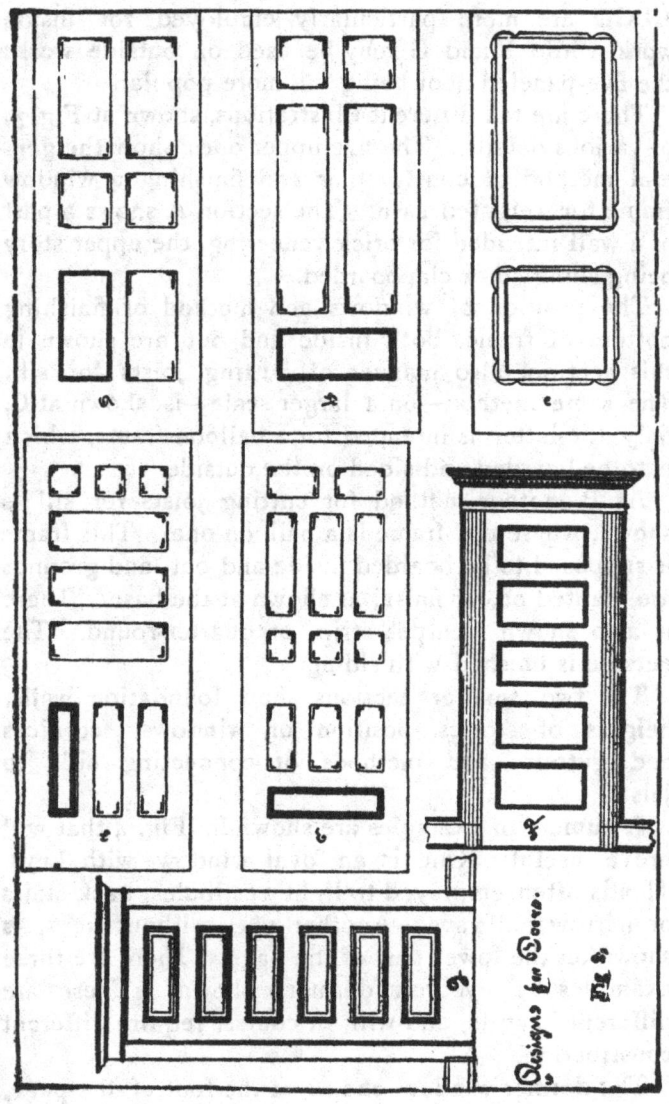

Designs for Doors.

FIG 3.

ABCD are more particularly employed for inside work, while F and G may be used on outside work; the five-paneled door being the more popular.

There are ten different illustrations, shown at Fig. 3, of various details. The five upper ones show the general method of constructing and finishing a window frame for weighted sash. The section A shows a part of a wall intended for brick veneering, the upper story being shingled or clapboarded.

The position of windows and method of finishing bottom of frame, both inside and out, are shown in this section, also manner of cutting joists for sill. The same method—on a larger scale—is shown at C, only the latter is intended for a balloon frame, which is to be boarded and sided on the outside.

At B another method for cutting joists for sill is shown, where the frame is a balloon one. This frame is supposed to be boarded inside and out, and grounds are planted on for finish, as shown at the base. There is also shown a carpet strip, or quarter-round. The outside is finished with siding.

The two smaller sections show foundation walls, heights of stories, position of windows, cornices and gutters, and methods of connecting sills to joists.

A number of examples are shown in Fig. 4 that will prove useful. One is an oval window with keys. This is often employed to light vestibules, back stairs or narrow hallways. Another one, without keys, is shown on the lower part of the page. There are three examples of eyebrow dormers shown. These are different in style, and will, of course, require different construction.

The dormer window, shown at the foot of the page,

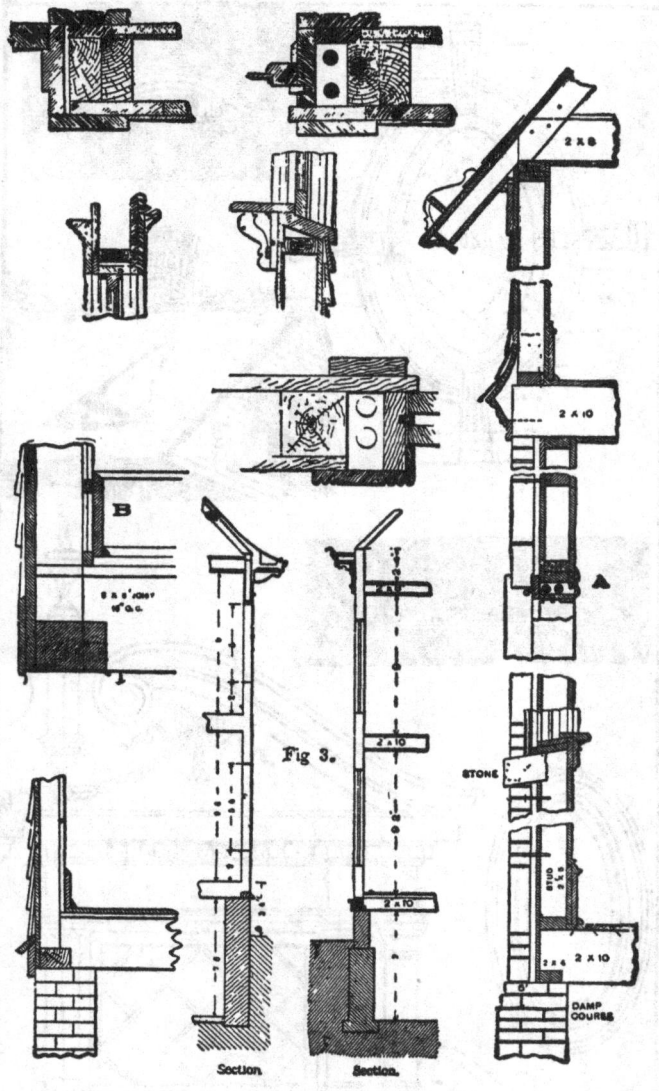

Fig 3.

Section. Section.

Fig. 4.

Dormer Window

is designed for a house built in colonial style, but may be adapted to other styles.

The four first examples in Fig. 5 show the sections of various parts of a bay window for a balloon frame. The manner of constructing the angle is shown, also the sill and head of window, the various parts and manner of working them being given. A part of the section of the top of the window is shown at E, the inside finish being purposely left off. At F is shown an angle of greater length, which is sometimes the case in bay windows. The manner of construction is quite simple. The lower portion of the page shows some fine examples of turned and carved work. These will often be found useful in giving ideas for turned work for a variety of purposes.

Six examples of shingling are shown in Fig. 6. The first sketch, A, is intended for a hip, and is a fairly good example, and if well done will insure a water-tight roof at that point. In laying out the shingles for this plan the courses are managed as follows: No. 1 is laid all the way out to the line of the hip, the edge of the shingle being planed off, so that course No. 2, on the adjacent side will line perfectly tight down upon it. Next No. 3 is laid and is dressed down in the same manner as the first, after which No. 4 is brought along the same as No. 2. The work proceeds in this manner, first right and then left.

In the second sketch, B, the shingles are laid on the hip in a way to bring the grain of the shingles more nearly parallel with the line of the hip. This method overcomes the projection of cross-grained points. Another method of shingling hips is shown at C and D. In putting on shingles by this method a line is snapped four inches from angle of hip on both sides

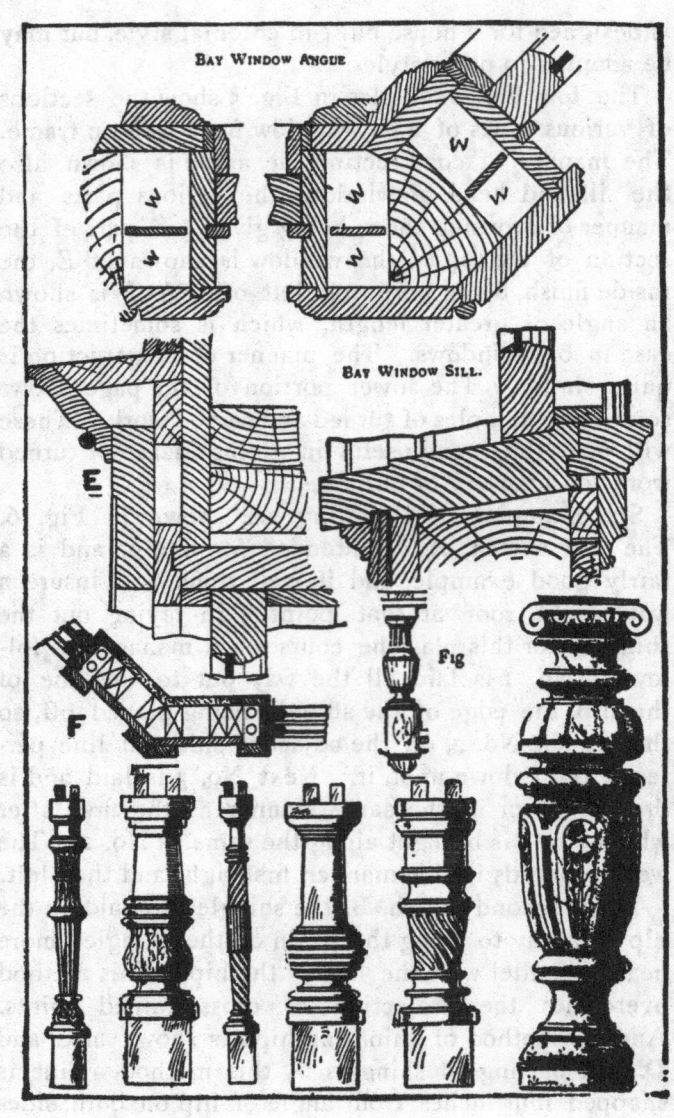

BAY WINDOW ANGLE

BAY WINDOW SILL.

of the ridge, as indicated by the dotted lines in **C**, then bring the corner of the shingles of each course to the line as shown. When all through with the plain shingring, make a pattern to suit, and only cut the top to shape, as the bottoms or butts will break joints every time, and the hip line will lay square with the hip line, as shown at **D**; thus making a first-class watertight job, and one on which the shingles will not curl up, and it will have a good appearance as well.

At **E** a method is shown for shingling a valley, where no tin or metal is employed. The manner of doing this work is as follows: First take a strip 4 inches wide and chamfer it on the edges on the outside, so that it will lay down smooth to the sheeting, and nail it into the valley. Take a shingle about 4 inches wide to start with and lay lengthwise of the valley, fitting the shingle on each side. The first course, which is always double, would then start with the narrow shingle, marked **B**, and carried up the valley, as shown in the sketch. Half way between each course lay a shingle, **A**, about 4 or 5 inches wide, as the case requires, chamfering underneath on each side, so that the next course will lie smooth over it.

If tin or zinc can be obtained, it is better it should be laid in the valley, whether this method be adopted or not.

The sketch shown at **F** is intended to illustrate the manner in which a valley should be laid with tin, zinc or galvanized iron. The dotted lines show the width of the metal, which should never be less than fourteen inches to insure a tight roof. The shingles should lap over as shown, and not less than four inches of the valley, **H**, should be clear of shingles

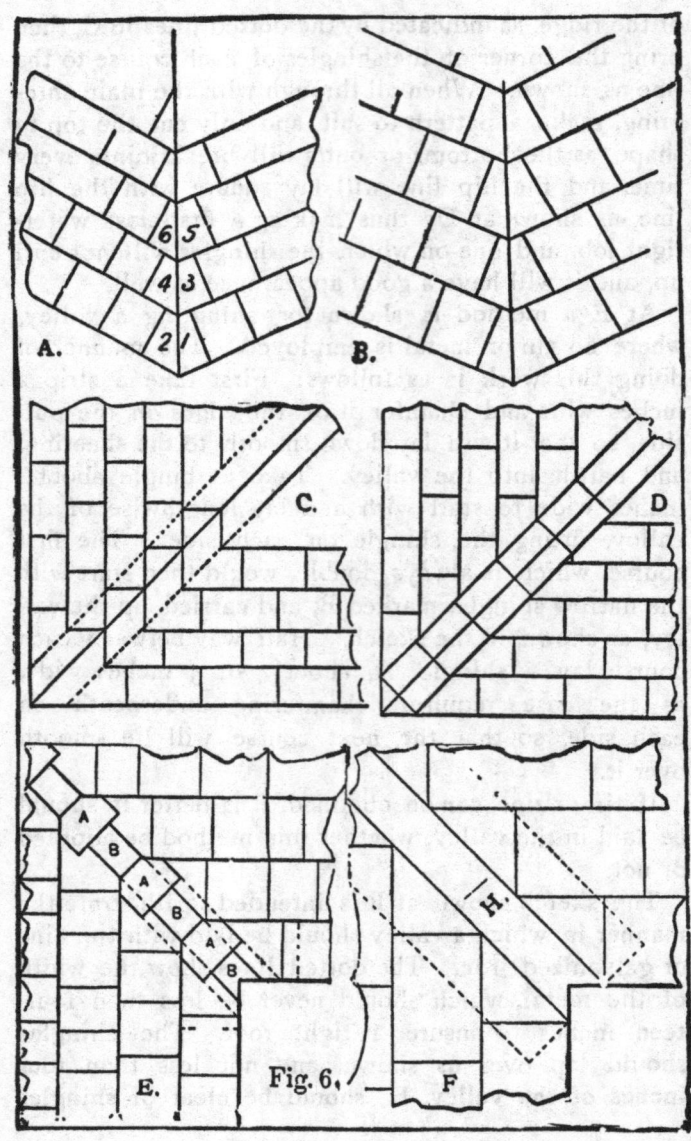

Fig. 6.

in order to insure plenty of space for the water to flow during a heavy rain storm. A great deal of care should be taken in shingling and finishing a valley, as it is always a weak spot in the roof.

PART IV

USEFUL TABLES AND MEMORANDA FOR BUILDERS

Table showing quantity of material in every four lineal feet of exterior wall in a balloon frame building, height of wall being given:

Length of Studs.	Size of Sills.	Size of Studs, Braces, etc.	Quantity of Rough Lumber	Quantity of Inch Boarding.	Siding in sup. feet.	Tar Paper in sup. feet.
8	6x 6	2x4 studs.	42	36	40	74
10	6x 8	4x4 braces	52	44	50	80
12	6x10	4x4 plates.	62	53	60	96
14	6x10	1x6 ribbons.	69	62	70	112
16	8x10		82	71	80	128
18	8x10	studs.	87	80	90	144
20	8x12	16 inches from	98	88	100	160
22	9x12	centers.	109	97	110	176
24	10x12		119	106	120	192
18	10x10	2x6 studs.	122	80	90	144
20	10x12	6x6 braces.	137	88	100	160
22	10x12	4x6 plates.	145	97	110	176
24	12x12	1x6 ribbons.	162	106	120	192
26	10x14		169	114	130	208
28	10x14	studs 16 inch centers.	176	123	140	224
30	12x14		198	132	150	240

Table showing amount of lumber in rafters, collarpiece and boarding, and number of shingles to four lineal feet of roof, measured from eave to eave over ridge. Rafters 16-inch centers:

Width of House, Feet.	Size of Rafters.	Size of Collarpiece.	Quantity of Lumber in Rafter and Collarpiece.	Quantity of Boarding, Feet.	No. of Shingles.
14	2x4	2x4	39	61	560
16	2x4	2x4	45	70	640
18	2x4	2x4	50	79	720
20	2x4	2x4	56	88	800
22	2x4	2x4	62	97	880
24	2x4	2x4	67	106	960
20	2x6	2x6	84	88	800
22	2x6	2x6	92	97	880
24	2x6	2x6	101	106	960
26	2x6	2x6	109	115	1040
28	2x6	2x6	117	124	1120
30	2x6	2x6	126	133	1200

A proper allowance for waste is included in the above. Roof, one-fourth pitch.

Table showing the requisite sizes of girders and joists for warehouses, the span and distances apart being given:

Distance apart.	Span of Girders.				Joists.	Remarks.
	6 Feet.	8 Feet.	10 Feet.	12 Feet.		
Feet.	Inches.	Inches.	Inches.	Inches.	Inches.	Girders to have a bearing at each end and joists 6 in.
10	8x12	12x13	12x16	14x18	2½x10	
12	9x12	12x14	12x18	16x18	3 x10	
14	10x12	12x15	14x18	....	3 x12	

Table as before, adapted for churches, public halls, etc.

Distance Apart.	Span of Girders.				Joists.	Remarks.
	6 Feet.	8 Feet.	10 Feet.	12 Feet.		
Feet.	Inches.	Inches.	Inches.	Inches.	Inches	
12	6x10	8x12	12x14	12x16	2 x 8	
13	9x11	9x12	11x15	12x17	2 x 9	Bearings of
14	6x12	10x12	12x15	11x18	2 x 9	girders and
15	7x12	11x12	11x16	12x16	2 x10	joists as
16	8x12	12x12	12x16	13x18	2 x10	above.
17	8x12	9x14	12x17	14x18	2 x12	
18	9x12	10x14	11x18	....	2 x12	
19	9x12	11x14	12x18	....	2½ x12	Both tables
20	10x12	12x14	13x18	....	2½ x12	are calcu-
21	10x12	11x15	14x18	....	2½ x12	lated for yel-
22	11x12	12x15	....	....	3 x12	low pine.
23	11x12	11x16	....	....	3 x12	
24	10x13	12x16	....	....	3 x13	
25	10x13	12x17	....	....	3 x13	
26	10x14	12x18	....	....	3 x14	
27	10x14	12x18	....	....	3 x14	

Table showing quantity of lumber in every four lineal feet of partition, studs being placed 16 centers, waste included:

Height of Partition, Feet.	Quantity of Studs 2x4 Feet.	If 2x6 Feet.
8	20	30
9	23	34
10	26	38
11	29	42
12	32	46
13	35	51
14	38	55
15	41	59
16	44	64

Lumber Measurement Table

2x4		2x6		2x8		2x10		3x6		3x8	
Length.		Length.		Length.		Length.		Length.		Length.	
12	8	12	12	12	16	12	20	12	18	12	24
14	9	14	14	14	19	14	23	14	21	14	28
16	11	16	16	16	21	16	27	16	24	16	32
18	12	18	18	18	24	18	30	18	27	18	36
20	13	20	20	20	27	20	33	20	30	20	40
22	15	22	22	22	29	22	37	22	33	22	44
24	16	24	24	24	32	24	40	24	36	24	48
26	17	26	26	26	35	26	43	26	39	26	52

3x10		3x12		4x4		4x6		4x8		6x6	
12	30	12	36	12	16	12	24	12	32	12	36
14	35	14	42	14	19	14	28	14	37	14	42
16	40	16	48	16	21	16	32	16	43	16	48
18	45	18	54	18	24	18	36	18	48	18	54
20	50	20	60	20	27	20	40	20	53	20	60
22	55	22	66	22	29	22	44	22	59	22	66
24	60	24	72	24	32	24	48	24	64	24	72
26	65	26	78	26	35	26	52	26	69	26	78

6x8		8x8		8x10		10x10		10x12		12x12	
12	48	12	64	12	80	12	100	12	120	12	144
14	56	14	75	14	93	14	117	14	140	14	168
16	64	16	85	16	107	16	133	16	160	16	192
18	72	18	96	18	120	18	150	18	180	18	216
20	80	20	107	20	133	20	167	20	200	20	240
22	88	22	117	22	147	22	183	22	220	22	264
24	96	24	128	24	160	24	200	24	240	24	288
26	104	26	139	26	173	26	217	26	260	26	312

Strength of Materials

Resistance to extension and compression, in pounds per square inch section of some materials.

Name of the Material.	Resistance to Extension.	Resistance to Compression	Tensile Strength in Practice	Comp. Strength in Practice.
White pine...	10,000	6,000	2,000	1,200
White oak....	15,000	7,500	3,000	1,500
Rock elm......	16,000	8,011	3,200	1,602
Wrought iron	60,000	50,000	12,000	10,000
Cast iron	20,000	100,000	4,000	20,000

In practice, from one-fifth to one-sixth of the strength is all that should be depended upon

Table of Superficial or Flat Measure

By which the contents in *Superficial Feet*, of Boards, Plank, Paving, etc., of any *Length* and *Breadth*, can be obtained, by multiplying the decimal expressed in the table by the length of the board, etc

Breadth inches	Area of a lineal foot.	Breadth inches.	Area of a lineal foot.	Breadth inches.	Area of a lineal foot.	Breadth inches.	Area of a lineal foot.
¼	.0208	3¼	.2708	6¼	.5208	9¼	.7708
½	.0417	3½	.2916	6½	.5416	9½	.7917
¾	.0625	3¾	.3125	6¾	.5625	9¾	.8125
1	.0834	4	.3334	7	.5833	10	.8334
1¼	.1042	4¼	.3542	7¼	.6042	10¼	.8542
1½	.125	4½	.375	7½	.625	10½	.875
1¾	.1459	4¾	.3958	7¾	.6458	10¾	.8959
2	.1667	5	.4167	8	.6667	11	.9167
2¼	.1875	5¼	.4375	8¼	.6875	11¼	.9375
2½	.2084	5½	.4583	8½	.7084	11½	.9583
2¾	.2292	5¾	.4792	8¾	.7292	11¾	.9792
3	.25	6	.5	9	.75	12	1.0000

Round and Equal-Sided Timber Measure

Table for ascertaining the number of Cubical Feet, or solid contents, in a Stick of Round or Equal-Sided Timber, Tree, etc.

¼ girt in in.	Area in feet.	¼ girt in in.	Area in feet	¼ girt in in.	Area in feet.	¼ girt in in.	Area in feet.	¼ girt in in	Area in feet.
6	.25	10¾	.803	15½	1.668	20¼	2.898	25	4.34
6¼	.272	11	.84	15¾	1.722	20½	2.917	25¼	4.428
6½	.294	11¼	.878	16	1.777	20¾	2.99	25½	4.516
6¾	.317	11½	.918	16¼	1.833	21	3.062	25¾	4 605
7	.34	11¾	.959	16½	1.89	21¼	3.136	26	4.694
7¼	.364	12	1.	16¾	1.948	21½	3.209	26¼	4.785
7½	.39	12¼	1.042	17	2.006	21¾	3 285	26½	4.876
7¾	.417	12½	1.085	17¼	2.066	22	3.362	26¾	4.969
8	.444	12¾	1.129	17½	2.126	22¼	3.438	27	5 062
8¼	.472	13	1.174	17¾	2.187	22½	3.516	27¼	5.158
8½	.501	13¼	1.219	18	2.25	22¾	3.598	27½	5.252
8¾	.531	13½	1.265	18¼	2.313	23	3.673	27¾	5.348
9	.562	13¾	1.313	18½	2.376	23¼	3.754	28	5.444
9¼	.594	14	1.361	18¾	2.442	23½	3.835	28¼	5.542
9½	.626	14¼	1.41	19	2.506	23¾	3 917	28½	5.64
9¾	.659	14½	1 46	19¼	2 574	24	4.	28¾	5 74
10	.694	14¾	1.511	19½	2 64	24¼	4.084	29	5.84
10¼	.73	15	1.562	19¾	2.709	24½	4.168	29¼	5 941
10½	.766	15¼	1.615	20	2 777	24¾	4.254	29½	6.044

Shingling

To find the number of shingles required to cover 100 square feet deduct 3 inches from the length, divide the remainder by 3, the result will be the exposed length of a shingle; multiplying this with the average width of a shingle, the product will be the exposed area. Dividing 14,400, the number of square inches in a square, by the exposed area of a shingle will give the number required to cover 100 square feet of roof.

In estimating the number of shingles required, an allowance should always be made for waste.

Estimates on cost of shingle roofs are usually given per 1,000 shingles.

Table for Estimating Shingles

Length of Shingles.	Exposure to Weather, Inches.	No. of Sq. Ft. of Roof Covered by 1000 Shingles.		No of Shingles Required for 100 Sq. Ft. of Roof.	
		4 In Wide.	6 In Wide.	4 In. Wide.	6 In. Wide.
15 in.	4	111	167	900	600
18	5	139	208	720	480
21	6	167	250	600	400
24	7	194	291	514	343
27	8	222	333	450	300

Siding, Flooring, and Laths

One-fifth more siding and flooring is needed than the number of square feet of surface to be covered, because of the lap in the siding matching.

1,000 laths will cover 70 yards of surface, and 11 pounds of lath nails will nail them on. Eight bushels of good lime, 16 bushels of sand, and 1 bushel of hair, will make enough good mortar to plaster 100 square yards.

Excavations

Excavations are measured by the yard (27 cubic feet) and irregular depths or surfaces are generally averaged in practice

Number of Nails Required in Carpentry Work

To case and hang one door, 1 pound.

To case and hang one window, ¾ pound.

Base, 100 lineal feet, 1 pound.

To put on rafters, joists, etc., 3 pounds to 1,000 feet.

To put up studding, same.

To lay a 6-inch pine floor, 15 pounds to 1,000 feet.

Sizes of Boxes for Different Measures

A box 24 inches long by 16 inches wide, and 28 inches deep will contain a barrel, or 3 bushels.

A box 24 inches long by 16 inches wide, and 14 inches deep will contain half a barrel.

A box 16 inches square and 8⅝ inches deep, will contain 1 bushel.

A box 16 inches by 8⅝ inches wide and 8 inches deep, will contain half a bushel.

A box 8 inches by 8⅝ inches square and 8 inches deep, will contain 1 peck.

A box 8 inches by 8 inches square and 4¼ inches deep, will contain 1 gallon.

A box 8 inches by 4 inches square and 4⅜ inches deep, will contain half a gallon.

A box 4 inches by 4 inches square and 4⅜ inches deep, will contain 1 quart.

A box 4 feet long, 3 feet 5 inches wide, and 2 feet 8 inches deep, will contain 1 ton of coal.

Masonry

Stone masonry is measured by two systems, quarryman's and mason's measurements.

By the quarryman's measurements the actual contents are measured—that is, all openings are taken out and all corners are measured single.

By the mason's measurements, corners and piers are doubled, and no allowance made for openings less than 3' 0"x5' 0" and only half the amount of openings larger than 3' 0"x5' 0".

Range work and cut work is measured superficially and in addition to wall measurement.

An average of six bushels of sand and cement per perch of rubble masonry.

Stone walls are measured by the perch (24¾ cubic feet, or by the cord of 128 feet). Openings less than 3 feet wide are counted solid; over 3 feet deducted, but 18 inches are added to the running measure for each jamb built.

Arches are counted solid from their spring. Corners of buildings are measured twice. Pillars less than 3 feet are counted on 3 sides as lineal, multiplied by fourth side and depth.

It is customary to measure all foundation and dimension stone by the cubic foot. Water tables and base courses by lineal feet. All sills and lintels or ashlar by superficial feet, and no wall less than 18 inches thick.

The height of brick or stone piers should not exceed 12 times their thickness at the base.

Masonry is usually measured by the perch (containing 24.75 cubic feet), but in practice 25 cubic feet are considered a perch of masonry.

Concreting is usually measured by the cubic yard (27 cubic feet).

A cord of stone, 3 bushels of lime and a cubic yard of sand, will lay 100 cubic feet of wall.

Cement, 1 bushel, and sand, 2 bushels, will cover 3½ square yards 1 inch thick, 4½ square yards ¾ inch thick, and 6¾ square yards ½ inch thick; 1 bushel of cement and 1 of sand will cover 2¼ square yards 1 inch thick, 3 square yards ¾ inch thick and 4½ square yards ½ inch thick.

Brick Work

Brick work is generally measured by 1,000 bricks laid in the wall. In consequence of variations in size of bricks, no rule for volume of laid brick can be exact. The following scale is, however, a fair average

```
7 com. bricks to a super. ft.  4 in. wall.
14   "       "    "    "    "   9  "   "
21   "       "    "    "    "   13 "   "
28   "       "    "    "    "   18 "   "
35   "       "    "    "    "   22 "   "
```

Corners are not measured twice, as in stone work. Openings over 2 feet square are deducted. Arches are counted from the spring. Fancy work counted 1½ bricks for 1. Pillars are measured on their face only.

A cubic yard of mortar requires 1 cubic yard of sand and 9 bushels of lime, and will fill 30 hods.

One thousand bricks closely stacked occupy about 56 cubic feet.

One thousand old bricks, cleaned and loosely stacked, occupy about 72 cubic feet.

One superficial foot of gauged arches requires 10 bricks.

Pavements, according to size of bricks, take 38 brick on flat and 60 brick on edge per square yard, on an average.

Five courses of brick will lay 1 foot in height on a chimney, 6 bricks in a course will make a flue 4 inches wide and 12 inches long, and 8 bricks in a course will make a flue 8 inches wide and 16 inches long.

Slating

A square of slate or slating is 100 superficial feet.

In measuring, the width of eaves is allowed at the widest part. Hips, valleys and cuttings are to be measured lineal, and 6 inches extra is allowed.

The thickness of slates required is from $\frac{3}{16}$ to $\frac{6}{16}$ of an inch, and their weight varies when lapped from $\frac{4}{8}$ to $6\frac{3}{4}$ pounds per square foot.

The "laps" of slates vary from 2 to 4 inches, the standard assumed to be 3 inches.

To Compute the Number of Slates of a Given Size Required per Square

Subtract 3 inches from the length of the slate, multiply the remainder by the width and divide by 2. Divide 14,400 by the number so found and the result will be the number of slates required.

Table showing number of slates and pounds of nails required to cover 100 square feet of roof.

Sizes of Slate	Length of Exposure.	No. Required.	Nails Required.
14 in. x 28 in.	12½ in.	83	.6 lbs.
12 x 24	10½	114	.833
11 x 22	9½	138	1.
10 x 20	8½	165	1.33
9 x 18	7½	214	1.5
8 x 16	6½	277	2.
7 x 14	5½	377	2.66
6 x 12	4½	533	3 8

Approximate Weight of Materials for Roofs

Material.	Average Weight, Lb. per Sq Ft.
Corrugated galvanized iron, No. 20, unboarded	2¼
Copper, 16 oz. standing seam	1¼
Felt and asphalt, without sheathing	2
Glass, ⅛ in. thick	1¾
Hemlock sheathing, 1 in. thick	2
Lead, about ⅛ in. thick	6 to 8
Lath-and-plaster ceiling (ordinary)	6 to 8
Mackite, 1 in. thick, with plaster	10
Neponset roofing felt, 2 layers	⅛
Spruce sheathing, 1 in. thick	2½
Slate, 3/16 in. thick, 3 in. double lap	6¾
Slate, ⅛ in. thick, 3 in. double lap	4½
Shingles, 6 in. x 18 in., ⅛ to weather	2
Skylight of glass, 3/16 to ½ in., including frame	4 to 10
Slag roof, 4-ply	4
Terne Plate, IC, without sheathing	½
Terne Plate, IX, without sheathing	⅝
Tiles (plain), 10½ in. x 6¼ x ⅝ in.—5¼ in. to weather.	18
Tiles (Spanish) 14½ in. x 10½ in.—7¼ in. to weather.	8½
White-pine sheathing, 1 in. thick	2½
Yellow-pine sheathing, 1 in. thick	4

Snow and Wind Loads

Data in regard to snow and wind loads are necessary in connection with the design of roof trusses.

Snow Load.—When the slope of a roof is over 12 inches rise per foot of horizontal run, a snow and accidental load of 8 pounds per square foot is ample. When the slope is under 12 inches rise per foot of run, a snow and accidental load of 12 pounds per square foot should be used. The snow load acts vertically, and therefore should be added to the dead load in designing roof trusses. The snow load may be neglected when a high wind pressure has been considered, as a great wind storm would very likely remove all the snow from the roof.

Wind Load.—The wind is considered as blowing in a horizontal direction, but the resulting pressure upon the roof is always taken normal (at right angles) to the slope. The wind pressure against a vertical plane depends on the velocity of the wind, and, as ascertained by the United States Signal Service at Mount Washington, N. H., is as follows:

Velocity. (Mi. per Hr.)	*Pressure.* (Lb. per Sq. Ft.)	
10	0.4	Fresh breeze.
20	1.6	Stiff breeze.
30	3.6	Strong wind.
40	6.4	High wind.
50	10.0	Storm.
60	14.4	Violent storm.
80	25.6	Hurricane.
100	40.0	Violent hurricane.

The wind pressure upon a cylindrical surface is one-half that upon a flat surface of the same height and width.

Since the wind is considered as traveling in a horizontal direction, it is evident that the more nearly vertical the slope of the roof, the greater will be the pressure, and the more nearly horizontal the slope, the less will be the pressure. The following table gives the pressure exerted upon roofs of different slopes, by a wind pressure of 40 pounds per square foot on a vertical plane, which is equivalent in intensity to a violent hurricane.

UNITED STATES WEIGHTS AND MEASURES

Land Measure

1 sq. acre =   10 sq. chains = 100,000 sq. links = 6,272,640 sq. in.
1 "   "   = 160 sq. rods =   4,840 sq. yds. =   43,560 sq. ft.

Note.—208.7103 feet square, or 69.5701 yards square, or 220 feet by 198 feet square=1 acre.

Cubic or Solid Measure

1 cubic yard = 27 cubic feet.
1 cubic foot = 1,728 cubic inches.
1 cubic foot = 2,200 cylindrical inches.
1 cubic foot = 3,300 spherical inches.
1 cubic foot = 6,600 conical inches.

Linear Measure

12 inches (in.)..................... = 1 foot ....ft.
3 feet............................... = 1 yard ....yd.
5.5 yards .... = 1 rod...............................rd.
40 rods.............................. = 1 furlong ....fur.
8 furlongs .... = 1 mile...................... ....mi.

in.	ft.	yd.	rd.	fur.	mi.
36 =	3 =	1			
198 =	16.5 =	5.5 =	1		
7,920 =	660 =	220 =	40 =	1	
63,360 =	5,280	= 1,760	= 320 =	8	= 1

Square Measure

144 square inches (sq. in) = 1 square foot ....sq. ft.
9 square feet.................. = 1 square yard ....sq. yd.
30¼ square yards .... = 1 square rod ....sq. rd.
160 square rods .... = 1 acre ....A.
640 acres .... = 1 square mile.................sq. mi.

Sq. mi.	A.	Sq. rd.	Sq. yd.	Sq. ft.	Sq. in.
1 =	640 =	102,400 =	3,097,600 =	27,878,400 =	4,014,489,600

Miscellaneous Measures and Weights

1 perch of stone = 1 ft. × 1 ft. 6 in. × 16 ft. 6 in. = 24.75 ft. cubic.
1 cord of wood, clay, etc., = 4 ft. × 4 ft. × 8 ft. = 128 ft. cubic.
1 chaldron = 36 bushels or 57.25 ft. cubic.
1 cubic foot of sand, solid, weighs 112½ lbs.
1 cubic foot of sand, loose, weighs 95 lbs.
1 cubic foot of earth, loose, weighs 93¾ lbs.
1 cubic foot of common soil weighs 124 lbs.
1 cubic foot of strong soil weighs 127 lbs.
1 cubic foot of clay weighs 120 to 135 lbs.
1 cubic foot of clay and stone weighs 160 lbs.
1 cubic foot of common stone weighs 160 lbs.
1 cubic foot of brick weighs 95 to 120 lbs.
1 cubic foot of granite weighs 169 to 180 lbs.
1 cubic foot of marble weighs 166 to 170 lbs.
1 cubic yard of sand weighs 3,037 lbs.
1 cubic yard of common soil weighs 3,429 lbs.

Safe Bearing Loads

Brick and Stone Masonry.	Lb. per Sq. In.
Brick Work.	
Bricks, hard, laid in lime mortar...........................	100
Hard, laid in Portland cement mortar....................	200
Hard, laid in Rosendale cement mortar.................	150
Masonry.	
Granite, capstone...	700
Squared stonework..	350
Sandstone, capstone...	350
Squared stonework..	175
Rubble stonework, laid in lime mortar..............	80
Rubble stonework, laid in cement mortar..........	150
Limestone, capstone...	500
Squared stonework..	250
Rubble, laid in lime mortar.............................	80
Rubble, laid in cement mortar.........................	150
Concrete, 1 Portland, 2 sand, 5 broken stone...........	150

Foundation Soils.	Tons per Sq. Ft.
Rock, hardest in native bed................................	100 —
Equal to best ashlar masonry.............................	25-40
Equal to best brick..	15-20
Clay, dry, in thick beds......................................	4- 6
Moderately dry, in thick beds...........................	2 4
Soft...	1- 2
Gravel and course sand, well cemented...................	8-10
Sand, compact and well cemented........................	4- 6
Clean, dry...	2- 4
Quicksand, alluvial soil, etc...............................	5- 1

Capacity of Cisterns for Each 10 Inches in Depth

Twenty-five feet in diameter holds...............................3059 gallons
Twenty feet in diameter holds....................................1958 gallons
Fifteen feet in diameter holds....................................1101 gallons
Fourteen feet in diameter holds.................................. 959 gallons
Thirteen feet in diameter holds.................................. 827 gallons
Twelve feet in diameter holds.................................... 705 gallons
Eleven feet in diameter holds.................................... 592 gallons
Ten feet in diameter holds....................................... 489 gallons
Nine feet in diameter holds...................................... 396 gallons
Eight feet in diameter holds..................................... 313 gallons
Seven feet in diameter holds.................................... 239 gallons
Six and one-half feet in diameter holds........................ 206 gallons
Six feet in diameter holds....................................... 176 gallons
Five feet in diameter holds...... .... 122 gallons
Four and one-half feet in diameter holds...................... 99 gallons

Four feet in diameter holds	78 gallons
Three feet in diameter holds	44 gallons
Two and one-half feet in diameter holds	30 gallons
Two feet in diameter holds	19 gallons

Number of Nails and Tacks per Pound

NAILS. Name.	Size.	No. per lb.
3 penny, fine	1⅛ inch	760 nails
3 "	1¼ "	480 "
4 "	1½ "	300 "
5 "	1¾ "	200 "
6 "	2⅛ "	160 "
7 "	2¼ "	128 "
8 "	2½ "	92 "
9 "	2¾ "	72 "
10 "	3 "	60 "
12 "	3¼ "	44 "
16 "	3½ "	32 "
20 "	4 "	24 "
30 "	4¼ "	18 "
40 "	5 "	14 "
50 "	5½ "	12 "
6 " fence	2 "	80 "
8 " "	2½ "	50 "
10 " "	3 "	34 "
12 " "	3¼ "	29 "

TACKS. Name.	Length.	No. per lb.
1 oz.	⅛ inch	16,000
1½ "	3-16 "	10,666
2 "	¼ "	8,000
2½ "	5-16 "	6,400
3 "	⅜ "	5,333
4 "	7-16 "	4,000
6 "	9-16 "	2,666
8 "	⅝ "	2,000
10 "	11-16 "	1,600
12 "	¾ "	1,333
14 "	13-16 "	1,143
16 "	⅞ "	1,000
18 "	15-16 "	888
20 "	1 "	800
22 "	1 1-16 "	727
24 "	1⅛ "	660

Wind Pressures on Roofs

(Pounds per Square Foot.)

Rise, Inches per Foot of Run.	Angle with Horizontal.	Pitch. Proportion of Rise to Span	Wind Pressure, Normal to Slope.
4	18° 25′	$\frac{1}{6}$	16.8
6	26° 33′	$\frac{1}{4}$	23.7
8	33° 41′	$\frac{1}{3}$	29.1
12	45′ 0′	$\frac{1}{2}$	36.1
16	53° 7′	$\frac{2}{3}$	38.7
18	56° 20′	$\frac{3}{4}$	39.3
24	63° 27′	1	40.0

In addition to wind and snow loads upon roofs, the weight of the principals or roof trusses, including the other features of the construction, should be figured in the estimate. For light roofs, having a span of not over 50 feet, and not required to support any ceiling, the weight of the steel construction may be taken at 5 pounds per square foot; for greater spans, 1 pound per square foot should be added for each 10 feet increase in the span.

SUPPLEMENT TO

MODERN CARPENTRY AND JOINERY.

The aim in preparing this has been to supply necessary information for enabling a practical joiner to become a competent airtight-case maker, without the
tedium of waiting, perhaps for years, until chance brings
him into contact with one who has made a specialty of
this class of work. I have endeavored, by means of
illustrations, to elucidate as clearly as possible the points
which are so frequently the cause of failure to those
who, while having a good knowledge of wood-working,
have not had the advantages of direct practical tuition
in the intricacies of airtight-case making.

Before proceeding with the explanations, I would
point out that the first and most important rule in joinery is to have the stuff planed up true, and gauged
accurately to size.

I. AIRTIGHT WALL CASE WITH GLASS OR WOOD ENDS.

The general drawings of the airtight wall-case with
glazed ends are given in Figs. 1 to 5 and the details in
Figs. 6 to 9.

Framework. Figs. 6 and 7 give the width of the top
and bottom rails for the front frame of the case, and, by
adding the width of the top and bottom door-rails to
each we determine the width of the rails required for
the ends of the case, as shown in Fig. 5. The angle-
stile must be ¼ inch more in thickness than the thick-

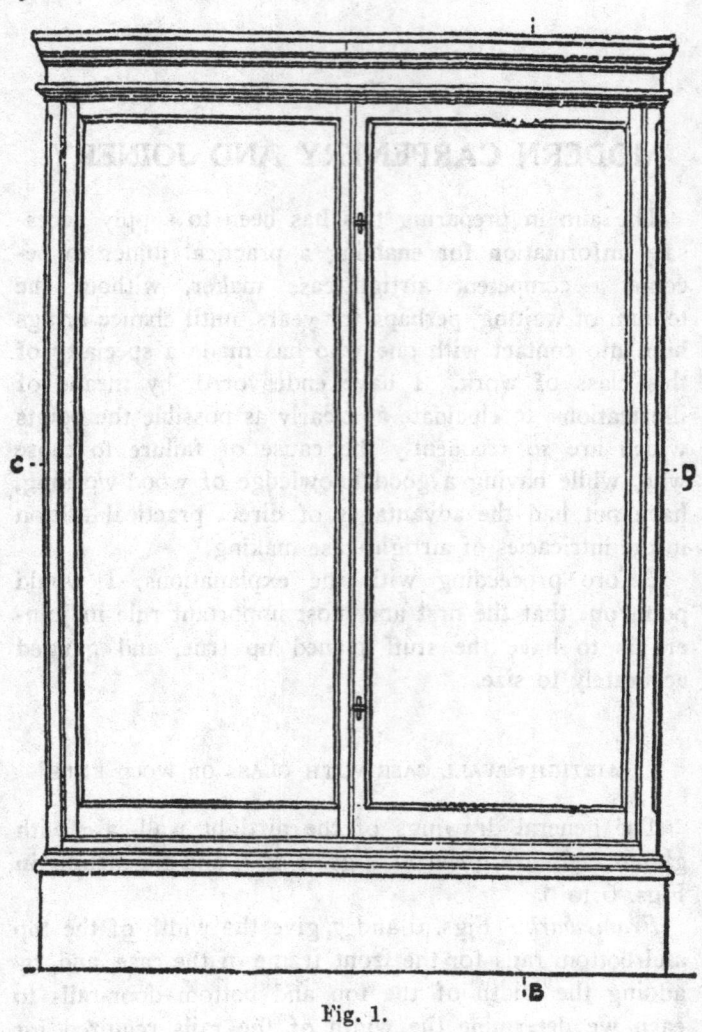

Fig. 1.

ness of the doors, in order to allow of a rebate being formed to receive the glass at the ends of the case. (See M Fig. 8.)

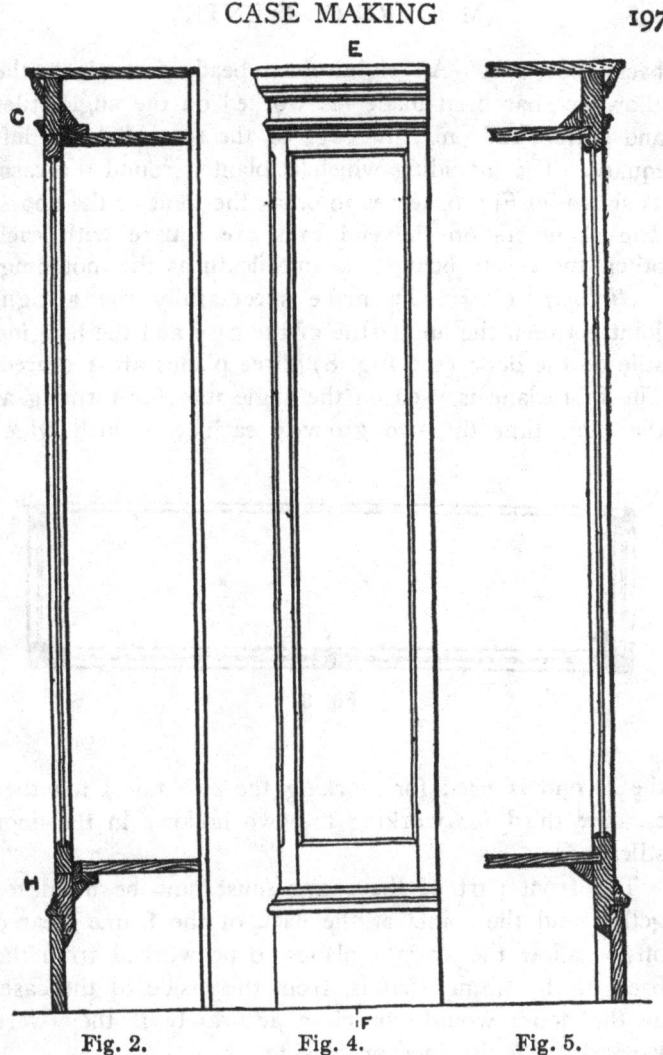

Fig. 2.　　　　　Fig. 4.　　　　　Fig. 5.

In setting out the framework (which is mortised and tenoned together in the ordinary way) the face shoulders of the front rails should be ⅛ inch longer than the back shoulders. An eighth inch bead—for which the allowance has been made—is worked on the angle-stiles and bottom rail only, the edge of the top rail being left square. The moulding which is planted round the case, as shown in Fig. 6, serves to break the joint of the doors. The shoulders on the end rails are square with each other, the rebate being the same depth as the moulding.

Airtight joints. To make successfully the airtight joint between the angle-stile of the case and the hanging stile of the door (see Fig. 8) three planes are required. The first plane is used on the angle-stile for forming at the same time the two grooves, each 3/16 inch wide;

Fig. 3.

the second is used for working the two fillets together and the third for working the two hollows in the door stiles.

The front part of the frame must now be fitted together and the joints at the back of the frame cleared off, to allow the airtight planes to be worked from the back of the frame, that is, from the inside of the case, as the doors would not close accurately if they were worked from the face or outside.

After the front frame has been fitted together as described, it must be taken apart, and the angle-stiles worked with plane No. 1 When this has been done,

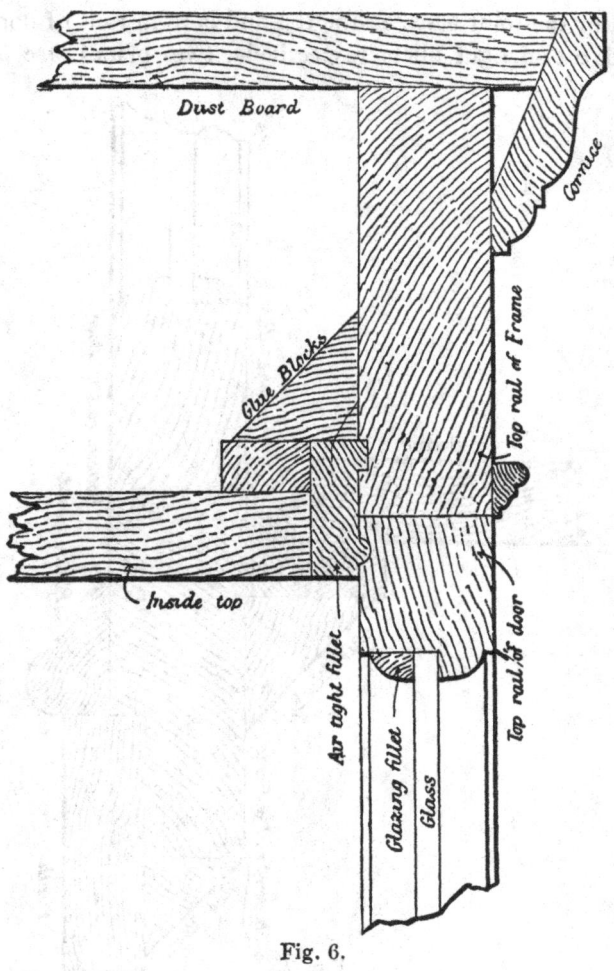

Fig. 6.

the fillets must be glued in the grooves, and, when set, rounded over with plane No. 2. The fillets will not require to be taken to the exact width before rounding over, as plane No. 2 works all surplus stuff away.

For the joint between the top and bottom rails of doors and the airtight fillets respectively, two planes are re-

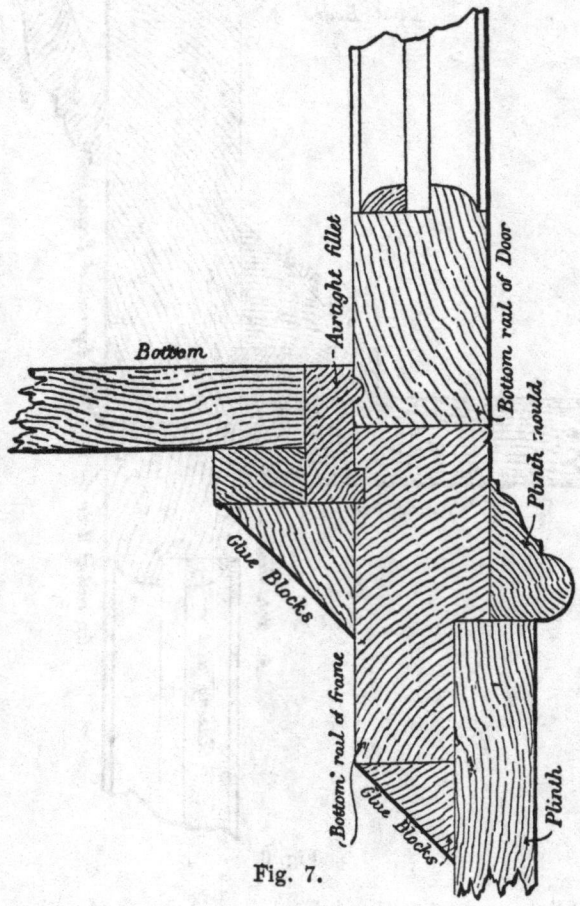

Fig. 7.

quired; the first for sticking the airtight fillet, and the second for working the small hollow on the door rails to match the fillet.

Continuing with the framework. After rounding the fillets in the angle-stiles, groove the top and bottom

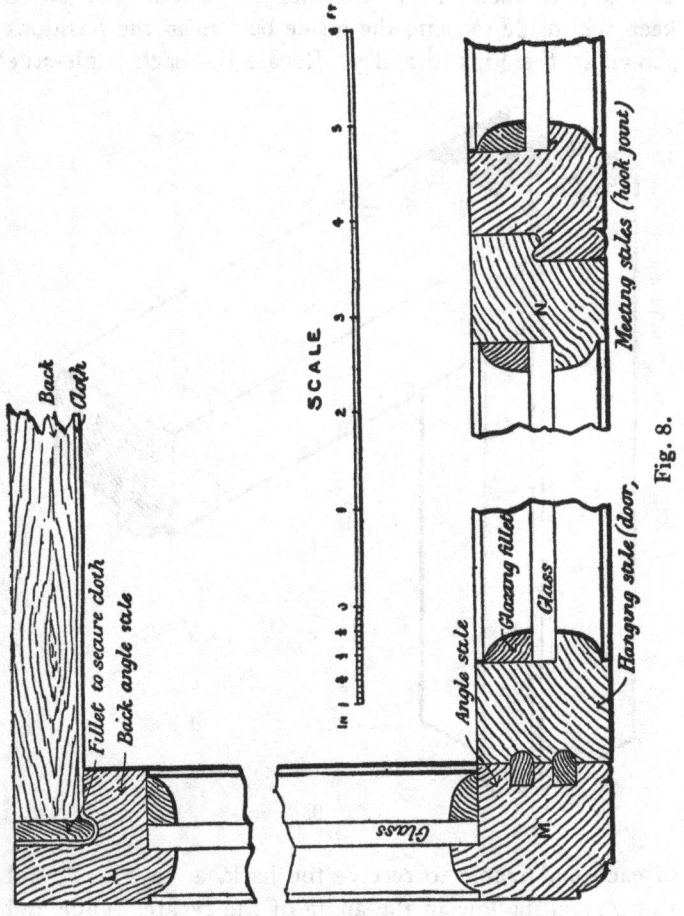

Fig. 8.

rails to receive the tongue on the airtight fillets as shown in Figs. 6 and 7 and rebate the bottom rails to rest on the plinth, Fig. 7. The top and bottom rails at each end of the case are trenched to receive respectively the ends of the inside top and inside bottom, Fig. 5. Care must be taken to make these trenches in such a way as to keep the inside top and the inside bottom in the positions shown in the Figs. 6 and 7. Rebate the back angle-stile

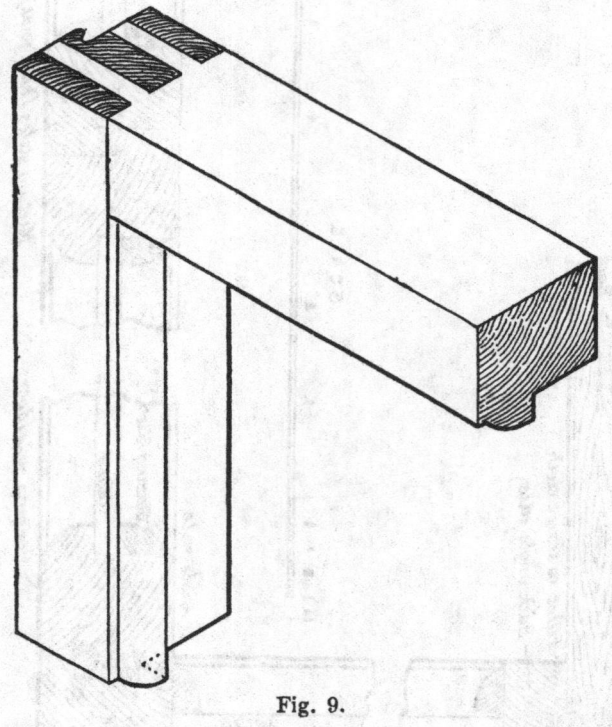

Fig. 9.

of each end frame to receive the back, as in Fig. 8, and run a small hollow in the angle of the rebate. Glue and pin the airtight fillet on the front edges of the inside top and bottom respectively; also glue the fillet on the back of each in order to strengthen the airtight fillet, and make out the thickness to receive the glue-blocks as shown. An ovolo or other moulding is now worked on the external angles of the two front angle-stiles as shown in Fig. 8, the moulding being stopped in a line with the top and bottom rails respectively of the doors, Fig. 1.

The body of the case must now be put together, care being taken to glue-block the front frame and ends securely to the bottom and top, as well as behind the plinth, which is screwed to the bottom rails from the back.

Match-boards are used for the back, the boards being run to the floor, as shown in Fig. 2. Mitre the cornice round the front and ends, screwing it from the back of the top rails; cut the dust-board to fit on the top edges of the rails and bevel against the cornice; having previously rebated it to receive the back of the case. Before the back is fastened, the cloth, Fig. 8, should be placed in the rebate of the stile, the fillet placed on top of the cloth and pressed into the hollow, and then fastened to the stile with screws, the cloth thus being securely held between the fillet and the stile. The cloth can now be stretched taut and fixed at the other end in the same way, and the boards fastened in.

Doors. In planing up the stuff for the doors, the same gauge must be used as that for the frame of the case. When setting out for the doors, take the width and height accurately, and allow 1/16 inch on the height for fitting in. The width is set out as for ordinary folding doors, viz.: allowing half the hook-joint on each door, and ⅛ inch for jointing and fitting in. The best way to allow for fitting is to have each stile 1/16 inch greater in width than the finished size required.

The rails abutting against each angle-stile are single-mortised and tenoned together as in ordinary work, but double mortises and tenons must be used at the top and bottom of each meeting stile, as shown in Fig. 9. The reason for using the double tenon is, that if a single tenon were used, the ends of the tenon would slip off after the hook-joint had been made.

Presuming the doors to be wedged up, level off the joints at the shoulders, when the doors will be ready for jointing together and fitting to the case.

Hook-Joint. The following is the best method of making a well fitting joint. First rebate the stiles (the rebate being $\frac{1}{8}$ inch less in width than the thickness of the doors, and 5/16 inch deep), and next bevel the edges of the doors, bringing the rebate to a depth of $\frac{1}{4}$ inch, Fig. 8. The doors must now be worked with a hollow and round on the edge of the rebate to form the hook-joint. For this purpose a hook-joint plane is required. There is an adjustable depth-gauge on the side of the plane, which can be easily set for working different thicknesses of stuff. Before working the doors with the plane, it is advisable to work a piece of stuff of the same thickness as the doors. Cut the piece thus worked into two, and put the joint together. This will test the accuracy of the setting of the plane. If the faces do not come flush with each other, the gauge on the plane must be raised or lowered accordingly.

Having fitted the meeting stiles, place the doors together across the bench, as they can thus be more easily taken to the exact width and height of the frame of the case. After the doors have been fitted in the opening, work with the airtight planes as previously instructed, always remembering to hold the fence of plane No. 3 on the back side of the door while forming the hollows on the hanging stiles. With plane No. 2 the small hollow on the top and bottom rails to match the airtight fillet is worked.

After working the doors as described, clean off the back side, place the doors in position, and clean off the face to the level of the frame. Take the doors out and

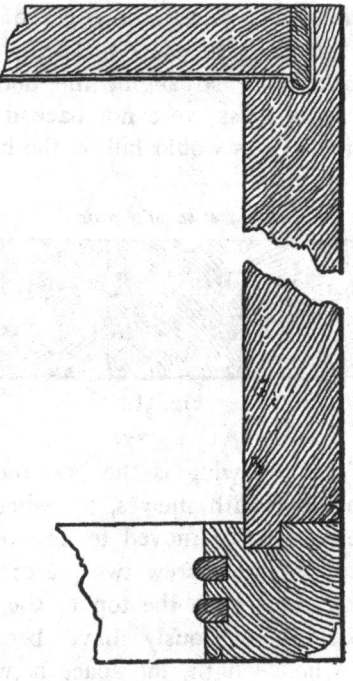

Fig. 10.

work the bead on the joint between the doors, Fig. 8. This bead is flatter than usual and has a very small quirk.

The doors are hung to the frame, each by three hinges. The top and bottom hinges are usually kept their own depth from he top and bottom edges of the doors respectively, e. g., a 2½ inch hinge will be 2½ inches from the edge. The handles on the meeting stiles are respectively about 9 inches from the upper and lower edges of door.

All glass in the doors must be carefully packed with small slips of wood between the edges of the glass and the frame of the door, in order to keep the frame rigid. The woodwork being so slight, the doors would sag when hung if the glass were not packed tightly, as all the weight of the glass would fall on the bottom rail.

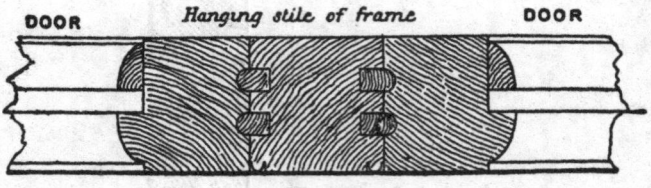

Fig. 11.

Shelves. The following is the best method to adopt for fitting the case with shelves, as, when fitted in this way, the shelves can be moved to any required height. To the back of the case screw two pieces of iron, one at each side, extending from the top to the bottom of the case. These must previously have been drilled and tapped their whole length, the space between each hole being ½ inch from centre to centre, and each hole being large enough to receive a 3/16 inch screw. A malleable-iron bracket about 3 inches long on the back edge—the length of the top edge being the width of the shelf—is now required, having a small piece projecting above the top edge in which is drilled a plain hole, and having a pin near the bottom edge. The pin at the bottom edge is placed in one of the holes in the tapped bar, and a 3/16 inch screw is passed through the hole at the top edge and screwed into the bar, thus securing the bracket firmly. Care must be taken to have the same distance between the centres of any two holes in the bar.

Fig. 10 shows a horizontal section through a show-case having solid ends.

Fig. 11 shows a horizontal section through the centre hanging stile in the front frame of a wide showcase, when two pairs of doors are required. It is worked in the same manner as previously described for hanging stiles.

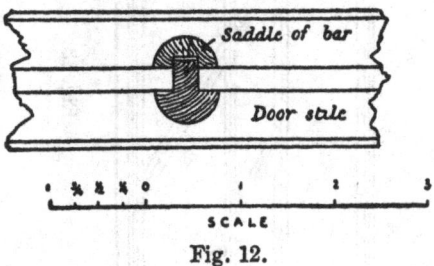

Fig. 12.

Fig. 12 shows a section of a cross bar in doors. This is only required where sheet glass is used. Each end of the bar is sunk into the moulding of the door-stiles. The saddle is cut between the rebates, and secured to the bar.

Plinths separate from the case. If the showcase is over 6 feet 6 inches in height, or the plinth is of a greater depth than 12 inches, it is advisable to make the plinth separate from the case. Instead of the bottom rail being rebated behind the plinth, as shown in Fig. 7, a frame must be made out of 1½ inch by 3 inch stuff dovetailed together at the angles; and two or three bearers should

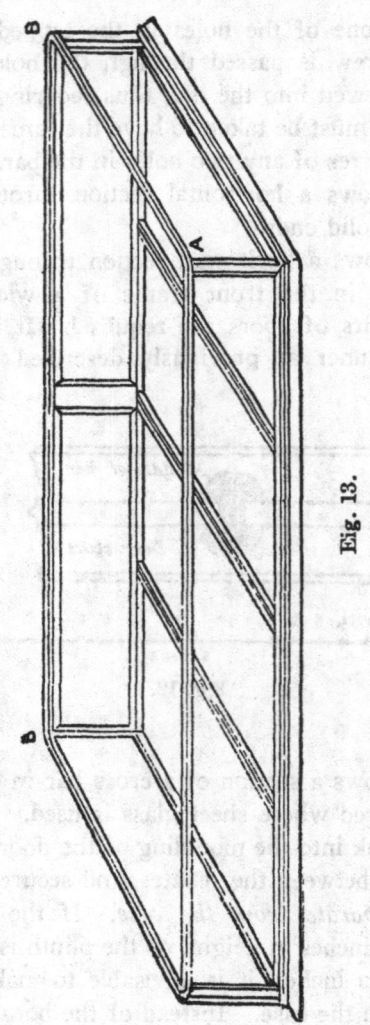

Fig. 13.

be mortised and tenoned between the front and back
rails (as the length of the case may require). At each
angle, and under each end of the bearers, a leg is stump-

tenoned into the under side of the rails to support the case. When this is done, the plinth should be mitred round the frame. It should be screwed from the back, and glue-blocks used in all the angles.

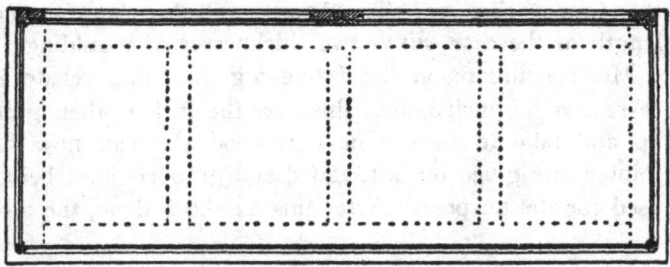

Fig. 14.

An isometrical projection of a counter-case is shown in Fig. 3. The top, sides, and front are of plate-glass. Mirrors are placed on the inside of the doors at the back of the case. The divisions on the bottom show the position of the trays.

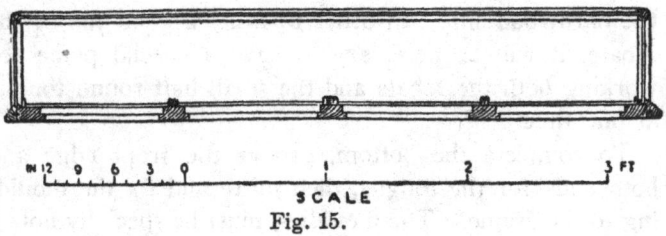

Fig. 15.

Before commencing work, it is absolutely necessary to draw Figs. 14 and 15 full size, to enable the taking off and working to an exact size of the various parts required to be done.

Bottom of case. Commence with the frame, which should be made out of well-seasoned pine. The width of the bottom frame will be the extreme width of the case less the thickness of the moulding on the front edge and 1½ inch for a hardwood slip on the back edge of the frame, Fig. 17. The length will be the extreme length of the case *minus* two thicknesses of moulding.

Mortise and tenon the frame together, and rebatc it to receive ⅝ inch panels flush on the inside; then glue up and take to size. The hardwood slip can now be jointed and glued on, a tongued and grooved joint being used for the purpose. After this has been done, the air-

Fig. 16.

tight rebate to receive the doors should be worked on the hardwood slip. In order to make a good job of the rebate, it will be necessary to have a special plane for working both the rebate and the small half-round tongue at one time.

To complete the bottom, groove the front edge and both ends for the tongue, then mitre and fix the moulding to the frame. The moulding must be specially noted. It must project above the bottom 3/16 inch to form a rebate for the glass; and the first member, i. e. the part projecting, must be rounded to intersect with the upright angle-bars, Figs. 17 and 18, with mitre into the mouldings.

The panels in the bottom are to be screwed to the frame. Before putting the whole case together, they

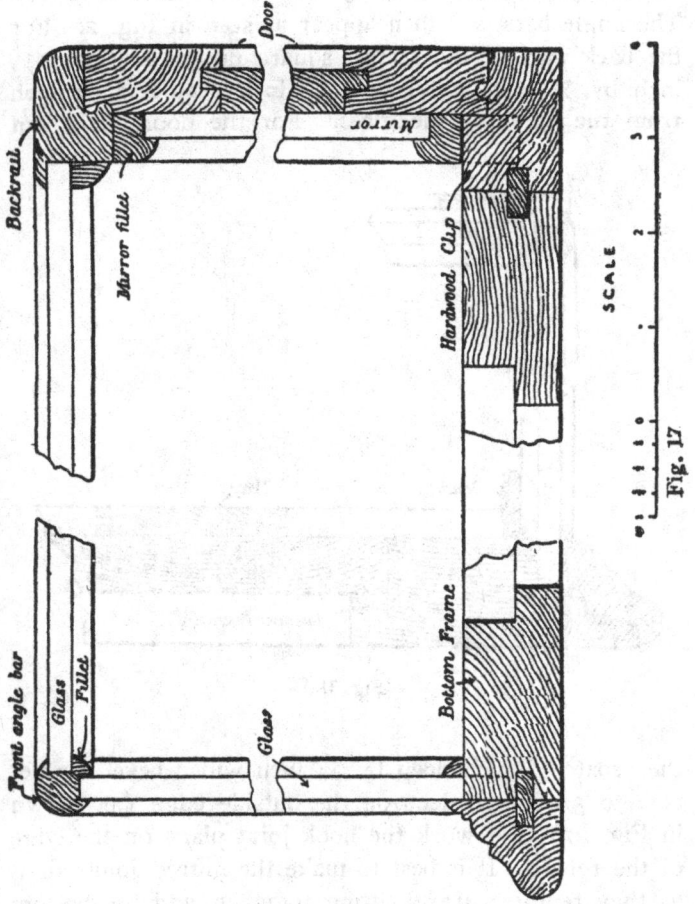

Fig. 17

must be taken out for enabling the small fillets which secure the glass to be easily screwed into their respective positions.

Framework for glass. Plane up the stuff for the round angle-bars, gauging it to 9/16 inch square, and rebate ⅛ inch deep and ⅛ inch from the face edges. The angle bars will then appear as seen in Fig. 2. For the back part of the frame, square up the stuff to 1½ inch by ¾ inch and rebate ¼ inch deep and ⅛ inch from the face for the glass. For the doors, take out

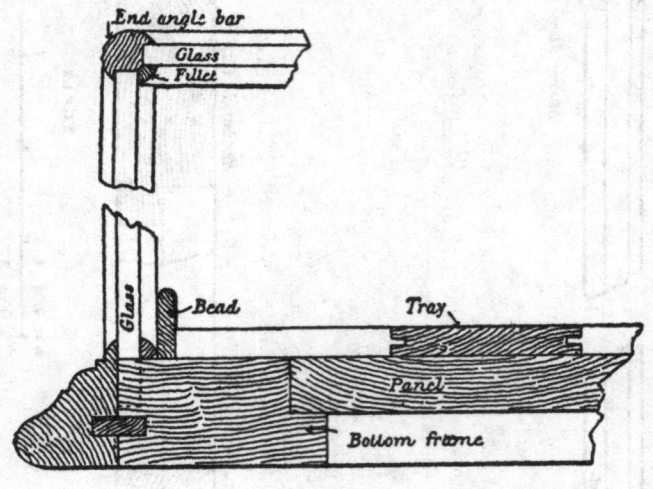

Fig. 18.

the rebate ¼ inch deep by ⅝ inch wide; bevel the rebate to 5/16 inch deep on the outside edge (as shown in Fig. 21), and work the hook-joint plane on the edge of the rebate. It is best to make the mitred joints first, as they require careful fitting together, and the bottom ends can be afterwards easily taken to the required length and cut.

Fig. 23 contains isometrical projections showing the

joints at the intersection of the front and the end angle-bars with the upright angle-bar. The position of the point is shown at A, Fig. 23.

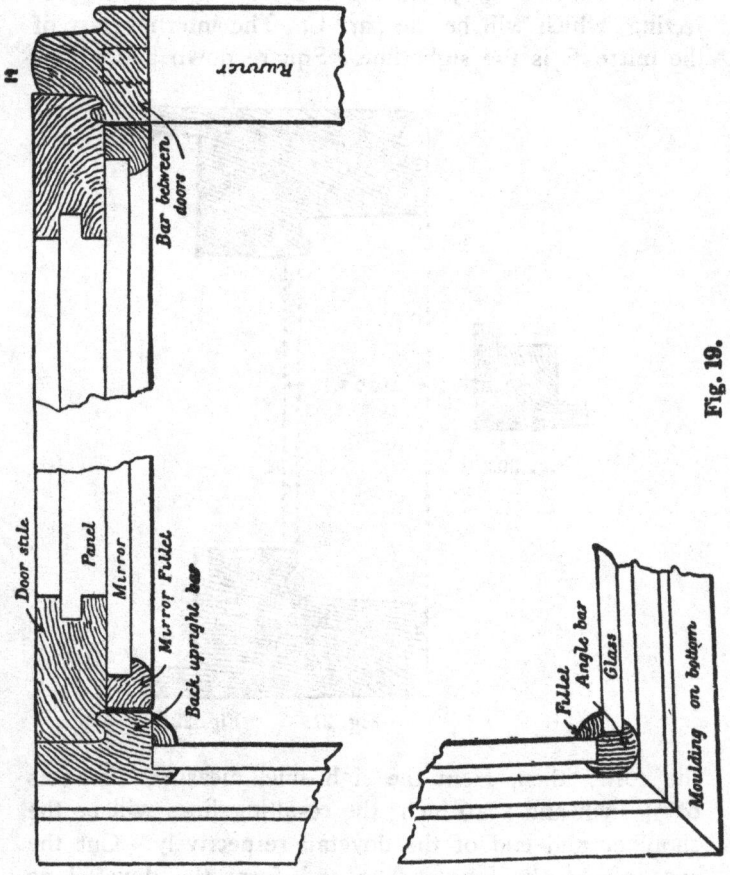

Fig. 19.

Three pieces of the required section, Fig. 20, should be got out, and the joint worked as follows:

Commence with the front and end angle-bars, cutting

a square mitre, 45 degrees on each outside face of both bars, bringing the external angle to a point, as shown in the sketch. Cut the mitre down to the rebate line and cut the surplus away, leaving the core of the bar projecting, which will be the part C. The internal part of the mitre E is the sight line. Square down and across

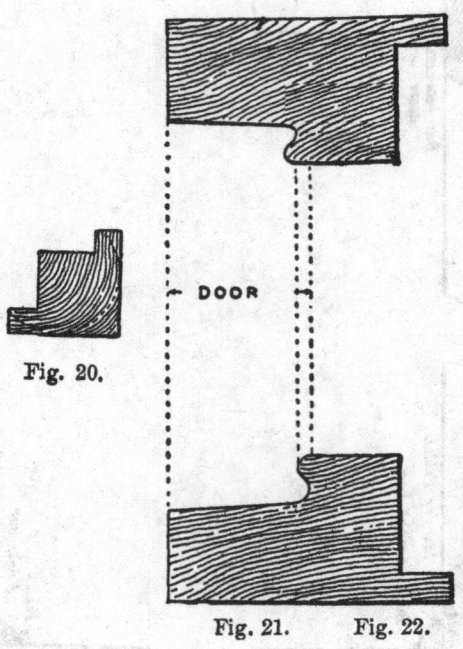

Fig. 20.

DOOR

Fig. 21.   Fig. 22.

the core; then, from the sight-line, measure distances of ⅛ inch and 7/16 inch; the resulting lines will be the shoulder and end of the dovetail respectively. Cut the core off at the longest line and form the dovetail as shown in the sketch, when the two bars can be fitted together.

Proceed with the upright angle-bar. Cut the square

mitre as before, but instead of cutting to the depth of
the rebate, it must be cut 1/32 inch less. From the

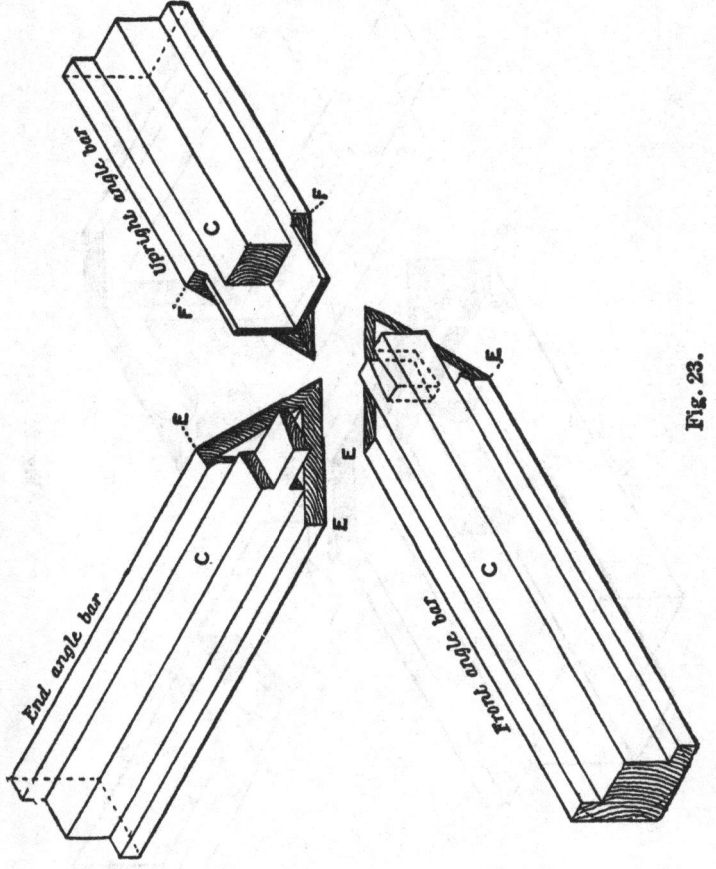

Fig. 23.

sightline F measure the same distances as before, viz.,
⅛ inch and 7/16 inch. Cut off at the longest line, taking care not to cut through the projecting point of the

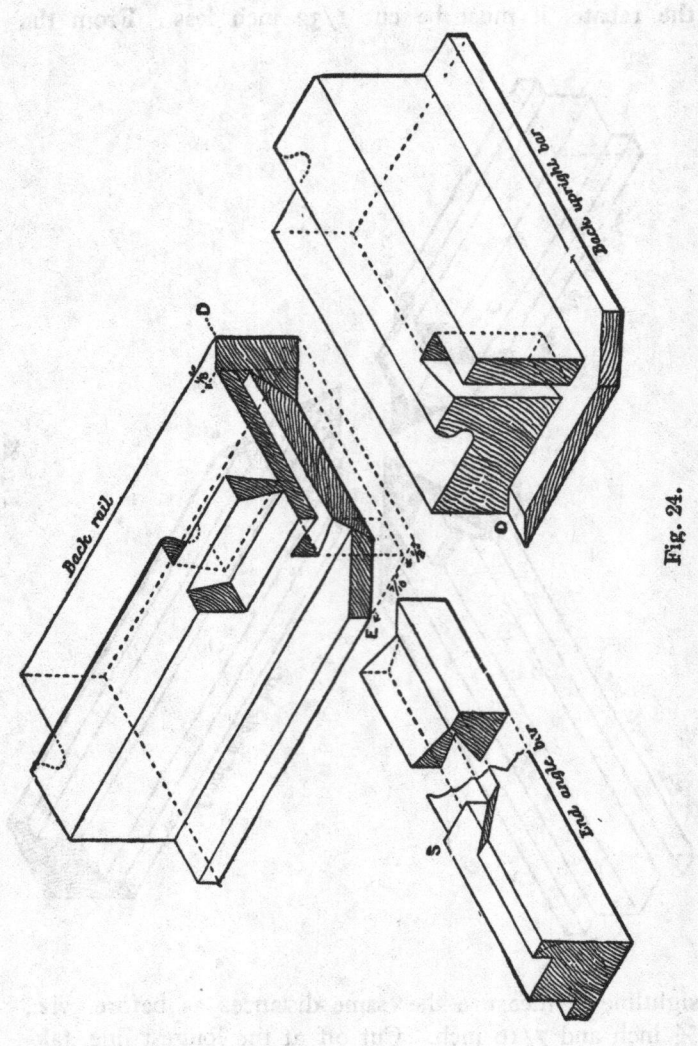

Fig. 24.

mitre, then take out the core C back to the shoulder line, thus leaving a thin tenon as seen in the sketch. Cut the tenon back 1/16 inch on each edge and continue the mitre through.

It will now be necessary to mortise the front and end bars to receive the tenon on the upright angle-bar. For the mortises, square a line across the mitre 1/16 inch from the sight line E. Gauge a line down the mitre 3/32 inch from the face of the bar, leaving 1/32 inch (the width of the mortise) between the core of the bar and the gauge line. The depth of the mortise will be to within ⅛ inch from the other face.

The work must be done very carefully, and great care taken to have the tenon on the upright angle-bar of the thickness stated, viz., 1/32 inch, as the result of having it of greater thickness would be that, when the bars were rounded, it would work through to the face.

The front angle-bar will have the same joint on both ends. The joint at the back of the case on the end angle-bar is cut as shown at Fig. 24. The joint at the bottom end of each upright angle-bar is simply a square shoulder cut to the depth of the rebate, leaving the core of the bar projecting to form a stump tenon. The bars are afterwards mitred with the moulding on both the front and the end, the projecting round of the moulding being cut away between the mitres in order to allow the shoulder to butt on the first square member, which will be flush with the bottom.

Fig. 24 contains isometrical projections showing the joints used to unite the back rail with the back upright angle-bar for forming the door opening; and also the end angle-bar. The position of the joint will be clearly understood by referring to B, Fig. 13.

It will be well to follow the same system as in the last
group of joints, i. e., to prepare a piece of the required
section of back rail, Fig. 21, which, when cut into two
parts, can be used for both the back rail and back angle-
bar; the only difference in the section of the two being
that the back rail is rebated 1/16 inch less than the
thickness of the doors instead of ⅛ inch less as in the back
upright bar, Fig. 22. The reason for this is to allow the

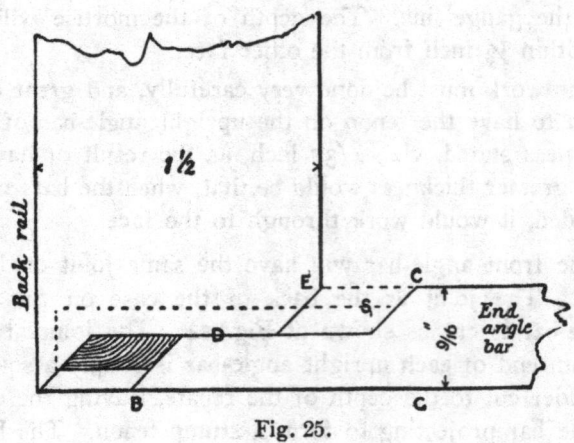

Fig. 25.

round of the hook-joint on the back upright bar to project
over the hook-joint on the back rail which butts against
it. It also allows a continuous hollow on the edges of
the doors, which would not be the case if the rebates
were kept flush with each other.

The end angle-bar is dovetailed into the back rail and
is also mitred both at the extreme end and at the rebate.
Fig. 25 shows the plan of this joint. It will be observed

that the joint has been left open to show the bevel from the shoulder line to the dovetail on the back rail, as at A Fig. 31.

The back rail is also dovetailed to receive the upright bar. If the reader will look at Fig. 24 and imagine the upright placed into position on the back rail, he will notice that D D meet and form the remaining part of the

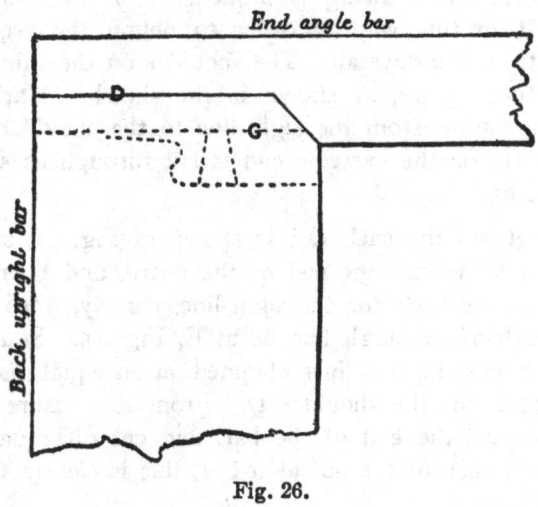

Fig. 26.

mitre, leaving a shoulder and mitre to join the end angle, bar when in position. The exact position of the latter is seen in Fig. 26, the dotted lines showing the position of the dovetail on the back rail.

We will now proceed to set out the work.

Commencing with the end angle bar, square off a line for the extreme end of the mitre at B, Fig. 25, and measure back the width of the back rail (namely 1½ inch) to C, which will be the sight line. From the sight line set off 5/16 inch for the shoulder of the dovetail as at S, Figs. 24 and 25; then set off 1⅜ inch from the sight-line to the end of the dovetail. Set a gauge to the centre of the angle-bar for the shoulders, as at D, Figs. 25 and 26. The shoulder at D, Fig. 25, is cut under on the bevel as shown in the section through the joint at A, and in the sketch of the end angle-bar, Fig. 24, where the drawing is broken. It is necessary to bevel it in this way in order to obtain the requisite strength in the dovetail. The shoulder on the side, Fig. 26, is cut square, as shown in the sketch. Mark the mitres, cutting from the sight-line to the shoulder line. The mitre on the extreme end is cut through as shown in Fig. 25.

To set out the back rail as shown in Fig. 24, square a line for the extreme end of the mitre, and from this line measure back for the sight-line, namely, 9/16 inch, the width of the angle-bar, as at E, Fig. 25. Square a line between the two lines obtained, at an equal distance from each for the shoulder D. From E measure 7/16 inch toward the end of the bar, and cut off square to within ⅛ inch of the outside edge; this is clearly shown in Fig. 24.

To mark the dovetail of the end angle-bar, make a thin hardwood or zinc pattern to fit the dovetail on the angle-bar and apply it to the rebate of the back rail, cutting the dovetail out very carefully to within ⅛ inch of the outside edge. On the top side of the rail mark the external mitre from the extreme point to the shoulder-line, and cut as shown in Figs. 24 and 25. Before the mitre can be completed, the bevel must be cut along the shoulder-line and edge of dovetail, and must work out against the mitre. The internal mitre is cut from the sight-line.

There now only remains the cutting of the dovetail to receive the upright bar. Referring to Fig. 24, it will be seen that it is necessary to obtain the shoulder-line only, which is accomplished by measuring from the extreme point of the mitre, D, Fig. 24, ¾ inch, the thickness of the upright bar. The position of the dovetail-joint between the back rail and the back upright bar is shown by the dotted line in Fig. 26.

Exact lines for setting out the back upright bar, Fig. 26, are found as follows: Square the shoulder-line D and set off for the back shoulder ¼ inch as shown by the dotted line G. The back shoulder is then cut off to within ⅛ inch of the face, as in the sketch, Fig. 24. Make a pattern to fit the dovetail on the back rail, and apply it to the back of the bar. Mitre the ¼ inch projection on the outside edge, and also mitre the inside as shown.

It is absolutely necessary that the whole of this work should be executed very carefully and very neatly. When the above mentioned joints have been fitted, make the bars to the required length.

To set out the bottom end of the back upright bar, cut the face shoulder square and mitre with the moulding as previously described for the front angle-bar. Allow the back-shoulder to be ¼ inch longer, so as to fit the rebate for the doors, the tenon being in the position shown by the dotted lines in Fig. 17.

After all the joints have been made, round the angle-bars and the back rail. The external angles of all upright angle-bars must have the rounding turned out about ½ inch above the bottom shoulder, leaving the bottom part of the bar square to follow the line of the moulding. The joints can now be glued together and cleaned off.

The double-rebated upright bar between the doors, as at H, Fig. 19, is cut to give both the top and bottom rebate, a small dovetail being cut at both ends in the positions shown by the dotted lines. The front edge of the bar is slightly rounded to break the joint between the doors. From the inside of the bar a runner of the same thickness as the bar is screwed to the bottom of the case to keep the trays in position.

Doors. There is nothing special to note in framing up the doors; they may be either tenoned or dowelled together. The panel is prepared flush on the inside.

Carefully fit the doors to the opening and work the hook-joint on the top edge and both ends. It will be remembered that the hook-joint must be worked through on each end; and also that it is deeper than the hook-joint on the top rail. In working the small hollow to fit over the fillet on the bottom edge, work the plane from the back side of the door.

Hinge the doors on the bottom edge, fixing the butts against the outside edge of the half-round fillet. When fixed thus the airtight joint will remain intact. The doors are fastened by a spring catch or lock let into the top rail.

When the doors are hung, the position of the mirror fillet can be marked by lining down the back of the doors round the frame. The fillets should be fixed 1/32 of an inch inside the lines to allow for clearing.

Trays. A cross section of the tray is shown in Fig. 18. The bottom is prepared for three pieces of ¼-inch pine. The grain of the centre piece runs from back to front of the case, the grain of the side pieces being at right angles to it, and the three pieces are tongued and grooved together as shown. Glue the pieces together, and, when set, mitre the bead round the bottom.

Another method of ensuring the bottom against warping is to have the bottom in three thicknesses, the grain of the centre lying across the two outside pieces, and the pieces being glued together.

The inside of the tray and over the bead are covered with velvet or some other material, which must be glued to the tray. Glue should be used sparingly so as to prevent it penetrating the material.

CIRCULAR-FRONTED COUNTER-CASE WITH GLASS ENDS.

Fig. 28 shows a cross section through a circular-fronted case with glass ends. The only difference in the construction of this case from that of the square case is the bent angle-bar, and, of course, the omission of the front angle-bar.

In making this case it is first necessary to have the glass bent to the shape required. For this purpose a pattern of the curve should be sent to a glass manufacturer. When the glass has been received make a mould of the same shape, on which to bend the angle-bar, as shown in Fig. 29. The convex side of the glass will give the rebate line from which to work the mould.

Use birch for the angle-bar, as it bends easily; it can be stained to match the other part of the case. Have the bar long enough to bend from the bottom of the case to the back rail.

To bend the bar successfully, cut the top side of the bar away down to the rebate line on the end required to be bent. The length of the part cut away will be from the bottom of the case to a little beyond the springing line. Care must be taken to cut the two bars for

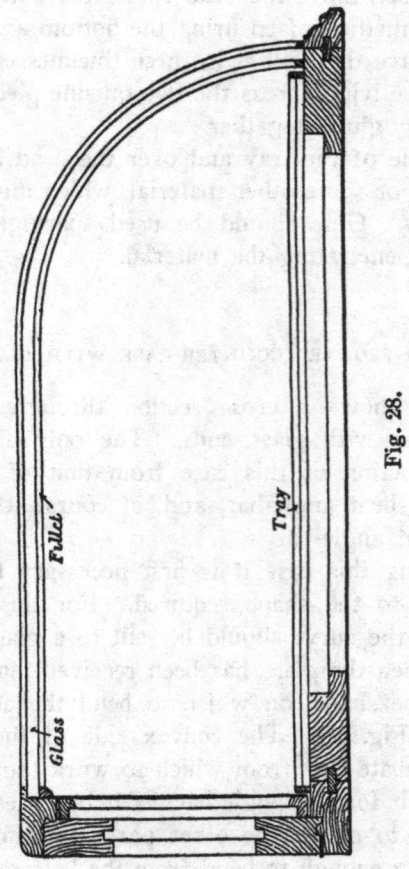

Fig. 28.

the case in pairs. Steam the bars for several hours and then bend them round the mould (Fig. 29) by securing the extreme end first with a cleat, as shown at A. Draw

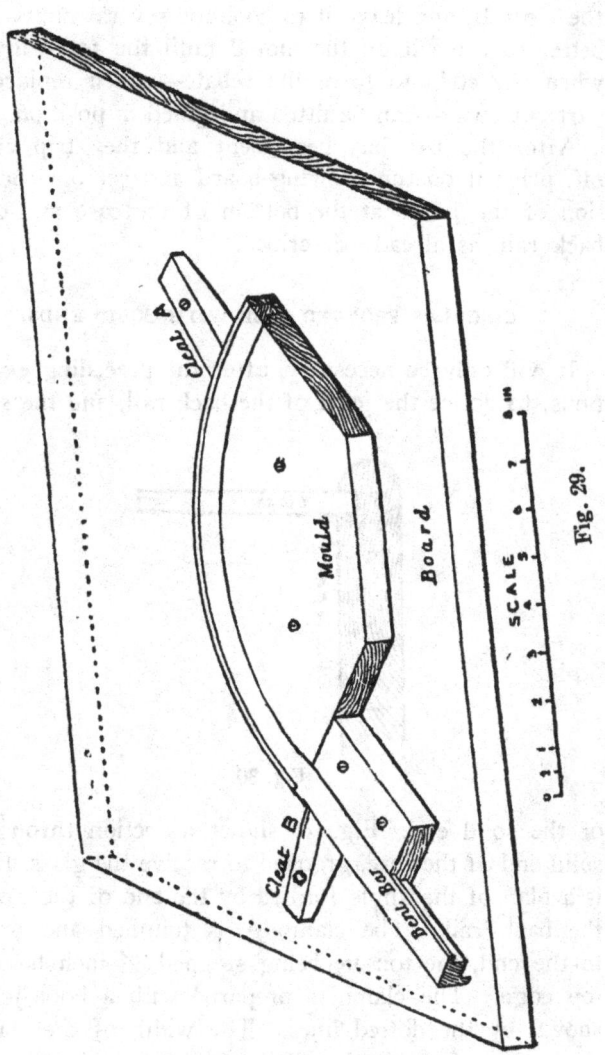

Fig. 29.

the bar gradually to the mould, secure it in position by the cleat B, and leave it to cool for several hours. It is better to leave it on the mould until the following day, when the strip to form the rebate—which replaces the part cut away—can be fitted and glued in position.

After the bar has been bent and the strip cleaned off, place it on the drawing-board and set out the position of the joints at the bottom of the case and on the back rail, as already described.

CIRCULAR-FRONTED CASE WITH SOLID ENDS.

It will only be necessary, after the preceding explanations, to notice the joint of the back rail, and the section

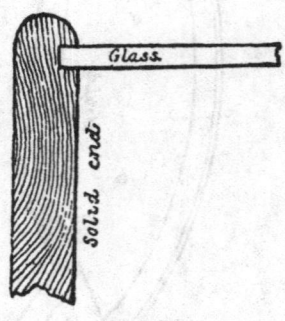

Fig. 30.

of the solid end. Fig. 30 shows a section through the solid end of the case, grooved to receive the glass. Fig. 31 is a plan of the angle formed by the end of the case and the back rail. The clamp A is tongued and grooved to the end, the tongue being stopped ½ inch below the top edge. The clamp is prepared with a hook-joint as shown by the dotted lines. The width of the clamp is the width of the back rail less the rebate for the glass.

Fig. 32 shows in isometrical projection the joint at the junction of the back rail with the solid end. Imagine

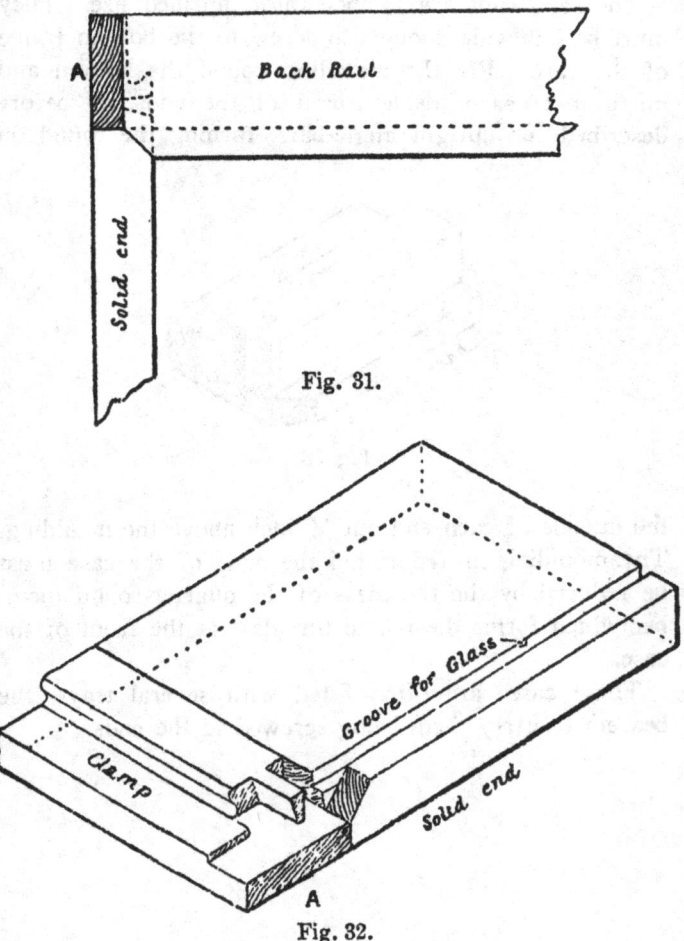

Fig. 31.

Fig. 32.

that A A are brought together. It will then be seen that they slide into position and present the appearance shown in the plan in Fig 31, and give the extra lines for setting work.

The solid ends are ⅝ inch thick, finished size. They must be left wide enough to screw to the bottom frame of the case. Fix the moulding round the bottom and mitre it at each inside round of the ends, as before described for upright angle-bars, turning the round on

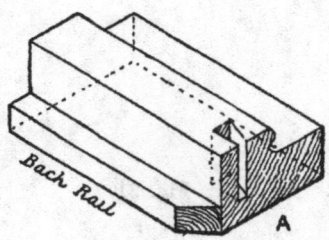

Fig. 33.

the outside of each end out ½ inch above the moulding. The moulding mitred round the ends of the case must be reduced by the thickness of the quarter-round member which forms the rebate for glass at the front of the case.

These cases are often fitted with several trays, the bearers to carry them being screwed to the ends.

SOME FORMS OF PANELS.

We conclude this Volume by giving some illustrations of panels. In Fig. 1 we give a "flush" panel for a front or entrance door, in which in front elevation a, b, are the two rails, d d, e e, the stiles, c c, g g, the panel with

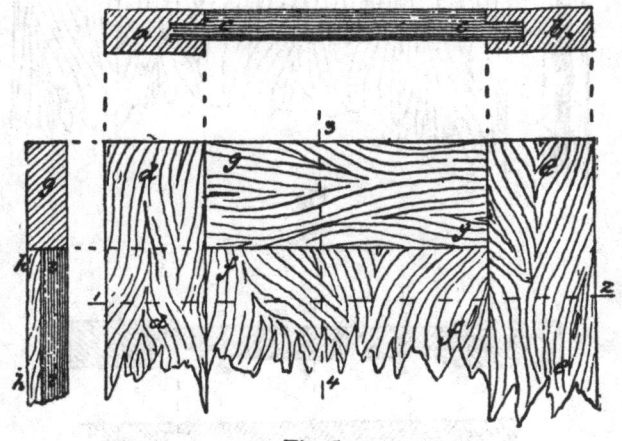

Fig. 1.

stuck-on mouldings all round and mitring at corners; g h is a vertical section in line 3 4. In this the recess between the stile and panel is one side only. Where there are recesses on both sides of the panel b b, Fig. 2, and the stiles a a, the panel is known as a "square" panel. In this figure the lower diagram is front elevation; that on the left is a section on line 3 4. In Fig. 3 we illustrate different forms of panels. In the upper diagram, a a, the stiles carry one "square panel,"

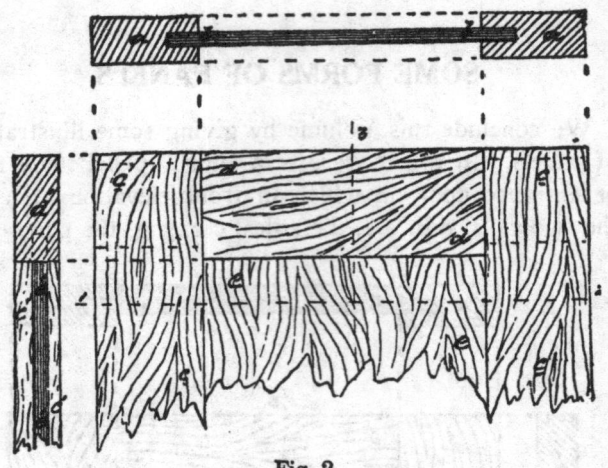

Fig. 2.

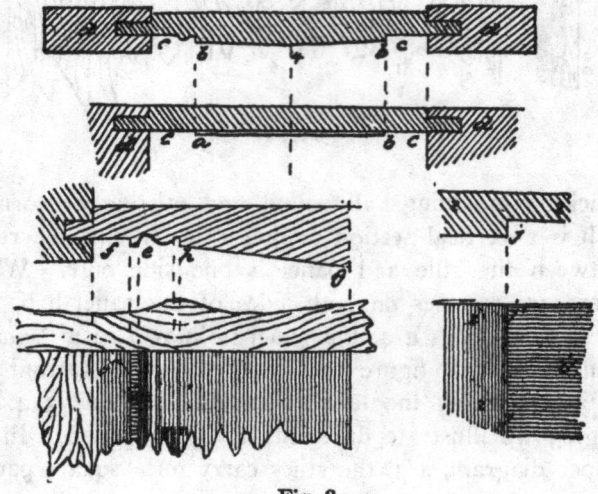

Fig. 3.

which is not flat, as in Fig. 2, on the inner side, but
tapers to the centre, which is thickest, to the sides,

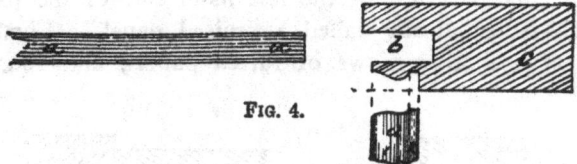

FIG. 4.

where it may be either square, as at the right hand,
or finished with a moulding, as on the left.

Resuming our description of the drawing named, the
second diagram shows a "flush panel," with stiles d d,

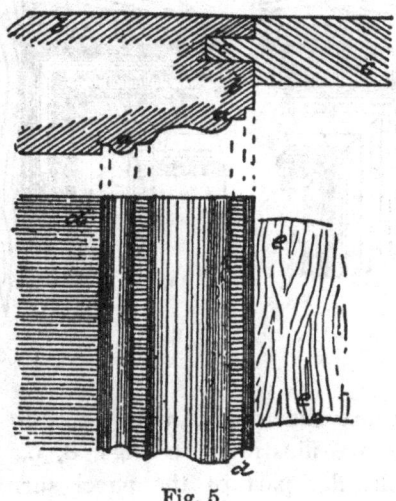

Fig. 5.

the panel having a raised position in the centre, as
shown at a b, with flat spaces as at c c, all round. The

lower diagram to the right is an enlarged view in section and elevation of the part of the panel of upper diagram to the right. The lower diagram to the left is an enlarged view of the left hand side of the panel, which is technically called a "raised panel." Figs. 12 and 13 are other views of raised panels, and diagram

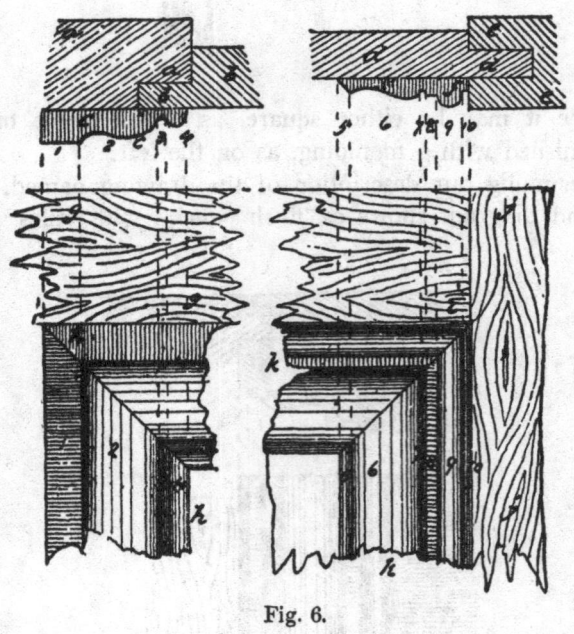

Fig. 6.

B in next figure shows a form of panel in the Gothic. Other forms are illustrated in Figs. 8, 9, 10, and 11. In Fig. 3 the flat part of the panel surrounding the raised central part is called the "margin." (See also Fig. 12 at b.) The panel, as in Fig. 3, is called a "moulded raised panel" when there is a moulding at the margin, as f e h. There are other distinctions in panel work, yet to be noticed. In "flush panels," as in Fig. 1, the "moulding" or "bead" is worked only on the two sides (vertical) of the panel, as at d d, Fig. 5, and these terminate at the rails, as at f f, no moulding being at the ends of the panel. This is called "bead butt" panel. When the panel has mouldings all round,

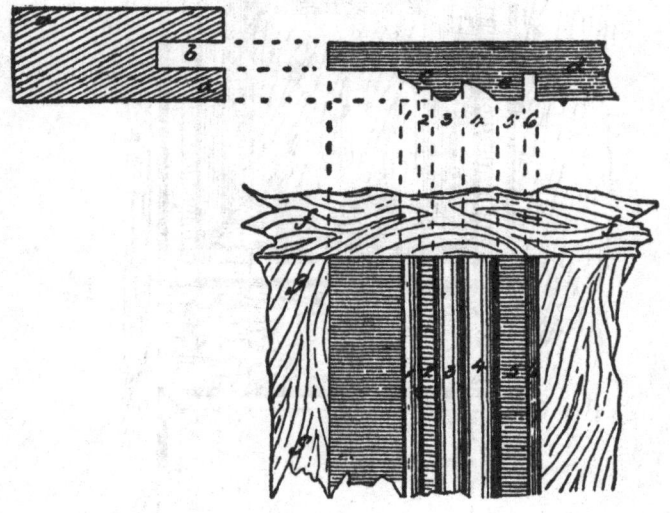

Fig. 7.

that is at top and bottom as well as at the sides, the mouldings meet at the corners and are mitred, as shown in the lower part of the diagram in Fig. 6, this is known as a "bead flush panel." In panel work where a moulding is worked out of the solid, as at b in Fig. 4, or at a a in Fig. 5 of the style, as c c or b b, the term "stuck on" (a corruption of "struck on," which is the true term) is applied. This is only applicable **to** "bead and butt" panel work vertically, as the mouldings would not mitre if struck horizontally on the rails.

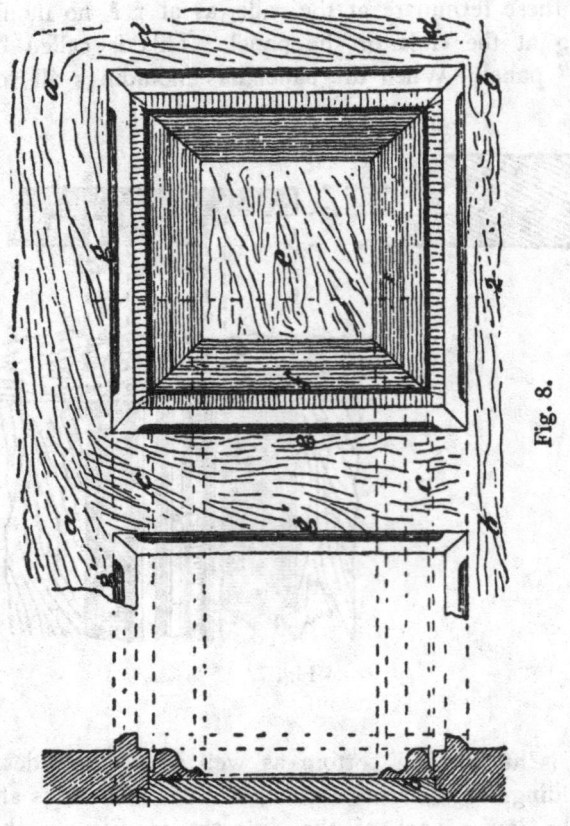

Fig. 8.

When the mouldings are made separately and nailed onto the stiles j j, and rails i i, Fig. 6, they are called "laid on" mouldings. They may be nailed on either to

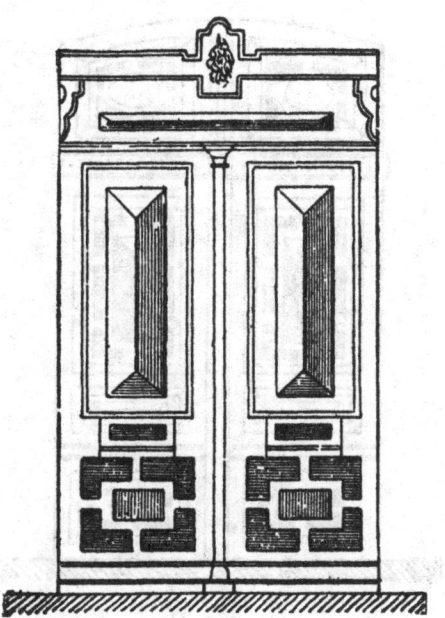

Fig. 9.

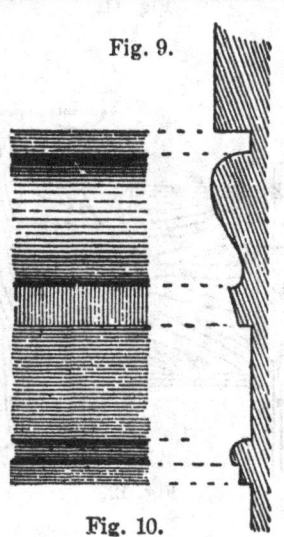

Fig. 10.

Fig. 11.

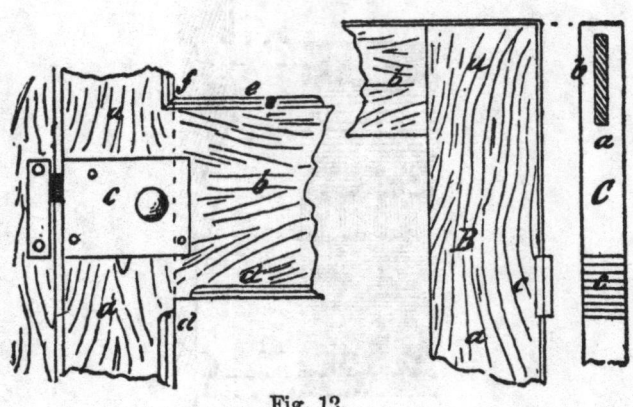

Fig. 12.

Fig. 13.

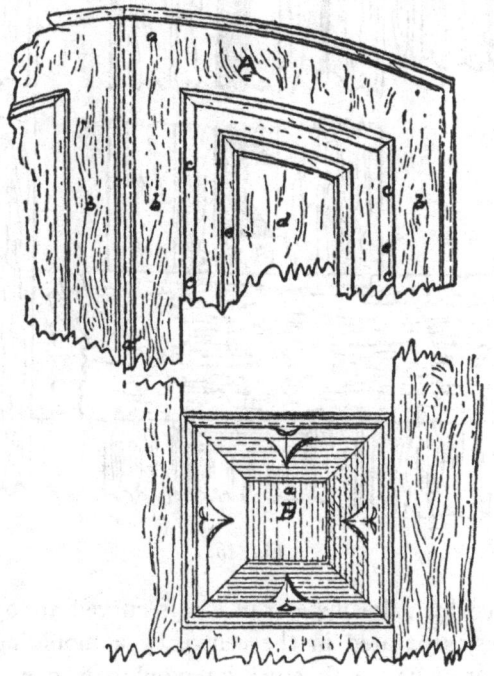

Fig. 14.

the stiles and rails or to the panels in "flush" work, or all around the panels in "square" panels. In Fig. 14 in diagram A, we give a panel at upper part of

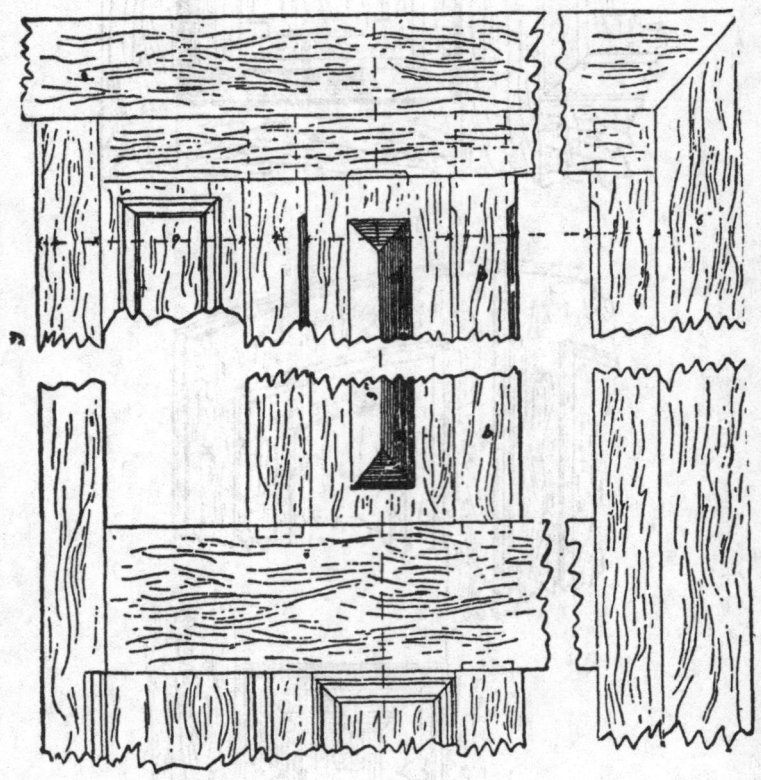

Fig. 15.

door, in which the upper rail a a is curved at top, b b b the stiles, separated in the centre by a moulding a a d the upper panel, with stuck-on mouldings c e e. Diagram B is front elevation of lower panel. In Fig. 13

we give a section of middle stile and panel; the middle
stile b b being provided down the centre with a stuck-
on moulding, as at b a, corresponding to the vertical
moulding a a in Fig. 15. A moulding as at c c is worked
in the margin of the stile corresponding to c c in Fig.
14. E shows the moulding in section stuck on the square
panel f g, the margin f being in this way wide. In Fig.
15, and in Figs. 8, 9, 10, 11 and 12 we give illustrations
of panel work, and in Fig. 9 section and elevation of
mouldings for a panel.

JOINERS' WORK IN THE CONSTRUCTION OF DOORS—DIFFERENT KINDS OF DOORS.

We now come to illustrate the different forms of doors, and various details of their construction. Doors are either external or internal and both may be con-

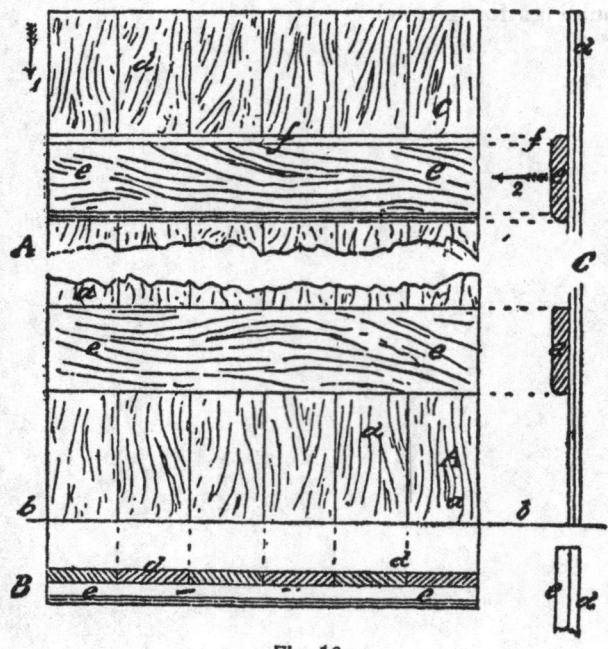

Fig. 16.

structed much in the same way. The chief difference between them, if difference may be made at all, is that external doors are heavier in their timbers—that is, thicker and broader—and are not quite so much ornamented with mouldings, or so highly and carefully finished, as internal or private room doors. Doors are of different classes, beginning with those adapted either for houses, of a simple character or for out-buildings, etc., where economy is carefully studied, and going up to the more elaborate forms, used in houses of the higher class.

The simplest form of doors is shown in part elevation at A, Fig. 16, in plan at B, looking down in direction of arrow 1, in C side elevation or edge view looking in direction of arrow 2. This form is what is called a "batten door." In elevation in diagram A, the lower part is a a, next to floor or ground line b b. The door is made up of flat planks, a a c d d, running vertically from foot or floor, or ground line b b up to head. These are either laid as in plan B in the cheapest class of work, edge to edge, and held together by cross pieces, or bars, e e. In better work, these and the vertical parts, d d, are secured by joints of different kinds. In the section C the cross bars e are simply laid flat and nailed to the upright planks, d d. The edges of the cross-bars, d d, may either be left square, or have the lines or corners planed off and "chamfered" or beveled off as at f f.

BATTEN AND BRACED AND BATTEN, BRACED AND FRAMED DOOR.

Fig. 17 is an elevation in diagram A of a "batten and braced" door. To the vertical and cross bars of the simple form in Fig. 16 the diagonal "brace" a a a a,

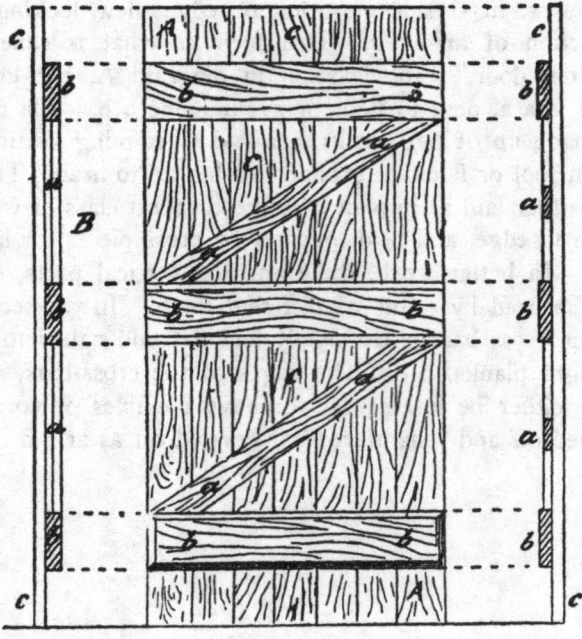

Fig. 17.

corresponding to the struts of a roof truss, are introduced; these butt against the cross bars or battens b b b b, while behind are the vertical boards c c c c,

Diagram B is side elevation or edge view and C vertical section. A still higher class of door is the "framed

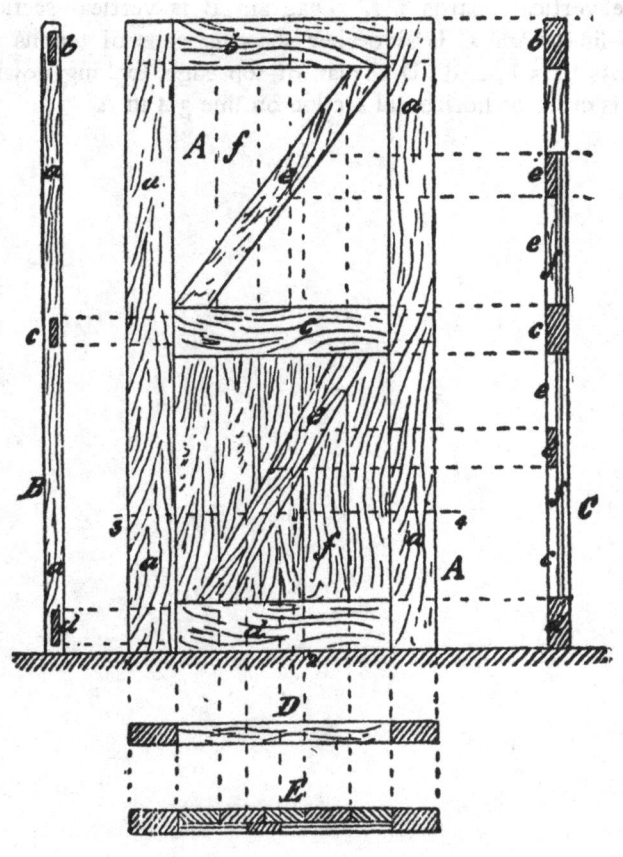

Fig. 18.

braced and battened" door, in Fig. 18, here as in elevation in diagram A, we have an outer frame vertical pieces, held together and secured by the cross-bars b, c, d, the ends of these being tenoned into the stiles a a. The central spaces are filled with braces e e, and the vertical boards f f. Diagram B is vertical section on line 2 and C is side view showing ends of tenons of cross bars b, c, d; D is plan of top edge, looking down; E is cross or horizontal section on line 3 4 in A.

PANELLED DOORS—NAMES AND OFFICES OF DIFFERENT PARTS—STILES—RAILS— MORTISES.

The transition from this form of door to the highest class, the "panelled door," is easy and natural. We have

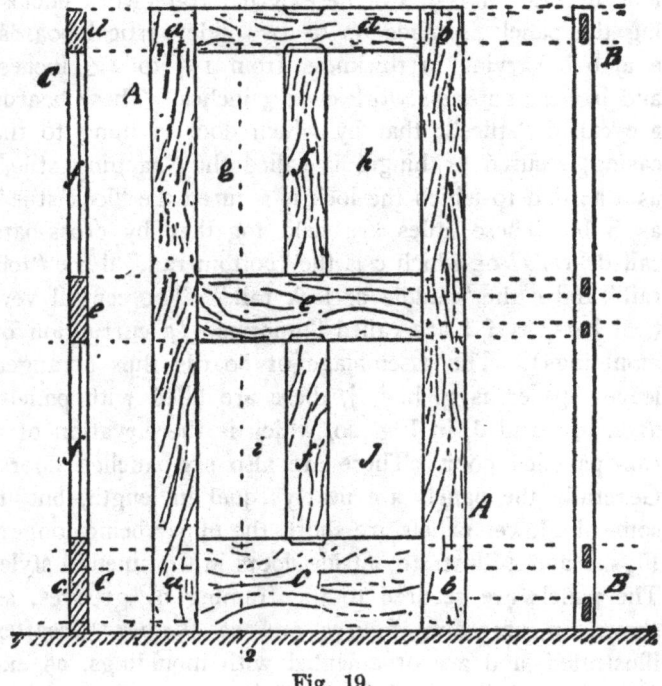

Fig. 19.

seen in the simplest timbers, which is the element of the "truss," and which gives the strongest form attainable.

In this view the panelled door, as in elevation in A, Fig. 19, is not so strong as the form in Fig. 18, fiom the absence of the diagonal braces, as e e, but those, if required in a door such as an external one, where strength is an object can be dispensed with in interior doors, which are always panelled in good houses.

Elegance or neatness of arrangement, with such ornamentation as mouldings, etc., can give, are what are looked for. In Fig. 19, the external framework enclosing the panels is made up of two side vertical boards, a a, b b varying in thickness from 1½ to 2½ inches, and in very superior work even 3 inches. These boards are called "stiles"; that by which door is hung to the casing, secured by hinges is called the "hanging stile," as a a; that to which the lock is secured the "lock stile," as b b. These stiles are held together by cross-bars called "rails" of which c is the "bottom rail," d the "top rail" and e the "middle or lock rail." The central vertical bars, as f f are called "muntins" (a corruption of mouldings). The assemblage of boards thus arranged leaves spaces as g, h, i, j, these are filled with panels, as a, b, c and d, in Fig. 20, which is the elevation of a *four*-panelled door. There are also six-panelled doors. Generally the panels are nearly equal in length, but in some the lower panels are short, the upper being longer. Figs. 2 and 4 illustrate outside doors in Continental style. The panels are secured to the framing by grooves, as shown in preceding figures and as further hereafter illustrated, and are ornamented with mouldings, as explained. In Fig. 19 diagram C is the vertical section, edge view of style b b. In Fig. 20 B is plan of top edge of door. The rails are secured to the styles by tenons, sometimes single, but more frequently in good work by double tenons, as in Fig. 21, in which is front elevation of rail, a a, b c two tenons. Diagram B is part of. stile a cut vertically in two to show the seats of the mortises b and c, diagram C and view of rail. In left-hand dia-

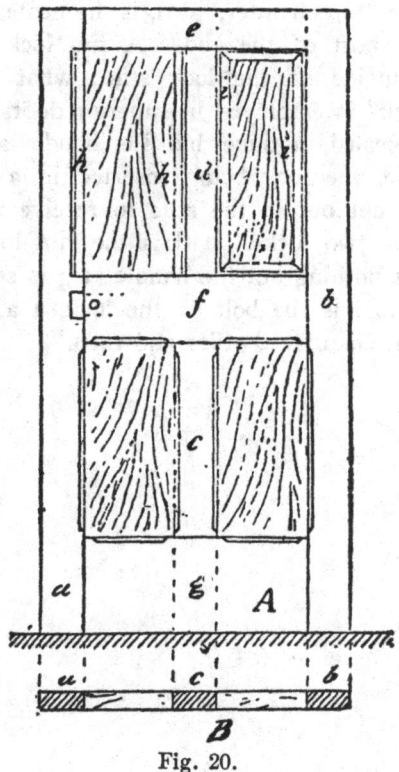

Fig. 20.

gram in Fig. 12 is elevation of part of "lock stile," a a and "lock rail," b of a bedroom door, with simple lock, c, known as a "rim lock." In diagram B, part of the "hanging stile," a a, of this door is given in elevation, b part of "top rail," a portion of upper "hinge" is shown at c. Diagram C is edge view. The inner edges of stiles, rails, and mortises are generally, in good work, "stop chamfered" as at d d, or beveled off from end to end, as at e f, the two edges meeting in a mitre, as shown. The "top chamfer," d d, is the neatest, stopping, as it does, short of the end. A rim lock is screwed onto the outside of the lock stile; what is called a "mortise lock" is employed in superior doors, where the lock is concealed, nothing but the handle and keyhole being visible, the lock being inserted in a mortise or vacant part cut out in the stile to receive it. Fig. 29 contrasts the two locks. c d is the rim lock. In the mortise lock nothing but the handle at g is seen, and the escutcheon h, i is the bolt of the lock, a a, b b, a' a', b' b'. are the chamfered stiles and rails.

DOOR CASINGS.

Doors are secured to "casings." These are of timber, and built into the walls, and are secured to wood, bricks or grounds. Fig. 23 illustrates in part elevation an outer "door casing." The sides b b, c c, are called "jambs," f f, the "head," into which the jambs are tenoned, the feet being also tenoned, at d, into the upper part of stone step a a. Fig. 22 is sectional plan showing arrangement and relative positions of various parts of a door and its casings. The door, l l, is hinged to the "jamb" b, this being secured to the "ground" or "wood brick" a a, bulit into the wall b b, c and j are the "architraves." The opposite "jamb," f f, is rebated as at m to allow of a space into which the "door lock stile" falls, as shown by the dotted lines, which represent the lines of the door. The outer edge of the jamb may be left plain, but is often finished off with a "quirked head," as at j; k, k, the hinge. The inner and outer architraves are at c and j; a a, the wood brick; b b, the wall; e, i, are the elevations of the architraves, d and h. The elevations of these two parts of sectional plan of door fittings are given in the under part of the drawing in Fig. 23. The edge of the door a, as looking at it from the inner side, is shown at p p, q q, being the ends of tenons of top rail, r r, the hinge, n n, from a view of architrave, o o the wall in the void of which the door is hung. In the under drawing to the right, part of front surface of door is shown, s s, the architrave, t t the wall.

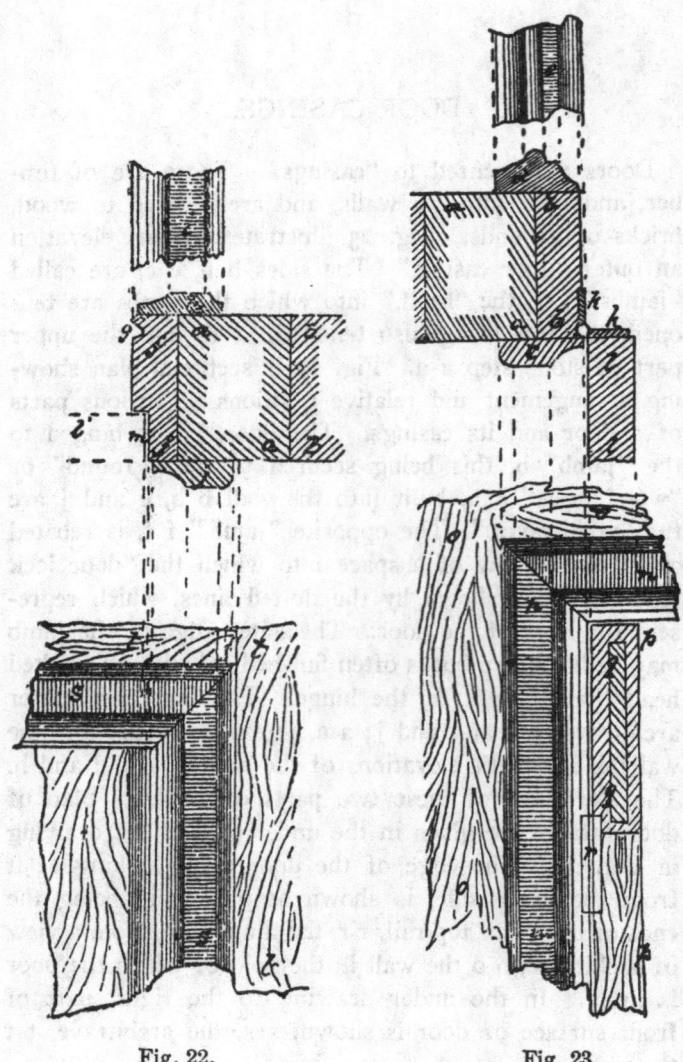

Fig. 22.   Fig. 23.

JOINTS OF STILES AND RAILS IN PANELLED DOORS.

Figs. 24 and 25 give illustrations of methods of joining rails and stiles, or rails and mortises. Let a b c d, Fig. 24, be the stile, with moulding stuck on edge; f g h is part of the rail, with tenon f, shown by dotted lines

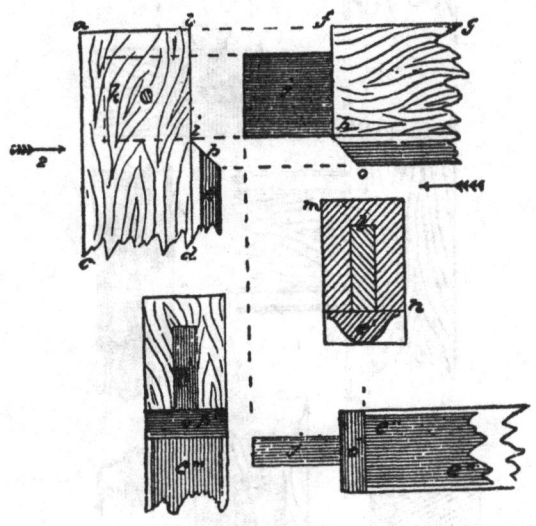

Fig. 24.

in stile a b c d. Front view of tenon are face of mitre of chamfer at p, looking at a b c d in the direction of arrow l, is shown in the lower diagram at k′, p′ and e″. The section of part f g looking at its end, in direction of arrow 2, is shown at l m n; the section of a moulding

251

is in this at e′. In lower diagram to the right is given a view of under side of rail f g. In Fig. 25, a a, is

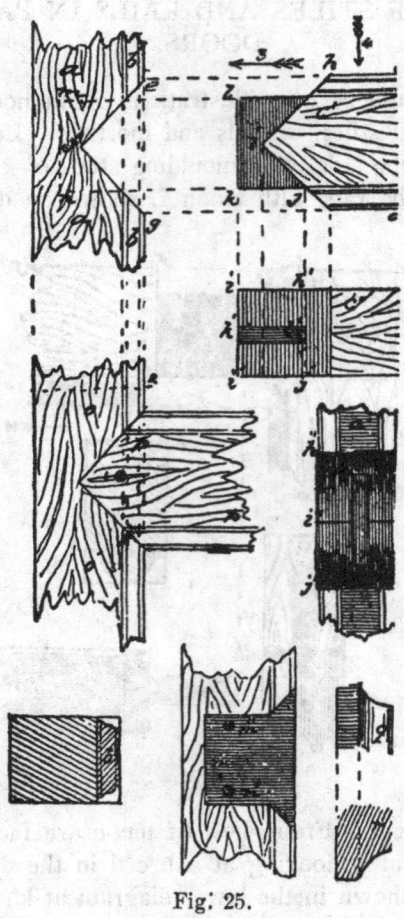

Fig. 25.

front view of part of stile with moulding worked on edge, at b b; part of rail is at c′ c′ d. The angular face of part cut out in stile e f, fg corresponds with angular end h i j of rail, but a tenon i l k is left on, or is inserted in end of piece c′ c′ d. The end view of the stile a a, looking at it in the direction opposite to that

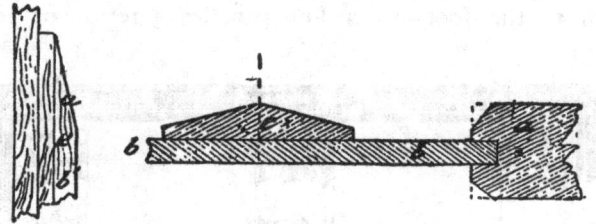

Fig. 26.

of the arrow 3, is shown in the middle diagram to the right with corresponding letters accented, showing corresponding parts. The line i″ i″ corresponds to the line at point in rail c′ c′ d d. The plan of under side of rail c′ c′ d is shown in diagram immediately below k′, l being edge view of tenon k l. The finished joint is shown at o o, p p; the diagram below to the left being cross

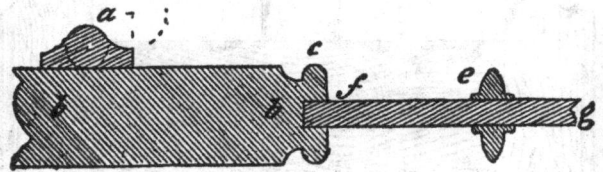

Fig. 27.

section to the line 1 2. Enlarged elevation q, and section r of moulding b b, or b″, is given at the two diagrams to the right at bottom of drawing. Another method of forming the junction is shown in the middle diagram at the foot of Fig. 25, the shaded part showing form of tenon with the ends of moulding united.

A FOUR-PANELLED DOOR.

In Fg. 28 I give a drawing—to a scale of ⅛, or 1½ inch to the foot—of a four-panelled interior or room

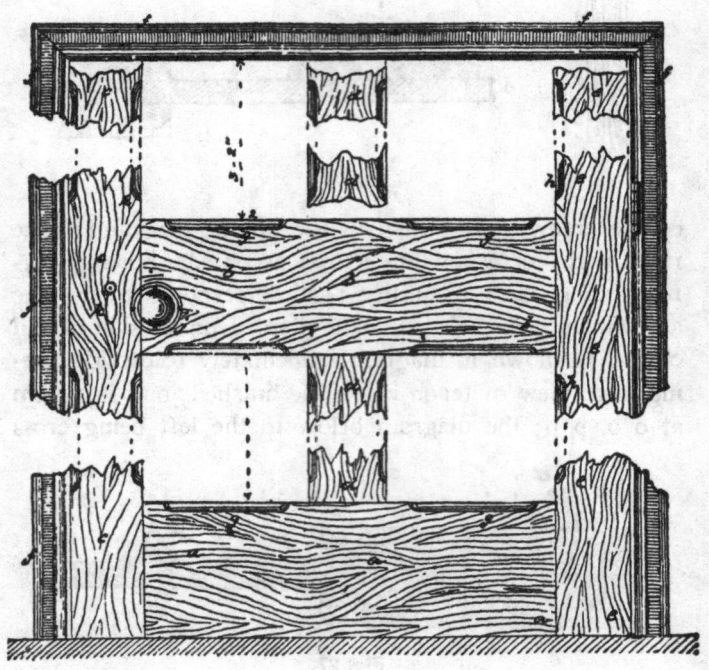

Fig. 28.

door, showing all the leading parts of the framework, with the exception of top rail, which is usually about half the breadth or depth of the middle of lock rail, marked b b in the drawing. The panels are not shown, but the dimensions of the spaces they occupy are given. The panels are plan "square," the only ornamentation in this example being a "stop chamfer" worked on the margin of stiles, and rails, as shown at g g and h h. In the drawing a a is the "bottom rail," b b the middle, or usually "lock rail," as it carries the "mortise lock," the handle of which is shown at j. The "key hole" is covered by a movable part, hung or jointed at upper end, called the "escutcheon," or more frequently in technical talk, the "scutcheon," or "skutcheon," shown at k. The stiles are at c c, e e—the stiles c c, termed the "lock stile," being that in which the lock is mortised. The stile e e is called the "hanging stile," being that on which the door is "hinged" or "hung" to the door casing. The vertical pieces, or "muntins," which divide the panels from each other, placing them in pairs on each side of the door, are shown at d d. The door framing thus constructed is surrounded on both sides and at top by the architraves f f f.

ARCHITRAVES OF A FOUR-PANELLED DOOR.

The section of architrave in relation to the door casing or check is in upper diagram to the left in Fig. 29, a a being part of the door casing, b b the section of architrave, of which part elevation is shown at c c, 1, 2, 3, and 4 showing similar parts in section correspondingly lettered. The edge view of the "lock stile" as a a f in the figure preceding, is shown at d d; e e shows the brass plate let into the edge and secured by screw nails as shown. This is part of the lock furniture of the door, f indicating position and section of the shooting or locking bolt of the lock, which passes into the aperture of a brass plate secured to the inner side or edge of the door casing. The bolt, which secures the door, being closed —not locked—f being the locking bolt, is shown at g, this being worked by the handle j of the lock. The part of the lock furniture attached to the door casing opposite to the edge, as d d d, of the door stile, is shown in the lower diagram to the right. The part 3 3 in this corresponds to the face of the recessed or rebated part p in drawing above, cut in the face of the door casing n n n, the door passing into and resting against the face of recess or rebate p. In the upper diagram to the right, o o o is the outer architrave secured to the door casing n n n, r part of the inner architrave. The part of the lock furniture secured to the door casing is shown at t t; it is a brass plate let into the face g, or 3 3 of recess or rebate p. The aperture in this into which the bolt f of the lock passes is shown at p; that into which the bolt

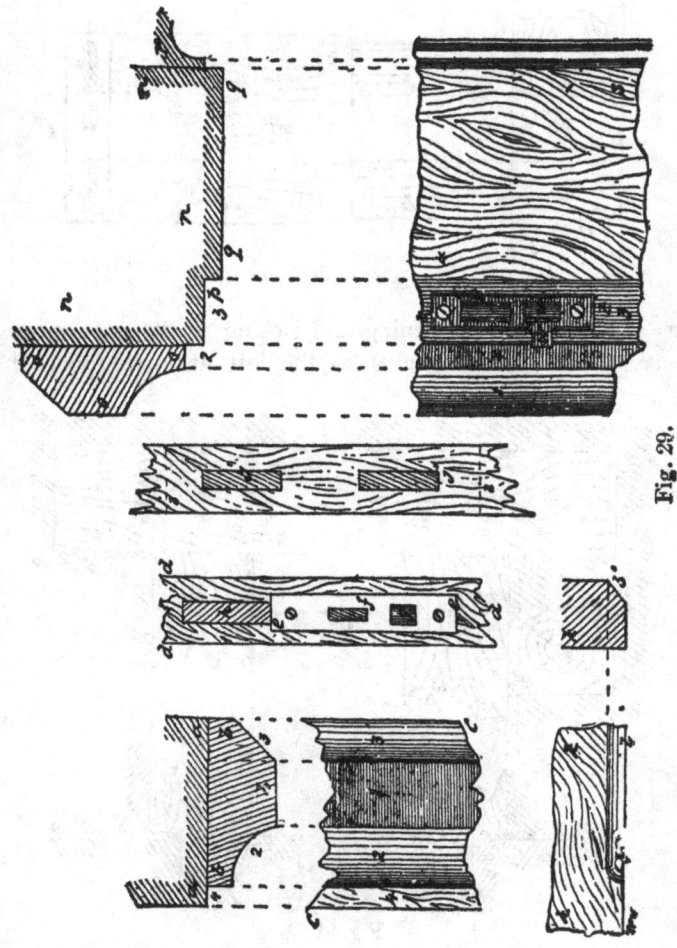

Fig. 29.

moved by the hand passes is at u, a spring w, cast onto the plate t t, being shown at w. A small projecting part

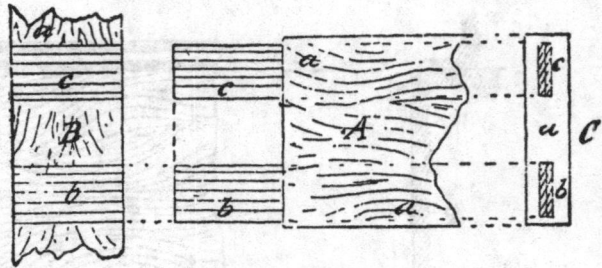

Fig. 30.

as w', to make the opening and closing of the door more easy. The two diagrams to the left at lower part of

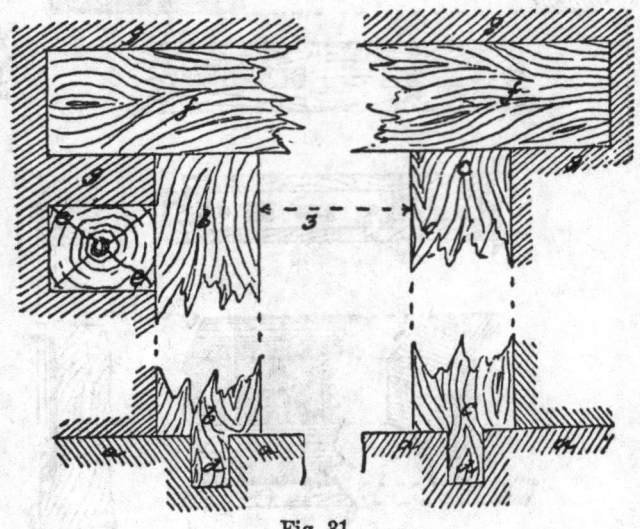

Fig. 31.

drawing show the elevation k l m, the chamfered part of framing with section at k' k'.

SOME EXAMPLES OF ORNAMENTAL WOOD-WORK.

The following examples are introduced in order to

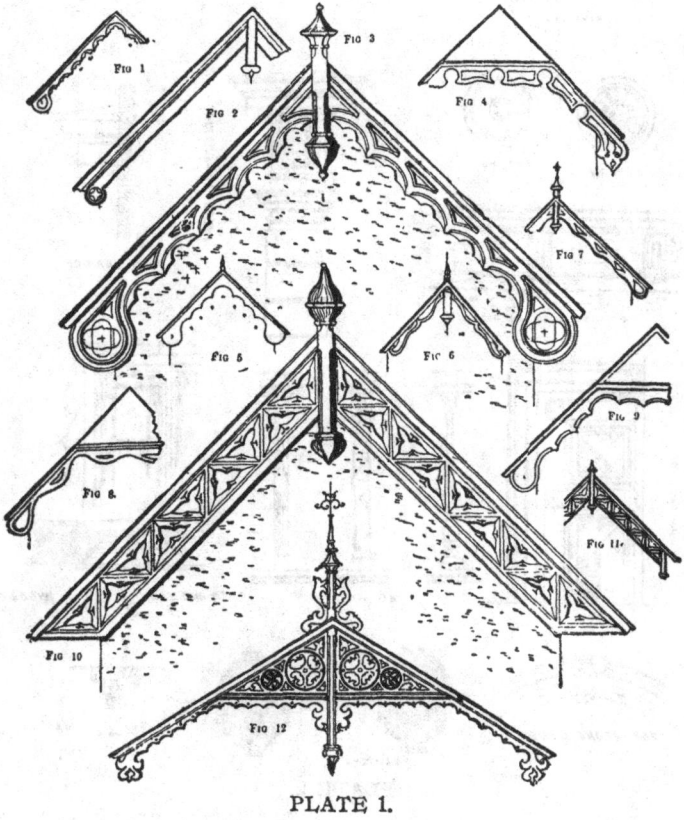

PLATE 1.

give the workman an idea of the shape and construction of low-cost ornamental wood-work. The figures

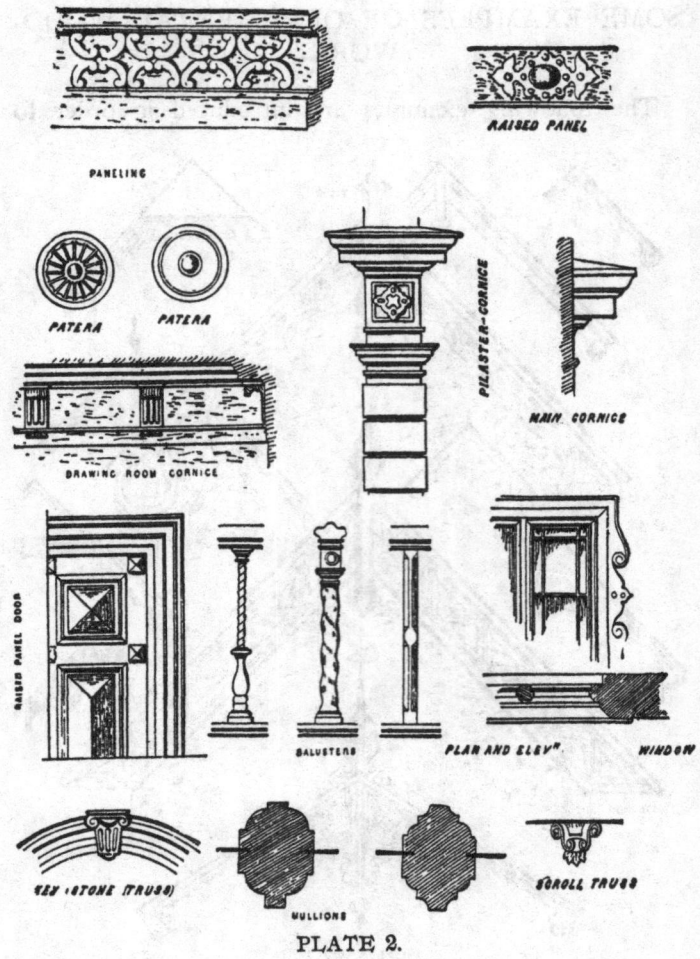

PANELING

RAISED PANEL

PATERA

PATERA

PILASTER-CORNICE

MAIN CORNICE

DRAWING ROOM CORNICE

RAISED PANEL DOOR

BALUSTERS

PLAN AND ELEV^N

WINDOW

KEY (STONE (TRUSS)

MULLIONS

SCROLL TRUSS

PLATE 2.

shown from No. 1 to No. 12, inclusive, exhibit a number of large boards, chiefly in Gothic style. Plate No. 2 is a style which was in vogue very much a few years ago and was generally known among carpenters as Ginger-Bread work. It is well adapted for sea-side cottages or

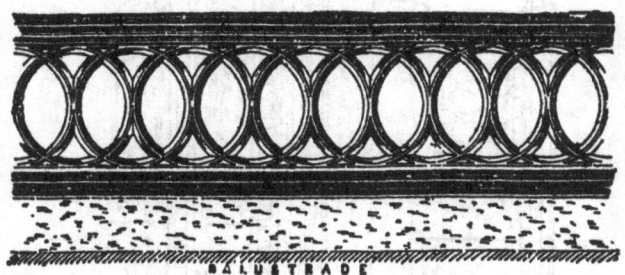

No. 13.

summer residences; it consists mostly of cutwork. Nos. 2, 5, 8 and 9 are well adapted for ordinary cottage

No. 14.

work. Nos. 13, 16 and 21 are well suited for balustrades, No. 16 being especially adapted for heavy balus-

No. 15.

trades on verandas or over bay windows. Nos. 14, 15 and 17 require no explanation, as they may be adapted

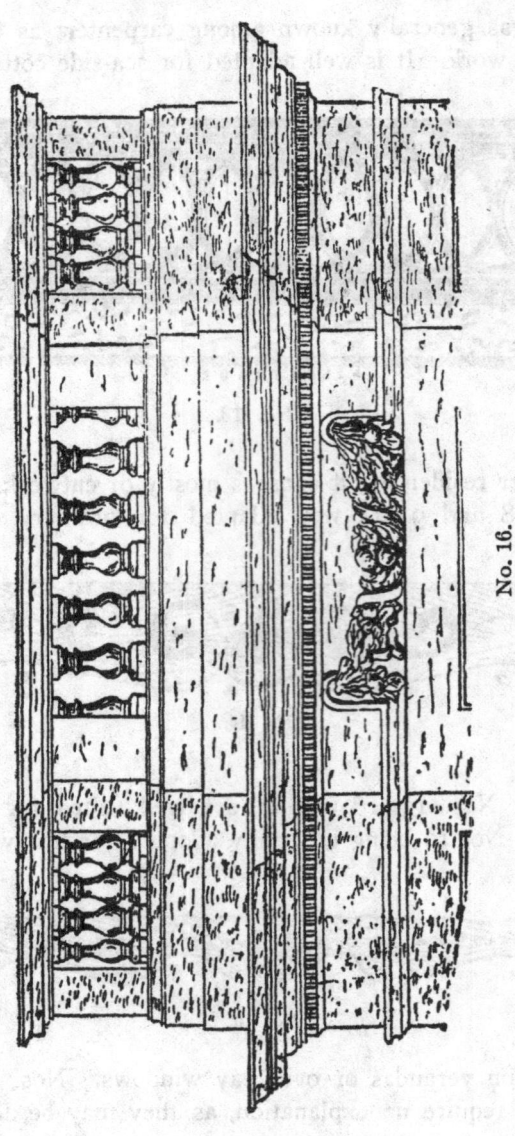

No. 16.

to a thousand different purposes. Nos. 18 and 19 make very handsome drops for verandas and other similar

No. 17.

work. No. 29 shows a single drop with the grain of the wood running vertically. A number of these placed

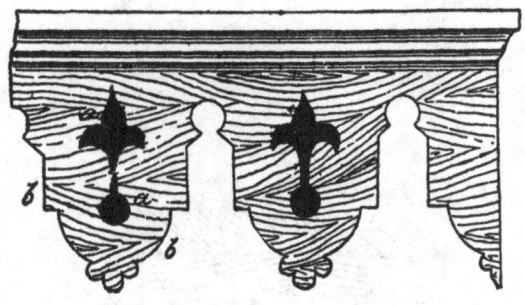

No. 18.

together edge to edge make a very nice trimming for verandas. No. 22 shows a cut bracket which will often

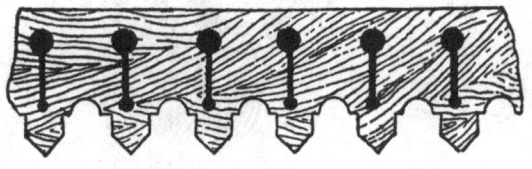

No. 19.

be found useful. No. 23 shows an elaborate railing suitable for a veranda or balcony. No. 24 exhibits a

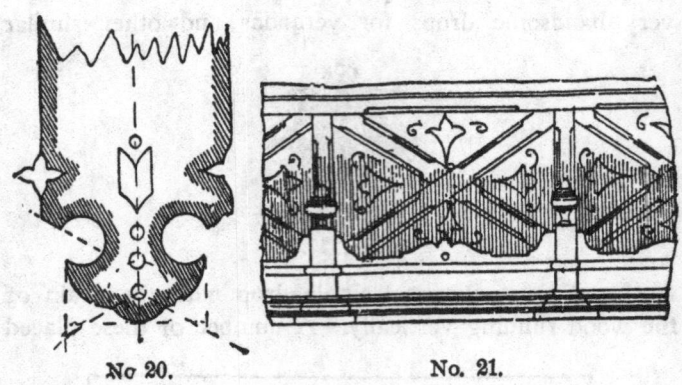

No 20.   No. 21.

No. 22.

No. 23.

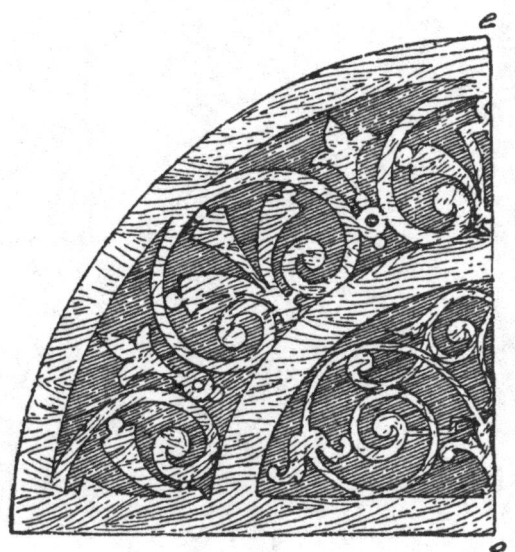

No. 24.

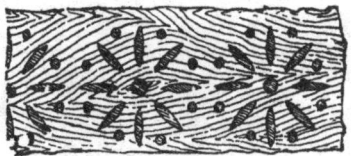

No. 25.

perforated panel suitable for many places. No. 26 shows a portion of a circular panel which may be perforated or the ornaments may be planted on, according to exigencies. See Plates. The balance of the examples shown speak for themselves. They offer a number of excellent suggestions to the progressive workman. These examples will doubtless prove of great value to the work man.

QUESTIONS ON MODERN CARPENTRY
VOL. I.

QUESTIONS.

1. Give definition of a "circle."

2. What term is given to a line that is drawn through center to circumference of a circle?

3. What term is given to a line drawn from center to circumference of a circle?

4. What term is given to a line (less than the diameter) that cuts the circumference of a circle at two points?

5. Give definition of a "tangent."

6. Give definition of a "segment of a circle."

7. Give sketch of a circle showing the "diameter," "radius," "chord," "segment" and "tangent."

8. Give sketch and describe how to find the center of a circle.

9. Into how many equal parts is the measurement of the circumference of a circle divided?

10. Give the three terms used in measurement of the circumference of a circle, and show how they are written.

11. What is a quadrant of a circle?

12. How many degrees are in a quadrant of a circle?

13. How many degrees are in a semi-circle?

14. What term is given to the angle of a circle that is half of a right angle?

15. Give sketch and describe how three right angles may be formed within a semi-circle.

16. Give sketch and describe how a hexagon may be formed within a circle.

17. Give sketch of a hexagon showing how an equilateral triangle may be formed.

18. Give sketch and describe how a right angle or quadrant may be bisected.

19. Give sketch and describe how to get a straight line that shall equal the circumference of a circle or part of a circle or quadrant.

20. Give sketch and show how quadrant may be divided into any number of equal parts, say thirteen.

21. Give sketch and show how equilateral triangle may be employed in forming the trefoil.

22. Give sketch and describe method of finding the "stretch out" or length of circumference of a circle.

23. Give rule by arithmetic of how to find the circumference of a circle.

24. Give sketch and describe how a curve having

any reasonable radius, may be obtained, if but three points in the circumference are available.

25. Give a practical illustration of how to find a place to locate a center, where the diameter is great.

26. What is a "polygon?"

27. Give the names applied to polygons having three sides, four sides, five sides, six sides, seven sides, eight sides, nine sides, ten side, eleven sides, and twelve sides respectively.

28. Give the two names under which polygons are classified.

29. Give sketch showing how a trigon may be constructed and how the miter joint may be obtained.

30. Give sketch and describe how a square may be formed.

31. Give sketch and describe how to construct a pentagon.

32. Give sketch and describe how a hexagon may be formed.

33. Give sketch and describe how a heptagon may be formed.

34. Give sketch and describe how an octagon may be formed.

35. Show practically how all regular octagons may be constructed.

36. Give a practical illustration of how a perpendicular line may be made on any given straight line.

37. Give a practical illustration of how to bisect an angle by the aid of the steel square alone.

38. Give a practical illustration of how to bisect an acute angle by same method—steel square.

39. Show practically how to get a correct miter cut, or angle of 45° on a board.

40. Show how to construct a figure showing an angle of 30° on one side, and on the other an angle of 60°.

41. Show how the diameter of a circle may be obtained through the aid of the steel square.

42. Show how an equilateral triangle may be obtained through use of the steel square.

43. Show how to describe an octagon by using the steel square.

44. Show how a near approximation of the circumference of a circle may be obtained by use of the steel square and a straight line.

45. Give illustration how a board may be divided into any given number of equal parts by aid of steel square or pocket rule.

46. Give the definition of an "ellipse."

47. Give an illustration of one of the simplest methods of describing an ellipse.

48. Give an illustration of projecting an ellipse by using a trammel.

49. Give illustration of describing an ellipse by the intersection of lines.

50. Give illustration of describing an ellipse by the intersection of arcs.

51. Show how radial lines may be obtained for arches and elliptical work.

52. Give an illustration how to describe a diamond or lozenge-shaped figure.

53. Give illustration how to describe a spiral or scroll by a simple method.

54. Give illustration of how a spiral may be described in a scientific manner, and which can be formed to dimension.

55. Give illustration of the method of obtaining a spiral by arcs of circles.

56. Give illustration and method of forming a "parabola."

57. Give illustration and method of forming an "hyperbola."

58. Give the names of the different kinds of arches in buildings.

59. Mention the names given to pointed arches.

60. What is the name given to the stones forming an arch?

61. What is the name given to the centre stone in an arch?

62. Give the names applied to the various divisions of an arch, namely, the highest point, the lowest point, and the spaces between respectively.

63. What is the name given to the under or concave surface of an arch?

64. What is the name given to the upper or convex surface of an arch?

65. What are the names given to the supports of an arch?

66. Show by illustration and describe how to obtain the curves and radiating lines of a semi-circular arch.

67. Show by illustration and describe how to obtain the curves and radiating lines of a segment arch.

68. Show by illustration and describe two examples of Moorish or Saracenic arches, one of which is pointed.

69. What is a "flatband"?

70. Give illustration and describe how to obtain the curves and radiating lines of the elliptic arch.

71. Give illustration and describe how the centers and curves of an equilateral arch may be obtained.

72. Give illustration and describe how the centers and curves of a lancet arch may be obtained.

73. Give illustration and describe how the center and curves of a low or drop arch may be obtained.

74. Give illustration and describe how the centers and curves of a Gothic arch with a still less height, may be obtained.

75. Give illustration and describe another four-centered arch of less height.

76. Give illustration and describe how to obtain an equilateral Ogee arch.

77. Give illustration and describe method of obtaining the lines for an Ogee arch, having a height equal to half the span.

78. Give some instances in carpenter work where half of the Ogee curve is employed.

79. Give a description of the steel square and its several divisions.

80. Give a practical illustration of how a board or scantling may be measured by use of steel square.

81. Give rule how to find hypothenuse of a right angled triangle.

82. Give an illustration of how length of braces may be obtained by use of the square.

83. Describe the use of the "octagonal scale" on the tongue of the square.

84. Show method how the pitch of a roof may be obtained by use of the square.

85. Show method to obtain bevels and lengths of hip rafters by use of the square.

86. Show method for finding the length and cuts for cross-bridging.

87. Show method for obtaining the "cuts" for octagon and hexagon joints.

88. Show by illustration the method of defining the pitches of roofs, and giving the figures on the square for laying out the rafters for such pitches.

89. Give a short description of what is known as balloon framing, and how the different parts are constructed.

90. Give illustration and describe a "hip-roof."

91. Give illustration and describe a "lean-to-roof."

92. Give illustration and describe a "saddle-roof."

93. Give illustration and describe a "mansard roof."

94. Give illustration and describe a simple hip-roof having a ridge.

95. Give illustration and describe an "octagon roof."

96. Give illustration and describe manner of construction of a "dome roof."

97. Give illustration and rules for construction of an octagonal spire.

98. Give a few illustrations of scarfing timbers.

99. Show a few examples of strengthening and trussing joints, girders and timbers.

100. Explain what is meant by the term "kerfing."

101. Give illustration showing how to determine the number and distances apart of saw kerfs required to bend a board round a corner.

102. Give illustration of how to make a "kerf" for bending round an ellipse.

103. Describe how to bend thick stuff around work that is on a rake.

104. Give illustration and describe how to lay out a hip rafter for a veranda having a curved roof.

105. Give illustration and describe how to obtain

the curve of a hip rafter, when the common rafters have an ogee or concave and convex shape.

106. Give illustration and describe how raking mouldings are used to work in level mouldings.

107. Describe the kind of mouldings called "spring mouldings."

108. Give illustrations showing plan and elevation of cluster column of wood for 4 columns and describe how constructed.

109. Give illustration of a hopper and describe how to be constructed.

110. Give illustration and describe how a conical tower roof may be curved.

111. Give illustration and describe how to cover a dome roof.

112. Give illustration and describe how the semi-circular soffit of a doorway may be made.

113. Describe how a circle soffit may be laid off into panels.

114. Give illustration and describe method for obtaining correct shape of a veneer for a gothic-splayed window or door head.

115. Give illustrations and describe two methods of dovetailing hoppers, trays and other splayed work.

116. Give description of how an ordinary straight flight of stairs may be constructed.

117. Give sketch showing part of a straight stair.

118. Give sketch showing stair with winders and landing.

119. Give sketch and describe a stair with brackets.

120. Give sketch showing stair with two newels and balusters, also paneled string and spandrel.

121. Give sketches of seven of the latest designs for doors.

122. Give five sketches showing methods of constructing and finishing a window frame for weighted sash.

123. Give sketches showing the various parts of a bay window for a balloon frame.

124. Give illustration and describe six examples of shingling roofs.

125. Show by sketch how panels are formed.

126. Describe the various kinds of panels named.

127. Make sketch of a four-panel door.

128. How are air-tight cases made? Describe the method of making.

129. What is meant by the word "stile'?

130. What is a rail in a door? What is a muntin?

131. What is a chamfer? Describe one.

132. Examine examples of sketches of ornamental wood-work, draw and describe a "baye-board."

133. Make a design of perforated insular panel.

INDEX

A

B

INDEX

W